GW01464837

**Young Writers** 2005 CREATIVE WRITING
COMPETITION FOR SECONDARY SCHOOLS

# T·A·L·E·S·

# From Northern Ireland
Edited by Laura Rogers

Disclaimer

Young Writers has maintained every effort
to publish stories that will not cause offence.

Any stories, events or activities relating to individuals
should be read as fictional pieces and not construed
as real-life character portrayal.

Young **Writers**

First published in Great Britain in 2005 by:
Young Writers
Remus House
Coltsfoot Drive
Peterborough
PE2 9JX
Telephone: 01733 890066
Website: www.youngwriters.co.uk

All Rights Reserved

© Copyright Contributors 2005

SB ISBN 1 84602 233 9

# Foreword

*Young Writers* was established in 1991 and has been passionately devoted to the promotion of reading and writing in children and young adults ever since. The quest continues today. *Young Writers* remains as committed to engendering the fostering of burgeoning poetic and literary talent as ever.

This year, *Young Writers* are happy to present a dynamic and entertaining new selection of the best creative writing from a talented and diverse cross section of some of the most accomplished secondary school writers around. Entrants were presented with four inspirational and challenging themes.

'Myths And Legends' gave pupils the opportunity to adapt long-established tales from mythology (whether Greek, Roman, Arthurian or more conventional eg The Loch Ness Monster) to their own style.

'A Day In The Life Of ...' offered pupils the chance to depict twenty-four hours in the lives of literally anyone they could imagine. A hugely imaginative wealth of entries were received encompassing days in the lives of everyone from the top media celebrities to historical figures like Henry VIII or a typical soldier from the First World War.

Finally 'Short Stories', in contrast, offered no limit other than the author's own imagination while 'Hold The Front Page' provided the ideal opportunity to challenge the entrants' journalistic skills, asking them to provide a newspaper or magazine article on any subject of their choice.

*T.A.L.E.S. From Northern Ireland* is ultimately a collection we feel sure you will love, featuring as it does the work of the best young authors writing today.

# Contents

**Ashfield Girls' High School, Belfast**
Lauren McCune (14)     1

**Christian Brothers' School, Belfast**
Barry Burns (13)     3
Connor Johnston (13)     4
Kevin Toner (13)     5
Paul Braniff (13)     6
Ciaran Brady (13)     7
Paul Claxton (13)     8
Stephen McCusker     9

**Clifton Special School, Bangor**
David Gordon (17)     10
Anika Johnston (17)     11
Patrick Potter (17)     12
David Morton (17)     13
Robyn Loyer (17)     14
Stacey Graham (18)     15

**Coleraine College, Coleraine**
Megan Wright (13)     16
Melissa Tannahill (14)     17
Simon Freeburn (14)     18
Tamara Kesterton (14)     19
Ruth Hyndman (14)     20
Courtney Aiken (14)     21
Sarah Mitchell (14)     22
Ruth Stevens (14)     23
Leanne Godfrey (14)     24
Laura Hall (14)     26
Hollie Hayes (14)     27
Jill Davis (14)     28
Henrietta Dickey (14)     29
Samantha Logan (13)     30
Becky Andrews (14)     31

## Friends' School, Lisburn

Carly Spratt  (13)  32
Marc Cairns  (14)  33
Stuart Allen  (13)  34
Kerrie Coyle  (14)  35
Debbie Cupples  (14)  36
Hannah Baxter  (14)  37
Ryan Woodburn  (14)  38
Lyndsey Shields  (14)  39
Elizabeth Wallace  (14)  40
Amy Traynor  (14)  41
Amanda Thompson  (14)  42
Glenn Whitten  (14)  43
Adam Woods  (14)  44
Stephen Uprichard  (11)  45
Susanna Elliott  (12)  46
Brendan Jacobson  (13)  47
Sarah Glasgow  (13)  48
Philip Harrison  (13)  49
Susannah Hylands  (13)  50
Rebekah Hanna  (12)  51
Adam Glass  (13)  52
Matthew Irwin  (13)  53
Bryan Hickland  (13)  54
David Cumins  (13)  55
Jessica Hughes  (13)  56
Nikki Gibson  (13)  57
Katie Payne  (13)  58
Katy Fair  (13)  59
Poppy Harvey  (13)  60
Niall Diffin  (12)  61
Camille Bonnel  (12)  62
Stuart Hughes  (13)  63
Laura Johnston  (13)  64
Shelley Henderson  (12)  65
Robyn Haskins  (13)  66
Clara Conn  (12)  67
Shane Brennan  (12)  68
Sophie Brackenridge  (12)  69
Lindsay Crockett  (12)  70
Helen Bell  (12)  71

| | |
|---|---|
| Sarah Aiken (12) | 72 |
| Victoria Coome (12) | 73 |
| Mark Campbell (12) | 74 |
| Andrew Carson (12) | 75 |
| Mark Campbell (12) | 76 |
| Andrew Brown (12) | 77 |
| Rachel Annett (12) | 78 |
| Usama Wain (14) | 79 |
| Stephen Smyth (13) | 82 |
| Kirsty Stretton (13) | 83 |
| Frances Thompson (13) | 84 |
| Rachel Walker (13) | 85 |
| Aoife Brown (13) | 86 |
| Timothy Bruce (13) | 87 |
| Michael Corr (13) | 88 |
| Emma Boles (13) | 89 |
| Julie Allan (13) | 90 |
| Collin Cleland (13) | 91 |
| Kyra Bothwell (13) | 92 |
| Amy Codd (13) | 93 |
| Laura Burns (12) | 94 |
| Amy Conn (13) | 95 |
| Marc Conlan (13) | 96 |
| Thomas Wilkinson (12) | 97 |
| Caroline Rodgers (12) | 98 |
| Chloe Smyth (12) | 99 |
| Sophie Wilson (12) | 100 |
| Lynne Smylie (14) | 101 |
| Judith Smyth (14) | 102 |
| Adam Tinson (14) | 103 |
| Conor Auld (14) | 104 |
| Lauren Watson (13) | 105 |
| Andrew Wylie (13) | 106 |
| Gary Uprichard (13) | 107 |
| Ralph Walker (13) | 108 |
| Hannah Wilson (12) | 109 |
| Jonny Steele (13) | 110 |
| Marcus Tinson (13) | 111 |
| Christopher Weir (12) | 112 |
| Becky Whittaker (13) | 114 |
| Steven Woods (13) | 115 |
| Matthew Morris (12) | 116 |

Olivia Pierce  (12)                                117
Mark Williams  (14)                                118
Sophie McCutcheon  (12)                            119
Jenna McQueen  (13)                                120
Ben Maze  (13)                                     121
Ross McCaughey  (13)                               122
Amie Johnston  (12)                                123
John McCulla  (13)                                 124
Ross McGarel  (13)                                 125
Nelson Lui  (13)                                   126
Kerry Logan  (12)                                  128
Matthew Rea                                        129
Sophie McDermott  (13)                             130
Tori Mallon  12                                    131
Emma Kennedy  (12)                                 132
Claire Jordan  (12)                                133
Alexandra Pengelly  (13)                           134
Rebecca Palmer  (12)                               135
Alexander McReynolds  (12)                         136
Hayley McKay  (11)                                 137
Sarah Mathewson  (12)                              138
Victoria Mayers  (12)                              139
Aimeé McCluskey  (12)                              140
Leah McCall  (13)                                  141
John McRitchie  (13)                               142
Stephen Johnston  (13)                             143
Jordan Owens  (12)                                 144
Joe Murphy  (12)                                   145
Jonathon Patterson  (12)                           146
Gareth Nelson  (12)                                147
Laura Montgomery  (12)                             148
David McGuigan  (13)                               149
Rachel Petticrew  (12)                             150
Kathryn Mercer  (11)                               151
Emily Wallace  (14)                                152
Nicole Burnett  (12)                               153
Christopher Young  (13)                            154
Jack Redpath  (12)                                 155
David Seeds  (12)                                  156
Josh McMullan  (12)                                157
Kathryn Magill  (12)                               158
Rebecca Lister  (11)                               159

David McCrossan (12)     160
Laura Killough (12)     161
Stuart Lightbody (12)     162
Rory McIvor (12)     163
Lee Livingstone (12)     164
Kirsty-Louise Knox (11)     166
Duncan Malcolm (13)     167
Craig Lewsley (13)     168
Nicola Laverick (13)     169
Emma Megoran (13)     170
Hannah Kearney (13)     172
Caroline Lloyd (13)     173
Oliver Armstrong (13)     174
Jenny Barr (13)     175
Steven Allen (12)     176
Hannah Downie (13)     177
Jonathan Bell (13)     178
Jonathan Swain (12)     179
Shauneen Toland (12)     180
Nicole Quinn (12)     181
Ruaraidh Sim (11)     182
Blair Treacy (13)     183
Lauren Walker (13)     184
Chin Mun Soong (13)     185
Ellen Morrison (12)     186
Hannah Clarke (13)     187
Kerri Mulholland (13)     188

**Oakgrove Integrated College, Londonderry**
Adam Donaghy (11)     189
Emer Curley (12)     190
Laura Phillips (13)     191
Jamie-Lee Fulton (13)     192
Amanda Doherty (13)     193
Christopher Devenney (13)     194
Emma Arbuckle (13)     195
Dervla O'Connell (12)     196
David Gourley (12)     197
Philip Sheerin (12)     198
Sean McElroy (12)     199
Caroline Thompson (12)     200

Natasha Buchanan  (11)     201
Martin Wilson  (16)     202
Tyler Stothard  (14)     203
Martin Kerrigan  (14)     204
Caoimhe Doherty  (12)     205
William Douglas  (12)     206
Luke O'Kane  (12)     207

## St Catherine's College, Armagh

Catherine McKinney  (14)     208
Eiméar McKinstry  (15)     209
Nicola Hart  (12)     210
Carina Oliver  (15)     211
Helen McCann  (15)     212
Katie-Mary Harvey  (15)     213
Joanne Caraher  (15)     214
Maeve Devlin  (15)     215
Lauren Hughes  (15)     216
Laura Hughes  (15)     217
Sarah Rath  (12)     218
Natalie Toal  (15)     219
Natalie McCreesh  (14)     220

## St Patrick's Academy, Dungannon

Michelle Devine  (12)     221
Niamh Doris  (13)     222
Corey Cassidy  (13)     223
Aaron O'Neill  (13)     224
Jamie Hughes  (12)     225
Michaela Cullen  (13)     226
Ciara McGrath  (13)     227
Conor Campbell  (13)     228
Niamh McCann  (13)     229
Sean-Michael McDowell  (13)     230
Niamh McGirr  (13)     231
Sarah-Jayne Campbell  (13)     232

## The Abbey CBS Grammar School, Newry

Christopher Price  (14)     234
Brian McArdle  (12)     235
Jonathan Rafferty  (14)     236

Christopher Duggan  (14)                 237
Eoin Murphy  (14)                         238
Cathal MacDhaibhéid  (13)                 239
Declan Price  (14)                        240
Dónal Daly  (14)                          241
Christy Carr  (14)                        242
Shane O'Hare  (14)                        243
Conal O'Hare  (14)                        244
David Fitzpatrick  (14)                   245
Owen Rice  (14)                           246
Keith Mackey  (14)                        247
Eugene McAteer  (14)                      248
Francis Agnew  (14)                       249
David Digney  (13)                        250
Christopher Harte  (14)                   252
Aidan Slevin  (14)                        253
John McAteer  (13)                        254
Niall McAteer  (14)                       255
Mark Rafferty  (14)                       256
David O'Hare  (14)                        257

# The Creative Writing

# A Day In The Life Of Marilyn Monroe

Arthur has finally persuaded me to go for the new Billy Wilder movie, 'Some Like It Hot'. I don't approve of the role. I wish people would take me more seriously. I am tired of getting 'dumb blonde' roles. I want to be a serious actress. Arthur thinks it will be great. I don't know. I am starring with Jack Lemmon and Tony Curtis. They are great actors. I guess it will be fun filming. I hope.

I have been sitting in my trailer for the past three hours. I always have a phobia of going on set before filming. I don't know why. My mind just goes blank. I am just going to have to pick up my feet and go. Everyone's waiting. Now that's scary!

*Phewww* just finished filming the train scene. I had to sing 'Running Wild', kind of the way I wanna be. Jack is great to work with, though Tony, not so much. He's a little dull. I don't think he likes me.

Second day of filming; I am quite enjoying my time here. Arthur is in London for a while. I miss him. But I have to concentrate on today. I'll worry about that tomorrow.

Milton Green has been fired from Marilyn Monroe Productions. That came as a shock to me. He was the only man I could ever trust. It will not be the last time I see him. We've been shooting for the past few hours. I'm on my break. I passed some ideas by Billy and you know, he shows great respect towards me and really listens to me. Paula Strasberg is my drama coach. I like her but she is a little too controlling.

Another day. Arthur's still in London. I was just thinking about how I've let my morals drop. The last time I worked with Billy was in 'The Seven Year Itch' and that resulted in my marriage to Joe ending. I really loved him. Kinda makes me question my marriage now. I want to make a good home and family with Arthur but I don't seem to have the time. Arthur constantly supports me to work. I've already had a miscarriage whilst filming 'The Prince And Me'. It was one of the hardest times of my life. I want a child so bad. But work starts at three so I better get going.

I have just heard from a camera man that Tony Curtis thinks I am the worst actress and kisser! Oh, what a scumbag. I'll show him.

I have had fun working with Jack these past couple of months. He makes me laugh. I hope we stay good friends.

Well that's it. My work is done. I've struggled through hard times which I'll never forget. Fellow cast criticising me, bossy people always correcting me, being alone at home, taking prescribed pills every day and night, depression and so on.

Time for me to go home and relax and wait for March when the movie is released. I hope it goes well.

**Lauren McCune (14)**
**Ashfield Girls' High School, Belfast**

# Another Win For The Celts

Last night Celtic took on Rangers in a Glasgow derby clash at Celtic Park. When the match started, Rangers had a wonder shot by Fernando Ricksen.

It all came from the kick off when Rangers had the advantage over Celtic.

The Rangers struck a wonderful 40-yard shot and it was over the bar. 20 minutes into the game it was now Celtic's game and John Harston started the score sheet 1-0 to Celtic. Exactly seven minutes later and Dianbobo Balde scored a lovely header from a corner kick, 2-0 Celtic. Just before half-time Rangers pulled one back by Petr Lovenkrands as he lobbed Rab Douglas from 38 yards. Yet again just two minutes later Rangers scored the equaliser with a tap in by Nacho Novo.

The second half started with a few changes in both of the teams. On the 54th minute Chris Sutton was badly tackled and it started a fight, which lead to two send-offs, both teams were down to 10 men. It was good right up to the 85th minute when Juninho struck one heck of a shot, which glided into the top corner of the net. With just half a minute left of the game Alan Thompson had a free kick. He struck a beautiful shot and it went into the net. The match was over and Celtic won 4 goals to 2 goals, and were now 5 points clear at the top of the league.

**Barry Burns (13)**
**Christian Brothers' School, Belfast**

# The Robbery

It was a cold, windy night, I was lying in my bed reading a book.

I heard a noise downstairs.

I sat up and listened, then I heard it again, I got out of bed and went to open the door of my room, I heard voices, I thought I knew them.

I listened, it was my friend's children. I didn't think they would do a thing like this to me, they were robbing my house.

They were taking everything, my trust was lost, I was so angry - I went to the cupboard and got a golf club and went to tackle. They came running towards me, so I hit Ryan over the head and he fell to the ground. Then Aaron came towards me and I hit him.

I went to my room and phoned the police. They arrived with the ambulance. They took Ryan and Aaron to the hospital.

The next day the forensics came and asked me questions about what had happened. They took fingerprints of the things they had touched and also the golf club I had.

They were both charged with robbery and they dropped the charges of assault, so I did not have to go to court.

They were both sent to prison for six months. Their parents came to see me, they could not believe that their sons would do this. They were so embarrassed and apologised for them.

**Connor Johnston  (13)**
**Christian Brothers' School, Belfast**

# Burglary

Jimmy and Paul are next-door neighbours and they're best friends, they do everything together and now they want to catch the burglar who burgled Jimmy's house.

They thought they knew who it was so they told Jimmy's parents that it was John Daley, but his parents said he was on holiday. So they had to think about who hated Jimmy or his family, they thought for a while.

Then it hit Paul, *'The bully out of school!'* he shouted, 'he always bullies you so he probably stole all the stuff because you got him a detention. He probably did it with his gang.'

So they went to his house which was a few streets away. At first it looked as if no one was home, then they heard laughing coming from the garage, it sounded like Matthew (he hated his name). Paul and Jimmy peered through the side window of the garage and then they saw all the stolen goods. So they ran to Jimmy's house and told his parents that it was Matthew from school and then they got their possessions back and Matthew got expelled from the school.

**Kevin Toner (13)**
**Christian Brothers' School, Belfast**

# Ali's Great Come-Back

Mohammed Ali will once again get into the ring to fight Amir Khan. Amir has just started his professional career in boxing.

He has just come back from the Olympics where he received a silver medal, beaten by 24 points to 36 points.

Khan said to our reporter Aaron Murphy, 'I am better than Ali and always will be.'

Ali replied to this comment saying, 'I haven't been in the ring in over 10 years, but when I was in the ring critics eventually said I was the best in the world.'

Ali also said, 'This young man has just started his professional career and if he wants to take on the best in the world he can do so on the 30th May 2005 in Madison Square Gardens. When I get into the ring I will float like a butterfly and sting like a bee.'

On the night of the fight Ali did do what he said, he floated like a butterfly and stung like a bee. In the seventh round Ali hit Khan with a body shot, Khan fell to his knees, the referee was on the count of seven when Khan struggled to his feet, but face first onto the canvas.

The crowd was stunned by Ali's performance. Khan was rushed to hospital, the doctor said he had four broken ribs.

Ali said after the fight, 'Khan shouldn't have got into the ring with the best in the world. If he hadn't he would not be lying in a hospital bed eating food through a tube.'

**Paul Braniff (13)**
**Christian Brothers' School, Belfast**

# A Day In The Life Of A Sabre-Toothed Tiger

I woke up this morning and noticed I wasn't my usual self. I had four legs and long sharp teeth, I looked outside my window and saw it wasn't AD2005, it looked like 2005BC. I went outside and saw my reflection in a pond and saw I was a sabre-toothed tiger.

I was hungry. I looked closely at the pond and saw a fish swimming past. I stuck my paw in tentatively and grabbed a fish and swallowed it whole.

I went back to the cave where I came from and saw it was covered with muck and dirt.

I was still hungry - I saw a dinosaur pass by so I dived outside and stuck my teeth into a baby Tyrannosaurus rex, king of the dinosaurs.

I left the skeleton on the grass and ran away because I saw a large female Tyrannosaurus rex coming my way and that was one of the animals I was most afraid of.

I fell into a large pit of muck, I saw a cave close by so I ran into it to get clean. I noticed that I cleaned myself like a cat or a tiger in AD2005.

Three hours later, I found a large plank of wood with lines carved into it. I put it beside my teeth to measure them. When I finished it marked it with my claw and reed. It was 20 points so I called it 20 centimetres.

I examined myself and tried to remember what I looked like. I went to bed and the next morning I woke up and saw I was me again. I remembered what I looked like and drew a picture of it.

**Ciaran Brady  (13)**
**Christian Brothers' School, Belfast**

# The Risen

Today Hitler has risen from the dead and so has his army. He has plotted revenge against the English. He said, 'I am going to blow up all of your football stadiums.'

The British Government said, *'We need to step up our security.'*

People have joined up to protect their football stadiums.

Tony Blair has asked the Americans to protect our country. 'We should worry in case this turns into a world war.'

Hitler has given Tony Blair the list of the football stadiums, which he and his army are going to blow up. Our newspaper has been given the first five stadiums. They are Old Trafford, Highbury, Stamford Bridge, Goodison Park and Anfield.

The British Army has put the top security all around the coast of England to stop the Germans and Hitler bombing them from the sky. They have also put ships out to sea and submarines under the water surface, so we should have no bother of being hit by bombs.

We have just been informed of the first sighting of a German ship, which is loaded with the newest equipment, and it looks like submarines protect the ships.

This looks like it could take a couple of days to finish. The head of the army has just said, 'We need backup, just in case we lose men.'

This day will probably go down in history because people rose from the dead and started a world war. If people die today, we will remember them.

**Paul Claxton (13)**
**Christian Brothers' School, Belfast**

# A Day In The Life Of A Cat

One morning I woke up. I was in my bed in my owner's room. I jumped up onto his bed. It was big, warm and soft. It was a lot better than my bed. He wasn't there. Then I heard and smelt a can of fish heads being opened. I heard, 'Tony', so I sprang up and I went down the stairs. When I got down there he had fed me and given me new water.

When I was eating my breakfast he was eating his too. He had bread buttered and toasted and he had a bowl of cereal.

After we were finished, he said, 'I have got to go to work, Tony. Bye-bye.' Then he said, 'I'll miss you, my black, furry cat with green eyes.'

I heard a *beep, beep*. It was his friend. He has a dog. I hate that dog Butch, he is a vicious dog.

Well, when James (my owner - I think he's cool) had gone, I was alone. I went out the cat flap. I met up with Stephen, Snowball and Mr Sprinkles - they're bad cats. Mr Sprinkles is the worst. My other friends are John, Sean and Tinkle. We go everywhere together. There is one woman who really hates us, especially when we go past her backyard on the fence. She was James' girlfriend until her dog bit me and made me bleed. James dumped her after that.

Later on I went back to my house and went to sleep. Then I heard a noise so I went to the door. It was James. I started crying.

He said, 'Where is Tony?'

He always will love me.

**Stephen McCusker**
**Christian Brothers' School, Belfast**

# Miss O'Connor Visits A Local School To Tell Pupils Of Her Visit To Peru

Miss O'Connor came yesterday to talk to pupils in ELCP about her trip to Peru. She took photos with her new disc camera and the pupils all watched it on the big screen. They saw all the poor people in the country of South America. Sometimes the weather was very hot and sometimes it was very wet with thunder and lightning. They get big floods over there, then all the roads are just mud. The buildings were everywhere, up the side of the big mountain. It was sad to see so many people living together. The houses were made from scrap wood and plastic. They only had one bedroom and a kitchen. The people had to carry their water from two tankers that came once a week. The poor people were hungry and thirsty in Peru, they went to the church to be fed.

Miss O'Connor showed the old church and then the new church getting built. She went there to help the poor children. She gave them money and clothes.

Their skin is a different colour. It could be white or brown and they speak a different language from us.

Miss O'Connor is fund-raising again to go back to help the poor children. The pupils had a good look at the photographs from Peru and she left some for them to use in a project. Stacey thanked Miss O'Connor for coming to the school and giving the interesting talk.

**David Gordon (17)**
**Clifton Special School, Bangor**

# The Castle

Long ago, a village lay between two mountains. On top of one sat the ruins of a grand old castle, which now sadly was uninhabited. The castle was subject to much speculation and rumour of being haunted.

The well-respected village had a bar, a shop for all needs and a doctor's surgery. The doctor's son, Rupert, had a harsh life as the doctor was bad tempered and Rupert always got the backlash. He spent all day up a tree picking apples and his evening by the window.

One night he could stand it no longer. He dressed, pulled on his highwayman's mask and a long cloak. He crept downstairs and into the night. Rupert climbed a mountain and there was the castle.

He had heard the rumours. Creeping along the hallway he saw a large mirror. Tiptoeing over he saw the reflection of a girl in a light pink dress with a dark purple sash placed neatly around her hips. Touching the mirror, it was like putting his hand into ice!

Rupert removed his mask.

'I am Princess Erica.'

'Rupert, Your Highness,' he said.

'What are you doing here?'

'I have run away.'

The doctor, drunk, as he often was, had returned to his surgery. Looking for Rupert he fell and knocked over a methylated lamp, turning the surgery into a sea of flames. The 'old bat' died.

Rupert returned and tried to rescue his father. Barely alive when pulled from the flames, Rupert recovered with a mug of hot whisky and a week in bed.

He then moved into the castle.

**Anika Johnston (17)**
**Clifton Special School, Bangor**

# A Day In The Life Of A Footballer

I am Owen Potter, I play for Real Madrid. I get up on a Saturday morning and have breakfast of Rice Krispies and two poached eggs on toast. I also have butter and jam on my toast. A good breakfast keeps me fit and gives me energy to play the match.

Then I go to the football ground to play football. I like it because it is good, it keeps me nice and healthy. I change into my white and black kit and I am ready for the match.

When I run out onto the pitch I see the other team, Chelsea. The crowd are cheering and singing. I kick the ball and the flag goes up. It is a corner. The ball has gone off the grass. The player takes a corner kick and kicks the ball hard. I try to score a goal in the net.

Just after half-time I scored a goal. The crowd all cheered loudly. I felt great.

My teammates said, 'Well done!' My team won the match.

I just like football because it is the best sport. I really enjoyed that match. I got a medal. The crowd all clapped and cheered as I ran around the pitch. Then I went back into the changing room to change and went out with my teammates to celebrate.

**Patrick Potter (17)**
**Clifton Special School, Bangor**

# David Morton Buys Townhouse

'My new townhouse is in South Street,' says David. 'A very good area of town and beside all the local amenities. I can walk to church, next door is a well-known hairdresser's, and the best chippy and pizza parlour are just along the street. One of the best eating houses and pubs is just across the road, so great for home entertaining. Who needs a cook?' adds David.

100 yards down the road is Derry Park, a great early morning training place for David. There's always a few children around to watch their hero practise his skills.

David says, 'I am enjoying my new home although sometimes I am disturbed in the night by the sound of fire engines, police cars, an ambulance in a hurry, or people walking home after a night in town.'

These are all new sounds to David who is more used to his country mansion where he goes to get away from the public.

'Inside, the house has been completely redecorated by the well-known designer Lawrence Llewelyn Bowen. All my new furniture arrived just before I moved in two weeks ago and I am finding everything very comfortable,' says David.

**David Morton (17)**
**Clifton Special School, Bangor**

# A Day In The Life Of A Vampire

Good evening, Robyn here. As you can see I just awoke about five minutes ago. All humans think we are monsters. We are flesh and blood, but human? I haven't been human for 200 years.

When we are made into a vampire it is only our body that dies, we are given another life.

Now that's enough about vampires, it's time to get started, don't you think?

Today you are going to see us feed on humans. I say this because you humans are food for us. I feel someone is coming here - a child? Oh yes. No, another vampire! Oh yes, Louis.

Now it's time to feed. Let's go out to eat. When we feed, we put our teeth into the neck of the person we are feeding from. I hope you can see us. Most people turn their head when we feed.

Good meal, now back to sleep for me. Good morning for you and goodnight for me.

**Robyn Loyer  (17)**
**Clifton Special School, Bangor**

# Clifton Move To New School

On the 19th April 2004, Clifton's new school opened on the Old Belfast Road. On the 26th April 2004 the pupils arrived for their first day. In the old school they had to pack their boxes, everyone in the school helped to move into their new school. The army offered to help them to move into their new school in April. The staff took one week to move in.

When the pupils moved into their new school, some of the pupils didn't know where they were.

When they first went inside the building it was strange to the younger ones, but the seniors were OK because they knew what they were coming to.

In their new school they have a new, big soft play area for the younger ones to play in when it's raining. If it's dry they can go out and play in their park. They have got a hydrotherapy pool to help the wheelchair users to exercise. There is an outside court for the senior end where they can play football, basketball and netball. They didn't have all this in their old school.

When I went to see Mrs Crowther to talk to her, Mrs Crowther said that she had had a word with the South Eastern Education Board to see if we could have a new school. The South Eastern Education Board said we could have a new school.

Everyone is very happy to have their new school.

**Stacey Graham  (18)**
**Clifton Special School, Bangor**

# Circle Of Magic

One day, four friends called Sarah, Megan, Ruth and Zoë were watching a programme on fairy circles when Sarah said, 'How about we all go up to the Black Glen tonight to see if it is true.'

'OK,' the girls chorused. So they each packed a backpack and got ready to go.

At 11.45pm the girls sneaked out of their bedroom windows and met at the Lions Gate. They finally arrived at the headland, where they set out a circle of stones and sat around it. It was dark and the girls were scared, but they wanted to find out the truth. 'We all have to join hands and count from one to seven repeatedly,' Megan informed the girls.

'Nothing's happened,' Zoë complained.

But while Megan was sitting, she felt something flicking her ear and then she saw a small glimmering light appear before her eyes. 'Fairies,' she said and when the four girls looked around, there were, of course, fairies flying above their heads. They had brought cameras, so they took pictures and when the fairies had all gone away the girls left too.

The next day the photographs were developed and the fairies were clearly visible. They showed their families and friends, went on television and became local celebrities. But of course, not everyone believed them. Do you?

**Megan Wright  (13)**
**Coleraine College, Coleraine**

# The Pot Of Gold

Once upon a time there was a little boy called Sam and a little girl called Katie. These two children were brother and sister. They lived in a cottage with their grandmother as their mother and father had died in a car accident a couple of years previous. Sam and Katie's grandmother didn't have a lot of money as she was poor.

Sam and Katie were put to bed and their grandmother would read them a story each night about leprechauns at the bottom of the garden, and how they would give a pot of gold at the end of the rainbow to anyone who caught one.

One day Sam and Katie decided to go hunting for a leprechaun so they could get the pot of gold for their poor grandmother. So off they went in search of the little green man. The two of them dropped down on all fours and started looking.

Two hours had passed and they still couldn't find one, but then suddenly, like a flash of lightning Katie saw a green figure move as swift as a cheetah behind a flowerpot. Katie crawled slowly towards the clay pot and grabbed the green figure. It looked like a leprechaun.

The leprechaun waved his arm and Katie saw magic dust fall from his tiny sleeve. Amazingly a huge pot of gold appeared and with that the leprechaun disappeared. 'Come quick Sam. Grandmother! I've found the pot of gold at the end of the rainbow!'

**Melissa Tannahill (14)**
Coleraine College, Coleraine

# The Phone Call

Every night since the first five years back, the night the first phone call was made. The night little Lindsay was scared out of her wits and the house empty. Lindsay's parents Mark and Louise had just gone out for dinner. But little did they know that this would be the last time they would see their daughter as she would be whisked away in the night.

It was 6.20 and the sky was losing the colours prevalent to early day. Lindsay was watching television, she lay back in the comfy armchair and relaxed.

*Ring, ring.* Lindsay removed herself from the chair and walked across the kitchen to pick up the phone. Lindsay picked up the phone, 'Hello?' she mumbled. A deep and unknown voice replied, 'I'm ten miles from your house.' The phone went silent and the mystery caller had hung up.

Lindsay remained in thought. She knew this was her big brother Martin playing tricks on her again as it was April Fool's Day. The clock had just struck 7pm; she turned off the television and went upstairs with the phone firmly clasped in her had.

*Ring, ring.* Lindsay held the phone to her ear. 'Hello!' she shouted.

The same voice replied, 'I'm outside your house.' No expression in what the mysterious caller said gave her any hints to the question of who he was.

The phone rang, 'I'm at your front door,' the voice screamed murderously.

Lindsay ran to the foot of the stairs and watched silently as the door handle turned. She turned left, her wardrobe, she could hide. She closed the wardrobe door too scared to utter a sound. Blood rushed through her ears, the absence of sound drowned out by the footsteps heard on the stairs. The phone shook in her hand.

'I know where you are!' that voice she could hear outside her room.

She tried to reassure herself this was a joke.

Screams tore through the house as she was brutally murdered. He had found Lindsay. Who would he find next?

**Simon Freeburn  (14)**
**Coleraine College, Coleraine**

# Once Upon A Concert!

Holly woke late on Saturday morning with a mammoth frown across her face. She always loved the weekends. Her and her friend Elle were especially looking forward to this weekend as they had finally got tickets to see Green Day in concert. But Holly's mum discovered they had skipped school to get them and grounded her daughter so she could not go to the concert.

The concert finally came and Holly was feeling even more downhearted. It did not help that her sister Leah was able to go. Holly was not in the mood to wait up and hear her boast about it so she decided to go to bed. When Holly was upstairs listening to her Green Day CD she heard a loud bang against her window. It was Elle, she had thrown a stone, Holly knew she would not be allowed out. The only answer was to sneak out and climb back in her window later. It would work if she could avoid Leah.

Holly could not see Leah at the concert but she did see Rio. Holly had fancied him for three years but thought he had never noticed her. Tonight Rio could not take his eyes off her. He came over to talk to her at the end of the concert.

In the haste to get home before Leah or her mum found her missing, she left, leaving her bag behind. Rio found it and gave it to her at school, along with a note inside asking her out. Holly said yes but they had to wait three weeks for a date as her mum had punished her even more for sneaking out.

**Tamara Kesterton  (14)**
**Coleraine College, Coleraine**

# Mermaid Girl

*(This story is about a girl called Susie who had always dreamed of being a mermaid.)*

There once was a little girl who was quite different from the rest of all the other girls in her class. Yes, she looked the same and she dressed the same, but when it came to asking the question of, 'What do you want to be when you grow up?' she replied, 'A mermaid.' Some people said she would grow out of it and she would forget about it, but when Susie was in second year she still wanted to be a mermaid. Susie got bullied for this, some people called her Mermaid Girl and some told her she couldn't even swim.

One day for a treat her class went to the beach and Susie loved the beach. They played games and had a picnic on the golden sand. The teacher told the class that if they were careful they could go for a walk along the pier. Nobody except Susie wanted to go, so off Susie went right to the end. Her teacher called her back, but instead of turning back Susie jumped in. Miss Hannah called the lifeguards and they searched the sea for her but they couldn't find her.

Her parents took it badly but they believe she is now a mermaid and they go every day to the beach to see if they can see her colourful tail flicking out of the water.

**Ruth Hyndman  (14)**
**Coleraine College, Coleraine**

# Dreams

This is an old legend where it is said that dreams really do come true. Do you believe in dreams? Well after this short but shocking tale of a young woman, you might think twice about what you believe in.

It was a beautiful day in Coleraine. The sun was shining like it was the last day it would ever shine again, but there was one person who was very unhappy. Mrs Faith was a lovely, kind and pleasant person who would never hurt a fly. Lately though she was having very strange dreams. Her dreams were so real to her though and sometimes she would wake up and think that they really happened to her. It made her very depressed.

Until one evening she was out at the beach paddling in the sea. When all of a sudden she was gone. Just like in one of her dreams she had dreamt the night before. Her friends and family searched everywhere for her, but all they found was her dream catcher necklace that she had worn everywhere in order to try and make her dreams go away.

It is said that if you go to that very same beach she disappeared at, you can see her reflection in the water and hear her trying to fight off her frightful dreams. Nobody knows what happened to the young, troubled woman but I tell you something, she didn't just fly away.

Are dreams just thoughts and visions or are they reality?

**Courtney Aiken (14)**
**Coleraine College, Coleraine**

# The Freedom Of Princess Ghana

Once upon a time there was an Indian fairy called Jasminda Rose. She lived in the jungle. Jasminda Rose was beautiful with long midnight black hair and twinkling green eyes. Wherever she flew a new blossom was born. Everyone knew her as kind and she danced all around the beauties of the Indian Jungle. Jasminda sang sweet songs to the other fairies as she braided wild flowers into their hair. At night the jungle was covered by a blanket of silver stars.

One day Jasminda met Princess Ghana who told her how sad she was. She sighed, 'I am no princess, I am not special,'

Jasminda soothed her, 'We are all special.'

Ghana looked upset, 'I have to marry Prince Sunjit as my father wishes, though I want freedom.'

Jasminda whispered, 'I will help you Princess,' while stroking the princess' hair. 'Now just eat this,' said Jasminda eagerly handing her a flower seed.

'What, why?' shrieked the princess.

'Trust me.' Ghana ate the seed.

'There's no more worries,' beamed Jasminda.

'No more worries?' said Ghana uncertainly.

The next morning Jasminda was pleased to find out the wedding had been cancelled as the king didn't want his son to marry a geranium! Jasminda Rose played the innocent as she rushed to see Princess Ghana, who sure enough, had a huge flower dancing on top of her head. Princess Ghana was looking so breathtakingly beautiful and so happy.

'Isn't that bizarre?' said her friend Nina Marie.

'Yes,' agreed Jasminda, 'totally bizarre!'

**Sarah Mitchell  (14)**
**Coleraine College, Coleraine**

# The Fairy Tree

Once upon a time Chloe and her family went to visit their mum's uncle Ronnie in his spacious house. Chloe had always loved visiting his house because it was a place to explore and also to see his cat, Sue.

When they arrived Chloe greeted her uncle and ran off behind the house to see his cat. She loved animals, especially cats, but was not allowed one herself because her dad hated animals.

Chloe said, 'I wish I had a kitten just like Sue.' Suddenly she heard something. It was a fairy and its wings glistened in the sunlight. 'Who are you?' Chloe asked.

'I'm a fairy from the fairy tree and I will grant you a wish if you give me something in return.'

Chloe grabbed a bunch of bluebells and handed them to her. She then asked, 'So fairies do really exist?'

'Yes and I want you to tell everyone because most people think we are make-believe.'

The fairy then flicked her magic wand and suddenly a kitten appeared. The fairy flew up into the tree and disappeared.

Chloe was very excited and grabbed the kitten and ran into the house. 'Look Mum, I have my own cat, I wished for a kitten and a fairy came down from the fairy tree and granted my wish.'

'Don't be stupid, stop fooling around.'

'No Mum, I'm telling the truth, the fairy made this lovely cat appear, can I keep it, please, please?'

'Well alright then.'

To this day Uncle Ronnie's house remains. If you search carefully you can still find the spot where Chloe sat ...

**Ruth Stevens (14)**
**Coleraine College, Coleraine**

# The Fairy God Maid

There was a beautiful young girl aged 15, her name was Faith and she had a twin sister called Morgan. They both lived in an extremely large mansion in Beverly Hills with their mum and dad. Faith was the prettier and more pleasant out of the two, Morgan was a spoilt brat.

One day at school the fittest lad came up to Faith, 'Hey, do you want to come to my huge party this weekend? You're first on my list,' asked Rick flirtatiously.

'Of course, see you then,' smiled Faith.

When Faith got home, 'Look what the cat dragged in,' smirked Morgan showing off in front of her sidekick Chloe. Faith just walked on past into the lounge to ring her friend and tell her. Her sister and Chloe overheard and Morgan went to the study to tell her mum. *'Mum,* Faith is going to a party and I want to go, and if I don't go, Faith isn't going either!' demanded Morgan.

'That's OK sweetie, you and Chloe can go too,' smiled her mum.

'Ha, I am gong to the party,' taunted Morgan.

Faith didn't say anything because she didn't care.

Morgan and Chloe went upstairs to plan how to get Faith in trouble so Morgan could get close to Rick. They got her dad's credit card and bought a million pound Gucci outfit.

It was the day of the party, *knock, knock,* their dad went to the door and got a shock. He was handed a form to sign. He signed it with anger. Suddenly Morgan appeared to blame it on Faith. Faith got grounded as planned.

While Morgan and Chloe were getting ready they were bickering over who was going to go with Rick. Faith was sitting in her room crying, knowing what her sister did. Morgan and Chloe went to the party, Morgan was pretending to be Faith and went to Rick and started flirting with him.

Back at home Faith was alone. Her mum and dad were out. The maid came upstairs to Faith with a D&G dress and a pair of gorgeous Gucci sandals and told her to go to the party as it was wrong that her sister had done.

'Thanks and all but how will I get there?' pleaded Faith.

The maid snapped her fingers and *bang* there was a flashy Mercedes and *snap* her hair and make-up were done. The maid hurried her along and warned her to be back before 12 o'clock, before her parents got home.

'Thanks, you're my Fairy God Maid!'

She arrived at the party. Her sister Morgan was at the ladies' room. Faith went up to Rick. 'Why did you change? You look different and prettier from a minute ago,' smiled Rick.

Faith just smiled and they started to dance and flirt. Her sister saw them together and stormed off in anger. Faith and Rick were really getting on. It was 11.55pm, Faith had to go. As Rick was about to kiss her, she just had to go. She ran out to the car park leaving her sandal behind her.

Next morning Rick came to the door with the sandal and Faith answered the door and smiled and apologised. Faith told him the whole story and he understood and they got back to where they started last night but didn't get to finish.

**Leanne Godfrey (14)**
Coleraine College, Coleraine

# The Pauper's Daughter

Once upon a time, there was a pauper called Adrian. He lived in an old log cabin in a clearing of Excalibur Forest. Adrian had a daughter called Arabella and her only wish was to find her true love. She had long blonde hair, cornflower blue eyes, a dazzling white smile and a peaches and cream complexion.

One day, Arabella was out in the forest picking wild berries for her father. She was having a wonderful time, strolling past gushing waterfalls, calm lakes, weeping willows and wild flowers. Deciding to take a break, she sat down on an old tree stump and was immediately surrounded by rabbits, birds and squirrels. Stroking the adoring animals around her, she noticed in the corner of her eye, three sparkling fairies. Looking again, she saw they carried tiny wands and had dainty wings on their backs. Bending down for a closer look, she saw one fairy was blue, one was red and one was yellow.

'We can grant you one wish,' squeaked the fairies.

Arabella thought for a moment and said, 'I wish I could find my true love.' The fairies waved their wands in unison and disappeared. Startled, she looked around and saw a handsome young man coming towards her. Sweeping her up into his arms, he walked towards his horse.

Arabella knew her wish had come true and was very happy.

**Laura Hall (14)**
**Coleraine College, Coleraine**

# Magical Match

*(Based on a Cinderella's story)*

Becky woke up at 6 o'clock on the dot and sneaked out of her bedroom window and went to meet her friend Tori. They were going to get a train to Manchester to watch the Manchester United match.

Becky had to sneak out as her mum grounded her as she skipped school to get the tickets.

They made it safely to the Manchester stadium and they entered a competition to win tickets to the annual team dance. Becky really wanted to win as she fancied Cristiano Ronaldo.

The match began, Man United were playing Chelsea. Half-time and United were winning 1-0 and the results of the competition were called out, 'Seats 55B and 56C.'

'That's us,' Becky cried, she was so excited, she was finally going to meet her footballing heroes.

The match ended, United won 3-0. Becky and Tori were so excited, she was going to meet her football heroes and get their autographs. Becky's heart skipped a beat when Cristiano asked her to dance. They got on well.

Just as he was going to ask Becky for her number, her phone alarm went off and as she took her phone out of her pocket, her match ticket fell out.

Becky had to go to be back home in time before her mum found out she was missing.

Cristiano wanted to see Becky again, so he took her ticket to the management to find out where she lived. He got her number and arranged a proper date.

**Hollie Hayes  (14)**
**Coleraine College, Coleraine**

# The Man And The Crow

Long, long ago in the heart of Ireland lived an old man and a crow. The man was called Tom. He always kept to himself and was always on his own except for the company of a crow. Tom lived in a big house in the country. Roots and weeds would grow in the garden and the house was nearly falling apart. As people walked past they could see Tom sitting by the window, just staring at anything he could see.

Day in day out all that was heard was the sound of the crow flying and squawking around the house, inside and out. Until one day something strange had happened. Tom was nowhere to be seen in his corner by the window. This was very unusual. The crow was still squawking but only inside. A strong farmer was chosen amongst the curious crowd standing outside to go into the house. He walked to the door but it was locked. So the farmer walked round to a window and broke the glass. When the glass was broken a strong smell quickly came from the house, which nearly made the farmer sick. As strong as he was, he covered his nose with his hand and climbed inside. The crow started to fly around his head squawking louder and louder trying to peck at his face. The farmer got away from the crow and ended up in the kitchen where the smell was very strong. The farmer let out a scream, which the crowd outside could hear very clearly. In front of the farmer lay Tom as white as a ghost and as stiff as a board with no movement at all. It was clear to the strong farmer that Tom was dead.

100 years later the legend still continues changing each time it is told. People say that when you walk by Tom's old house the squawking of the crow can still be heard and Tom can be seen sitting alone staring out the window. True or false? We will never know.

**Jill Davis (14)**
**Coleraine College, Coleraine**

# The Queen's New Shoes

*(Inspired by The Emperor's New Clothes)*

My story is like the Emperor's New Clothes only it's about the Queen's new shoes.

The Queen of England always had nice shoes. She had lots of shoes that had been designed especially for her. She had her own shoemaker. Her shoes were unique. It was coming up to Christmas and the Queen ordered her shoemaker to have her new blue shoes ready for Christmas Day. She wanted the new shoes ready for her annual Christmas Day speech.

The shoemaker listened to her ideas and worked night and day on the shoe design.

Finally he had the design. Now all he needed was the material.

The next day he went into Harrods to purchase the material. He was keen to get started. In his workshop he measured the material and cut the material to the size of the Queen's petite feet. It was two weeks to Christmas and the shoemaker thought he had plenty of time to make the shoes. He carefully stitched the shoes and hammered the heels into place.

Two days before Christmas and the shoes were finished. The Queen had an engagement in Wales so the shoemaker was going to leave the shoes at the palace on Christmas Eve.

Christmas Eve came and the shoemaker had lost a shoe. What was he going to do? The Queen couldn't wear just one shoe. He searched high and low for the shoe but still couldn't find it.

The day had come and the Queen was waiting on her new shoes. The shoemaker walked into the room where the Queen was sitting.

'Where are my shoes?' she questioned in an imperious voice.

'Your Majesty, can't you see them?' the shoemaker answered.

'Of course I can't see them,' Her Majesty replied.

'They're here in my hands,' the shoemaker said as he walked over to her.

The Queen looked puzzled. The shoemaker knelt down and put her shoes on.

The Queen of England walked down the hall and everyone told her that she looked amazing. At the end of the hall stood her youngest grandchild William, who looked at her feet and asked why she had no shoes on.

**Henrietta Dickey  (14)**
**Coleraine College, Coleraine**

# The Dreadful Sounds

It happened over fifty years ago, though you can still see and hear everything that went on that dreadful night. You can still hear the shouting from the girl and her boyfriend as they argued walking across the Bann Bridge. As the seemingly cheerful and likeable girl turned round to hit her boyfriend, he struck back accidentally pushing her over the wall of the bridge.

As she screamed, her boyfriend went to grab her hand. He was too late and with terrifying screams she landed with a huge splash in the river. His senses told him to jump in after her and as he leapt from the wall of the bridge into the water to save her, everything went black.

About an hour later he opened his eyes in horror to find himself alone on the bank. He knew his girlfriend was dead.

Though her boyfriend did call the police, he couldn't handle his loss so he decided to commit suicide by jumping back into the river. They searched for many days but the bodies were never recovered.

Now it's said that if you are standing on the bridge at night you can hear the terrible screams of the young girl falling in. You can also see her struggling against the current in the freezing water. Then you see her and her boyfriend walking hand in hand on the river. It is said he committed suicide because of a broken heart.

Would you chance walking across this bridge at night?

**Samantha Logan  (13)**
**Coleraine College, Coleraine**

# Cursed With A Kiss

This is the story of a Crystal Armstrong who was cursed by the witch of the Black Forest. Crystal was very beautiful and always got kissed by the men she desired.

The jealous witch who lived in the forest did not like this because Crystal was very vain.

One day while walking in the forest, Crystal heard a very unusual sound. She was very curious and followed this noise. She came to a tree but it was as black as night and its leaves, dead. She walked up and touched it and a voice yelled, 'You enjoyed being kissed but let's see how you like it when you cannot!'

The witch appeared in front of her and kissed her on the lips and with her magic pushed her away. Crystal fell to the ground and ran away in fear. She told her father of this and her father did not listen but instead brought in three men.

Forgetting what the witch said, she kissed each one of them. They reacted strangely. They choked, blood poured out of their mouths and their lips turned blue. In a quick ten seconds, they dropped dead.

She realised she could never kiss again or her beaus would drop dead. She went crazy and felt neglected.

Crystal never ate or slept. She died three years later. The witch of course had a terrible secret. All Crystal had to do, to get the curse lifted was ... to say 'please'.

**Becky Andrews  (14)**
Coleraine College, Coleraine

# A Day In The Life Of A Cavewoman

*(Revenge Is Sweet!)*

I woke up in my cave one morning, wearing my leopard-skin dress, as usual when I noticed that my family were still sleeping. So I got up quietly and went outside to get breakfast. I decided that I wanted fish so I walked to the lake.

When I got there I found a long stick on the ground and waited until I saw a fish then I fiercely stabbed the stick into the water and I caught the fish first time! When I lifted it out I shook it dry and brought it back to my cave.

Back home everybody had woken up and when they saw me with the fish they wanted some, but I refused and made them get their own. When they had all gone on the hunt for food I made a fire to cook my fish on but when I went to collect it, it was gone!

I knew that someone had stolen it and it was probably my sister, so I went out to the forest and collected red berries. Even though they looked tasty I knew that they were poisonous and would make me very sick if I ate them!

So I brought them home and set them on a leaf looking very tempting. Shortly after this my sister returned with a fish that looked exactly like mine but I didn't say anything. I left the berries on a rock (knowing that she would steal them too) and I went for a walk.

When I returned she told me that she felt sick! I told her, 'That's what you get for stealing my fish!'

**Carly Spratt (13)**
**Friends' School, Lisburn**

# The Beast Of Bree

The daylight faded away, darkness fell like a thick blanket laid down on top of the little village at the edge of Dark Wood Forest.

During the day, Bree was a lovely little village, with kind and welcoming people. But when darkness fell, everyone rushed back to their houses. There they locked the doors, bolted the windows and pulled the curtains. It suddenly became a ghost town, no movement and not a person to be seen anywhere.

For when darkness fell, it was rumoured that the forest became alive with movement and eerie noises. The villagers said, a couple of nights every year, strange creatures with human-sized bodies and wolf-like attributes came out of the deep, dark forest. It was rumoured that unsuspecting villagers disappeared from their homes in the middle of the night, and it is said that they were never seen alive again!

**Marc Cairns (14)**
Friends' School, Lisburn

# A Day In The Life Of John Terry

I raise the cup above my head and the crowd go wild as the sun glistens off the side of the wonderful trophy, and then, I wake. I take a few moments to wake up and then the thought crosses my mind, the real thing is today. I clamber down the stairs still drowsy but am happily refreshed by the sweet sound of 'Blue is the colour', echoing around my bedroom from my mobile phone. I said, 'Hello?' and the familiar voice of my brother Paul put my day into perspective.

Today was the day Chelsea FC would answer all critics, today was the day the name Chelsea FC would go down in history, today was the day we would lift the cup.

The trophy of the English first division had left Chelsea's trophy cabinet baron for fifty years, but today was the day it returned to the 'Bridge'. This day was special to me as I, John Terry would be the first captain to lift the trophy since Roy Bentley in nineteen fifty-five.

Since my glory days as a Chelsea youngster this was the day I had missed school and bled for. As I drove through the gates of the player's entrance at Stamford Bridge, the nausea in my stomach stunned my brain. It then fizzled with excitement as I saw the huge Chelsea badge on the wall of the 'Shed'.

My excitement was reimbursed when I pulled on my shirt and bounced into the heavenly atmosphere in Stamford Bridge. The match passed like lightning and when the final whistle blew to a one-nil Chelsea win, the crowd were ecstatic. As the ground staff prepared the presentation platform my body shivered with excitement and then the announcer called for me to approach the stage.

With one glance at the trophy I grasped it with both hands and threw it into the air. This would soon be normality, just a day in the life of *John Terry.*

**Stuart Allen  (13)**
**Friends' School, Lisburn**

# Self-Harm - Are You At Risk?

Imagine feeling so bad that you want to hurt yourself to feel better. When you ask for help, no one's listening and you cry yourself to sleep most nights. There's one thing you've found that seems to make you feel better, so you carry on doing it, in actual fact, you are addicted and can't stop. The problem is that you are injuring yourself and doing your body harm.

Self-harming can scar you for life or even leave you needing hospital treatment. More young people than ever before are harming themselves. Childline have actually reported that the number of young people calling in for help and advice on self-harm has risen by 30% in the past year. 62% of those callers (2,666 people) admitted to cutting themselves using razor blades, knifes or sharp pieces of broken glass. Others confessed to purposely burning or bruising themselves or pulling out their hair. With all the added pressures of teenage life, many turn to secretly hurting themselves, in order to cope with their feelings and emotions.

The idea that pain can make your situation better, may sound strange to some, but to those who do it, it is just a way of coping. Triggers may include low self-esteem, sexual, physical or emotional abuse, stress, anger, bullying or family pressures. They find it impossible to express their feelings openly, so instead they'll take it out on their bodies, to make themselves feel in control.

For people to stop hurting themselves, they have to deal with their feelings, without resorting to pain and they'll probably need your help. It may be difficult to know how to help them. Asking or telling them to stop won't work and may even make it worse, as it is another pressure to deal with. You should let them know that you are there if they need someone to talk to and that you are not judging them by offering support. It is a big issue for people to deal with on their own.

**Kerrie Coyle  (14)**
**Friends' School, Lisburn**

# In Your Skin Or Under Your Skin?

Am I too fat? Should I get a new hairstyle or wardrobe? These are questions teenagers ask themselves every day. Girls in particular are constantly worrying about their body image.

Now, there must be an influence somewhere that makes teenagers want to be anything but themselves. That influence is the media.

On TV, magazines, everywhere you go you see skinny, beautiful celebrities living a fabulous lifestyle. It seems that to girls it is a way of showing them what you have to look like. There is a certain stereotype which everyone likes. 'I think you'd look nicer if you went blonde like Scarlett Johannsen' or, 'Maybe you should exercise more often, to get a nice Hollywood figure'.

Those are comments that come up all the time, you never hear, 'I think you look great' or, 'Your hair is so nice, makes you stand out'.

No, it's always looking to a celebrity to complete your image. The pressures from the media make girls especially unhappy with their image. The number of anorexics and people with bulimia have gone up over the years and they say this increase is due to media influences.

What this world needs is to widen its categories of beautiful people, so that it isn't just skinny blondes.

There are many types of beautiful people but the sad thing is no one really notices it. Bridget Jones is still loveable even with her curvy figure and constant embarrassment! There are also lots of other stars who are beautiful who don't fit the stereotype.

I think the most beautiful people are the ones with beautiful hearts. Happy, friendly people who are happy with who they are. That's what the teenagers out there need to do, take a look at their inner beauty because in the end that is the most important thing.

Everyone has their flaws but, everyone can shine if they know they have a beautiful heart.

**Debbie Cupples (14)**
**Friends' School, Lisburn**

# Barbie: A Young Girl's Dream?

Who's that tall, blonde bombshell with the 16-inch waist and big blue eyes? It's Barbie of course! Everyone knows that young girls dream of being just like their idol - Barbie, but just how unrealistic is their dream? Many girls who long to fit this description start developing serious eating disorders, such as anorexia, at the tender age of seven. Children who are larger than average often feel worthless and have extremely low self-esteem. Being thin doesn't make you a better person.

Clothing manufacturers such as GAP also help to damage confidence because their children's clothing range is as follows: S, M, L, XL, XXL. An average 10-year-old would be wearing size XL which would make them feel fat even though they are perfectly normal. This is sending the wrong message to young girls about their body size. In Next, shoppers are able to buy the same outfit for a two-year-old and a thirteen-year-old. This means that children no longer have a defined childhood and can be wearing teenage clothes at age three.

Hopefully trends are changing, a new Barbie in the US has just been released in size 16, this could be a major breakthrough. In ten years time hopefully trends will have changed and young girls will not make themselves ill in order to be like their idols. If everyone in the world looked like Barbie it would be a very boring place to live, as they say variety is the 'spice' of life!

**Hannah Baxter  (14)**
**Friends' School, Lisburn**

# Use Your Head

Most of the tragic accidents that occur involving young children and quad bikes are mainly due to irresponsible actions. As these bikes are capable of speeds of approximately 50mph and are also quite heavy, *no one* should ever ride one unless they are properly protected and have been instructed on how to ride it. So if parents decide to buy their child a quad bike, they are the ones that must accept responsibility to ensure that they teach him/her to ride it within their capabilities, providing them with all the recommended safety gear and educate them to *always* wear their helmet - no excuses!

The best advice for first time quad riders (and non-swimmers) is: don't jump in at the deep end! There are many quad riding tracks all over Northern Ireland and I'm sure if you can't find one, your local dealer would be happy to give you the 'Idiot's Guide' to quad riding.

In conclusion, it's quite clear that if young riders aren't given guidance they won't take the right precautions. It is a proven fact that the greatest cause of serious injuries on ATVs is due to people not wearing helmets. Get into the habit of wearing one and never forget it. Okay, there will always be some foolhardy idiots willing to risk life and limb, but most respond positively to sensible advice. So our final and most important piece of advice to you is *never* go on a quad without a helmet.

**Ryan Woodburn  (14)**
**Friends' School, Lisburn**

# A Day In The Life Of A British Soldier
# On Bloody Sunday (30th January 1972)

Patrolling an anti-internment march in Londonderry, I watched with enthusiasm. Some three thousand people were marching. I watched them coming to a road block and a few of them were discussing matters with the RUC. Out of the corner of my eye I saw hooligans throwing stones at us. I shouted to my fellow colleagues. Fear crept up my body rapidly. First through my toes, next my knees started to tremble, a shiver was sent shooting up my back and my ears were ringing. Finally my eyes started to run. The hooligans amounted to around one hundred and fifty, the RUC brought in a water cannon. Stolen CS gas canisters were being forced under our noses. I remember feeling determined. I wanted peace in my country and the only way to get it was to fight for it. The RUC and some of my friends in the army made over fifty arrests in less than fifteen minutes. Those brave, brave men. Representing unionism in Northern Ireland.

I saw the crowds clearly. It was obvious they were making their way for an IRA sniper. Live rounds were being fired. I remember thinking of the people they were hitting, wondering how they felt. People ran amok. Within minutes people were falling to the ground like skittles. Were these innocent people? Was this sheer unadulterated murder? And was I to blame for somebody's death?

**Lyndsey Shields (14)**
Friends' School, Lisburn

# The Christmas Spoof

Ellie's arm was aching. It was Christmas Eve and she had spent all day putting up Christmas lights in her village. No one else would do it. They were all too scared. This village held an old and mysterious tale. Every year at Christmas no one stayed in the village.

The tale goes that as the mist comes over the town on Christmas Eve a man comes also. A man feared by every person he meets.

Ellie didn't believe in the ghost story and was determined to stay. She would be alone but would prove to everyone that there was no such thing as ghosts.

Everyone else had left. Ellie was just about to go home when she heard a footstep. She turned around, slowly, and there in front of her was a man who looked very ill.

He whispered into her ear, 'Come with me.' Immediately she felt very afraid. He took her to his car and when the door was shut he began to laugh.

'I had you there didn't I? You were petrified. This old town needs to wise up. I played a joke with my uncle when I was only six and they still believe in it!'

Ellie was amazed. She had been right. It was just a story. Ellie was safe and well.

She wasn't going to tell the secret but everyone would now spend Christmas at home.

After all, if a girl managed to stay there on her own everyone else would be safe as well.

Wouldn't they?

**Elizabeth Wallace  (14)**
**Friends' School, Lisburn**

# A Day In The Life Of Carl Barât

*I have written this in the style of a diary entry. It is based on a true event, but this is what I think could have happened beforehand. It is told from the point of view of Carl Barât, co-frontman of the band The Libertines. He is thinking about his best friend Pete Doherty who he hasn't spoken to in months, and who is due to be leaving prison that evening.*

I couldn't sleep much last night; the anticipation of the upcoming day was keeping me awake. I gave up at around 5.30 this morning so I went for a walk to clear my head. It was silent in a way you wouldn't think possible; it made me forget about everything. Sometimes you don't realise how quiet the world can be. No cars, no people, just birds and morning sun.

Though it was this thought that made me think of Peter. He couldn't see all this where he was. Silence was probably non-existent, the sun a novelty and certainly no birds. Being kept away from the things worth living for; Pete couldn't exist like that. I wondered how his experiences would have changed him.

I continued to walk until people began going to their normal jobs, their normal schools, doing whatever it is normal people do. I don't know what normal is. Ever since I'd met Pete, there'd been no such thing.

I began to think about what it would be like when we saw each other later. It had been ages since we'd so much as spoken to each other. I was thinking he wouldn't want to see me. I felt that he thought it was my fault he was in prison. The most I could do was go and greet him. As I thought about my motives I decided I had to go, show him that I still cared. He was the best friend I'd ever had.

**Amy Traynor (14)**
Friends' School, Lisburn

# Are We Obsessed With Celebrities

Every day, in the newspapers, on the news and in magazines, there is something about celebrities. From David Beckham's affair with Rebecca Loos to the royal family not being able to handle William and Harry. Many people have affairs but just because David Beckham is famous then it's front page news. It's the same with the royal family. Princes William and Harry are just having a good time while they're young but it seems to me like they are being penalised for doing so.

We must spend millions of pounds each year on buying gossip magazines about them. We never seem to leave them alone. The press follow them everywhere just to find a new exciting story from going to their homes and following them on holiday. I'm sure you'll agree with me when I say they have a right to their own privacy.

Having celebrities in the newspaper day after day may become a strain in female teenagers' lives.

When you are at this age you tend to dream of the 'perfect body' and you will go to any extreme to get it. Many younger people look at magazines and see these celebrities with the 'perfect body' and if they want it so badly they could go on diets which could turn serious.

I believe that we, as the public, love to read about celebrities' problems and embarrassing moments. It seems like it's a relief to hear that even famous people have their problems but when it comes down to it, their private life is their own business and we should really just leave them to it.

**Amanda Thompson (14)**
Friends' School, Lisburn

# Young People Need To Change. And Quick!

Young people today are increasingly becoming more and more obese. It is now a common fact that obesity is a rapidly growing problem among the younger generation and people need to wake up to the facts or serious problems will occur. These people need to do something to save their health and lives from being ruined.

From being obese the health issues are enormous and are potentially life threatening. The chance of having a heart attack is dramatically increased with having the extra fat in the arteries which supply the heart with the vital oxygen it needs. People who are so obese feel they can't socialise and take part in everyday activities so it would be in their best interests to lose weight.

Young people who are obese generally feel down and unhappy and this isn't good for them as it could effect schoolwork and anything they do.

These young people need to do something about their state if they want to have a happier life and a longer one, they need to take action. The best thing they can do is find an active interest they enjoy and join a club. This will help them lose their excess weight and will get them in better shape and they will most definitely feel a lot better and healthier.

They need your help and encouragement but they can definitely do it. If they want to save their lives and live a happier one they need to do something about it. And quick!

**Glenn Whitten (14)**
**Friends' School, Lisburn**

# City Of The Damned

*Jess had just woken up with a throbbing headache, her eyesight was blurred and she had no idea where she was. She couldn't remember anything, but her head felt as if it had just been hit with a sledgehammer. All she wanted was to get home!*

As Jess climbed to her feet, she heard a crackly, metallic voice behind her. Startled, she spun around.

'Who are you?' she said panicking, 'and where am I?' Slowly everything was starting to come back into focus. Quickly, she looked in the direction the robot was pointing.

In the distance she could see a cluster of buildings, which looked completely different than a normal town, but in an eerie way it was similar to pictures of New York she had seen on the TV.

'What's the date?' she asked the robot.

'22nd of August, 3005,' it replied.

'It couldn't be!' she said out loud, slowly realising that somehow she had travelled 1000 years into the future.

In that dark, silent night, Jess just sat down and she cried. She cried long into the night, then she realised, she couldn't just sit there forever.

She got up and walked in the direction of the city, for hours she walked, even as the sun got higher in the sky, bringing a horrible heat and a deep thirst.

As she came closer to the town, she worried more and more about what she would find there. Eventually she reached it, only to find it was completely deserted. She looked everywhere, when on the ground she noticed a faded newspaper.

Looking at the date she noticed that it was dated December 2994. Over 10 years before! 'Oh no!' she realised, 'this place must have been deserted ever since.'

Now, can she ever get home?

**Adam Woods  (14)**
**Friends' School, Lisburn**

# The Dog Lord Rinose

Rinose was 7 foot tall and had more teeth than a shark. It was pitch-black in colour and had fire-red eyes. Its main hatred was for cats, all cats. Not one cat has been in sight of the beast and lived to tell the tale.

The giant creature weighing in at 433 pounds can run at speeds of up to 1500mph! When it's hunting you don't see it move and when it strikes, one bite and you're dead, stone dead! The strange thing is that there is not one bite mark or even a drop of blood, it just looks like you're sleeping then one gulp and that's it, time for the next victim to be killed.

There is no dog like it, whenever it runs every dog within a mile starts howling then drops down to the floor like they're praising Rinose. Dogs have been known to sacrifice their pups to keep the lord of all dogs happy! But in a way you can't blame them for praising a 7 foot, 433 pound killing machine that in one swipe could kill a dog no problem then gulp it down like a drink of fresh water, can you?

The dog may be a myth to some eyes but the majority of the viewers believe in the massive beast, they may have only got a 5 second glimpse but in their hearts he exists and they fear when he will strike again.

**Stephen Uprichard (11)**
Friends' School, Lisburn

# War

I never asked to leave my home and family. It wasn't my decision to oust a regime which had condoned such genocide and terrorism. However, world history is shaped by the actions of ordinary people following the orders of those in authority, so like the many before me, I had no choice. Now my dreams are plagued by the corpses that seem to litter the streets of Basra, and the fearful eyes of Iraqi civilians haunt my steps. It is only now that I realise the extent of the power within my weapon. It is only now I see first hand the dread it can instil and the mutilation it may cause. Please forgive me and all the soldiers. In war it is easy to forget there is a human being in the cross-hairs.

We were only out on the street playing football. The fight broke out just behind us, and the bullets started flying. We tried to run. All but one of us succeeded. They say they are sorry. They say they never meant to do it, that the shot was not aimed at our friend. Our friend has a name. Mohammed. He has an identity. We each have our own identity. We are all different, with differing opinions and beliefs on important issues. We are losing our identities. The world sees us all as ruthless Muslims with a strong desire to destroy the western world. Somebody please realise that it's not like that. In war everything becomes distorted.

**Susanna Elliott (12)**
**Friends' School, Lisburn**

# A Day In The Life Of A Spider

I got up this morning at about 8 o'clock. I crawled out of my cobweb to look for something to eat when a colossal ogre with two legs and huge shapes hanging at either side walked past and tried to stand on me. I crawled hurriedly into a hole just in time as a second after I moved a foot came crashing down from above.

I couldn't find anything to eat so I gave up and crawled gloomily back home to my cobweb. When I got there, my children were already awake and had caught a few flies. I told my children that they would soon outsmart their master and they choked as they were eating because they couldn't stop laughing.

At lunchtime I took my children for a walk around the front garden. They loved the fresh air but it was soon wrecked. I went in to see how my wife was doing while leaving the children to their own devices. When I came back out however they were cornered by a giant bug. Even though we were poisonous spiders, their poison was still pretty harmless. I snuck up behind the bug and bit him. Within seconds he was dead.

That night we had a party. The ogres (humans) who lived in the house heard the party and since the children weren't used to living in a house the ogres squashed them all. We were going to have a funeral but the family dog got to them first.

**Brendan Jacobson (13)**
**Friends' School, Lisburn**

# The Piano Man

Why are they prodding at me? Have I done something wrong? How did I get here? Why do they care? I don't remember what happened. They don't understand what I say. I don't even have a name. I seem to have this gift … I can play the piano to my emotions since no one knows my identity. They call me 'The Piano Man' because of this gift. I don't know if I have a family, when my birthday is, where I live. Well I live here now.

My bedroom is quite a small space in the hospital. Have I always been there? They run tests on me, with ink on my fingertips, taking my blood from my arms, and attach things to my chest. I don't know whether I want to find out where I came from or who I am. I could be a homeless person, or a bus driver or even … no one.

After lunch they let me go round to the piano and play for people that all have the same dress/robe thing as me. We all look the same. They like my up-beat music, but the slow, lonely music is more realistic. I know I'll get through this but it feels more and more hopeless every day.

But as the sun goes down, I sit on my own in this empty room wondering why? When? How? Who? What if? But questions don't answer themselves so I'll wait, and I'll play, for I am 'The Piano Man'.

**Sarah Glasgow (13)**
Friends' School, Lisburn

# Escape

I kept running even though I felt like my lungs were about to explode. I glanced back to see if I was still being followed. I was. It wasn't even my fault. Nobody had told me the rock was magic.

I saw a rock, picked it up and thought nothing about it again until the alarms went off. It wasn't as if the rock was in a special box or anything like that. Just sitting on a table.

Well there I was, heart pumping, being followed by armed guards, trying to escape from one of the most confusing buildings I've ever been in in my life. I wheeled round the corner just too late and crashed through the window. I closed my eyes tight and waited for the impact of the ground that would surely bring death.

But none came. I cautiously opened my eyes and saw to my absolute amazement that I was hovering just outside the window! I was so astounded that for a moment I couldn't move but when I saw that the guards were firing at me my blood ran cold. I thought with all my might about being far away from that place when I found myself in a completely strange country!

It was then that I realised that I must've been using the rock's powers with my mind! I took it out of my pocket and, sure enough it was glowing a satisfying golden colour. I grinned, imagining all I could do with the rock.

**Philip Harrison (13)**
**Friends' School, Lisburn**

# War

Here I lie awaiting to fulfil my destiny. Death. I stare out at the grey haze of a world. My eyes rest upon my captain in command, still bleeding but unable to muster a breath, his gun is clenched tightly in his bleeding palms. They call this protecting our country, dying for valour. But this is the barbaric path, which I have not chosen to live and die in, but have been drafted into. A half life.

The sun will soon set, casting darkness over the land. My gaze reverts to the framed picture of my family, their smiles enclosed in my mind forever. I've been told that I was the bait, as I am but a lad. Seventeen years I've been on this Earth and it is still as unjust as it ever was. But I mustn't complain, as pawns in chess don't matter, why then would it be any different in war?

Everyone in the trench is tense and drawn, more so than myself. But I suppose it is always worse to witness a full-blown death than to be the victim. I suppose I shall never know. I feel no fear, only repressed anger at the thought of the enemy killing people, for the sheer joy they get out of it. The picture of my family rests under my shirt, close to my heart. My time has come.

*A man lies on the dry blood-stained earth, shards of glass surround him, a picture by his side.*

**Susannah Hylands  (13)**
**Friends' School, Lisburn**

# A Short Story On Blueberry

Blueberry is my 13.2hh grey gelding pony. Blueberry's life isn't all that great at the moment. When I got a different pony on loan, I lent Blueberry to my friend. This was in the summer. I got to see him lots, although my friend put him out in a field for a while and as it was far away from her house, I could only see him through the hedge. I missed him lots. When my friend was ready to give him back to me, I couldn't wait to ride him home from her house which was just around the corner, for the first time in five months.

The morning I was going to get him, I was so excited. Just before we left to drive up, my friend's mum called and said she thought I wouldn't be able to ride him down, as he seemed a bit stiff from coming out of the field. I was so disappointed.

They had to go out, so they put him in the stable, for us to collect him. When we got up there, his hooves were as long as flippers and he had chronic laminitis.

The vet said that he should recover, but that was in October. We are waiting on his blood test results to see if he has an even worse disease called 'cushings'.

I am hoping and praying he doesn't. If he does, the worst day of my life will come, because he will have to be put down.

**Rebekah Hanna  (12)**
**Friends' School, Lisburn**

# The Lufylap!

The Lufylap is a sort of cross between a duck and a kangaroo. The Lufylap lives in a world that is very different to this one, full of fields and trees with not a single city.

They're playful creatures but are also very timid!

This is a story of when one day a little Lufylap got lost exploring and managed to stray into my world.

It all started one day in the middle of spring and I was at home over Easter with nothing to do. I decided to play football in the garden and all of a sudden I heard a strange cooing noise, so I then went and looked to see what it was and there it was, the funny creature. As I approached it, it started to shy away, so naturally I stopped moving and I slowly started to pull back. I had some chocolate from the day before and I offered it to the cute, little thing. The Lufylap cautiously came and nibbled a small bit from my hand, its face lit up and it scoffed the rest in seconds. The little guy looked lost so I tried to discover where it came from. It then unexpectedly started to communicate with me (telepathically I think) through my mind. It said it was lost, so I tried searching the internet for information on him but found nothing so I had to keep him and look after him as a pet. I called him Biscuits after him eating the chocolate.

**Adam Glass (13)**
**Friends' School, Lisburn**

# A Day In The Life Of A Farmer

At 6am I get up and have my breakfast and get dressed for the day ahead. I then go outside and let my 12 cattle out of the barn, where they have spent the night, and lead them into the field.

After this tiring task, I jump on the tractor and drive round to my smaller farm to check that everything there is OK.

One day when I drove round I found that the cattle had somehow knocked down the fence, and were just about to wander out onto the main road. I had to call some of my farmhands quickly and we repaired the damage. Nothing like this has ever happened since, but I check just to make sure.

Also at this farm I unfortunately have the tremendously exciting job of mucking out the stables where I keep my 2 horses. This normally takes me up to about 12pm. Before lunch I collect a silage bale on the spikes of the tractor to take back to the main farm, so that the cattle will have something to eat at night.

I go back to my house and get some lunch. The afternoon is spent clearing out the barn where the cattle stay overnight. I put fresh hay down and fill up their water bowls. If there is time I will also carry out any repairs needed about the farm or on the machinery. At about 4.30pm I go and bring my cattle back to the barn for the night. I get to bed about 9.30pm, as I have to get up early the next morning.

**Matthew Irwin (13)**
Friends' School, Lisburn

# My Favourite Holiday

My favourite holiday would have to be Orlando in Florida. There is an endless amount of things to do. You can go to theme parks, go karts, mini golf and clothes outlets.

The flight going there would have been boring but the entertainment was excellent because I could watch all of the new movies that aren't even in the cinema yet. The flight lasted for six hours.

The most fun thing were the theme parks. I went to 'Blizzard Beach', 'Universal Studios' and 'Busch Gardens'. Going on the roller coasters and seeing the wildlife was amazing.

At night we would sometimes go to a place called 'Kart World' or go to miniature golf courses.

America is by far my favourite holiday destination because it is so cheap for clothes compared to Northern Ireland. I spent most of my money in the 'Tommy Hilfiger' and 'Ralph Lauren' outlets because the clothes aren't anywhere near as dear as they are at home.

I stayed in a complex called 'Berkeley Lake'. There were about one hundred villas and each one of them had a swimming pool.

I loved the food over there because of the atmosphere and the people in the restaurants. It was reasonably expensive but it was worth every cent.

There wasn't one thing that I didn't enjoy about the holiday. It was so good that I went back again to the exact same place. I had even more fun and bought even more clothes than the first time.

**Bryan Hickland (13)**
**Friends' School, Lisburn**

# Reporting For Duty

The last few weeks in May 1940 saw the German army (Axis) advance through Holland and with the Belgium army capitulating, the news reaching the home front looked bleak. The worry was that the Axis forces would then attack the south of England ...

*3rd June 1940.*

Many young men were gathered together at Clifton Street in Belfast to join the RAF, one of these men was my grandfather, he knew a lot of people in the building, and many of them were never seen again in Northern Ireland.

There was an anxious wait for a couple of weeks until my grandfather got his letter. He was immediately recruited to Padgate to get kitted out before he was moved on to Wilmslow in Cheshire, where he was taught how to perform square bashing (drills) for a few months. He was finally moved to RAF Halton in Buckinghamshire where he was finally taught how to fix fighter and bomber planes. At the end of the course they had a written exam to fill in, which he passed with flying colours.

One of my grandfather's most scary moments when he was on guard duty at Halton with a professional boxer corporal Remington when they heard the whistle of a bomb which landed a mere quarter of a mile away from the camp perimeter.

He was then sent home on leave for a fortnight. He was immediately recruited to Church Fenton in Yorkshire where he would practice engineering on Blenheim hummer bombers.

**David Cumins (13)**
**Friends' School, Lisburn**

# A Day In The Life Of Nikki Gibson

*Ding-a-ling-a-ling, ding-a-ling-a-ling!*
'Nicola! Get up!'
That's the first thing I hear when I wake up. 'Christopher, leave me alone!' I shout at my immature ten-year-old brother.
'But Nicola you have to get up, you have school. *Wake up!*' he screams in my ear.
Eventually after 10 minutes of shouting, I get up to face the day ahead of me. After I get dressed, grab my lunch, I run to get the bus where I meet up with my friends. I chat on the bus and we mess around, then we get to Smithfield and have to get off. I get to school all rosy-cheeked and flustered after being chased up the hill by my friends trying to pull me down by my schoolbag.
I quickly do my locker and get up to collect just on time to hear my name being called out. I sit with my friends and after a long day of school I get the bus home and go up to my room.
Usually after school I would phone my friends but I always get interrupted by my brother shouting, 'Nicola, are you still on the phone?' And I would reply, *'Yes!'* and he would shout again, 'Well get off it!' Then we would get into a big fight and I would end up having to hang up anyway. Then I would do my homework and get into bed.

**Jessica Hughes (13)**
**Friends' School, Lisburn**

# A Day In The Life Of Cinderella

The sound of the cockerel wakes me up on a typical Monday morning. I suppose I should go get everything ready, so I can be prepared for when the terrible two wake up.

I don't really have much time to do anything for myself, I'm usually cleaning or acting like a servant for my two step-sisters.

After the breakfast bells have been rung I help the terrible two get dressed. Their rooms are usually a mess so I have to tidy them before I start anywhere else.

All I ever do is clean, cook and wait hand and foot on my step-mother and step-sisters.

While I'm cleaning I usually sing a song or two and talk to the mice that dwell in the staircase. The rest of my family (my step-mother and step-sisters) are usually out socialising or shopping for fancy ornaments.

After I've cleaned the house from top to bottom, I then feed the animals and muck out the horse. By the time that's done the terrible twosome are home with my beloved step-mother.

Their demands come flooding in for what they want for dinner.

If I don't meet their demands I won't get to go to the ball.

The dinner is done and I'm left to do all the washing. Climbing up the stairs tired and weary, I go to bed, it's the only time I have when I can dream and have time to myself.

**Nikki Gibson  (13)**
Friends' School, Lisburn

# The Cave

I sat there battered and bruised from the fight. My mind was pounding. What was I going to do?

The three girls had done this to me before, but I had had enough.

I ran as fast as my legs could carry me, not knowing where I was going. I tripped and tumbled down what seemed to be a deep, muddy hole. I landed with a thud, on my back. I squirmed around on the muddy ground, trying to get rid of the cramp in my back. When the cramp had eased off I got to my feet, amazed how big this hole was. It was a cave!

I stumbled about trying to find something, anything. I knew I couldn't go back. I was lost in a cave.

Suddenly! As if from nowhere, I saw an amazingly bright light that glowed in the darkness. I walked towards it to see what it was. It seemed to take an age, step after step I just kept walking, but the light didn't get any closer.

Frustrated, I started to run, my feet crunching against the twigs and gravel on the ground.

Finally, I reached the glowing light when I realised it was a round sphere, floating in the middle of the room. I was astounded at the neon, glowing ball. I decided it would be my secret. I retraced my steps for what seemed an age, to finally see a glimmer of light at the end of a tunnel. I was free!

**Katie Payne  (13)**
**Friends' School, Lisburn**

# The Beggar

I stand here alone, nobody cares for me. There are people rushing around. They all hurry along the street with their many bags, having just spent hundreds of pounds shopping and not one of them sympathises with this poor beggar man. They probably all think that I'm some horrible, dirty criminal waiting to rob them of all the things in their highly strung lives. I've even heard pretentious mothers saying to their small children, 'Don't go near him, he's a *bad* man!' This hurts, it's unbearable.

I've suffered much in my life. I was born into a loveless family. My mother was always busy complaining about my father who, in turn, spent his time arguing with my mother and drinking. I was an only child. My first memories are of hiding behind the great armchair (or what seemed great) in the tiny, little council house that was ours. With the mould growing on the wall behind me I listened to my father's shouts and my mother's roars. I sobbed silently to myself and wished to be anywhere else. I ran away when I was 16. No one ever looked for me. I soon got hooked on drink and drugs.

Here I am now, a penniless, hopeless beggar with nothing to remember in his life but pain and misery. I can't afford food, let alone drink and drugs. I want to help myself, I want to start again. What can I do? I might as well be dead.

**Katy Fair  (13)**
**Friends' School, Lisburn**

# Four Steps To Insanity

I sit alone.

Twelve years ago I last saw my mum. Ten months ago my sister ran away. I'll never know why she left. Seven months ago, the last time I saw my dad, the pills lying beside his cold corpse; he wore a frown upon his face.

Four months I've been here, this 'home'. I feel like I'm on one of those reality TV shows, but there's no prize, just clipboards and monitoring. They're meant to help me; they give me quiet time, to think about everything.

I just see images, flashing, always haunting me. I can't sleep, they're in my dreams, I can't talk, they're in my mouth, horrible, sour vomit that will never be thrown up. Mum, in the cold bed, wires beeping, and then the one long beep. Dad on the sofa, one arm clutching the family photo, the other lying limply across his chest.

I shudder. A man walks past my door, he smiles, robotically, he's been grinning at 'problem children' for longer than I've been alive, his deep wrinkles tell no lies. I can't stand it; every noise freaks me out, bringing me one step closer to insanity.

I can't cope, I'm suddenly gasping for air, I run down the corridor, the emptiness so eerie, I run through the open door, the cold wind stings my face. Just across the road brakes squeal. Where should I go? I've no choice …

Heaven is great, they say, but Hell is the only thing I'll ever know.

**Poppy Harvey (13)**
**Friends' School, Lisburn**

# Thunder Cry

*Crash!* The sound of the thunder had continued on throughout that night. Inevitably, came the lightning. I was worried deeply as I had seen things that freaked me out throughout the duration of the day. The first and most disturbing sight was a cat eating a snake whole. This incident made me think that there was something wrong.

I was sitting, watching TV, with my younger brother and suddenly all we were watching was static. I went to check if the aerial was knocked out. The annoying thing was, it was pouring outside and the aerial was on the roof. I told my brother Michael to wait in the living room while I went outside up the wall to climb on to the roof. I fixed the aerial and went back inside. I went back into the living room.

No Michael, this is what really made my skin crawl.

I called out, 'Michael, Michael, where are you? This isn't funny. I'm really scared.' Suddenly the lights went out. I slowly paced back into the living room. In white letters, the TV screen spelt out, 'I know who you are'. I turned on my toes and standing in the doorway was Michael in the grasps of the man with a hook.

Later we found ourselves gagged and dreading the end.

**Niall Diffin (12)**
Friends' School, Lisburn

# The Mummification

My name is Papyrus and I am an embalmer. I live in Cairo and today my job is special. Pharaoh has died and I was called to prepare him for his new life in the next world.

Tutankhamun's body arrived yesterday. My first task is to clean it. I am sad to see my king dead but also very proud to be chosen for this job.

My friends and I have to eviscerate the body and to put the organs into canopic jars. After that, his body will be dried during 70 days with a product called natron.

My favourite task will be the last but not least: the mummification. I would like my pharaoh to be the most beautiful. I have done this job for a long time and know it perfectly. I am probably the best embalmer in all Egypt and this is the reason why I was chosen. Tutankhamun will be mummified with linen wrappings before being locked up for eternity.

In the country, people are in despair. A lot of offerings were given to him to be put with his body into the pyramid. It is amazing to see how loved he was.

But he was also a king who knew how to command respect. He was powerful and clever enough to keep his throne until his death.

And my opinion about that is different from the official version. Thanks to my job, I know exactly the reason why Tutankhamun died …

**Camille Bonnel  (12)**
**Friends' School, Lisburn**

# Labour Win Historic 3rd Term

Tony Blair recently became the first Labour Prime Minister in history to win a 3rd successive term even though it was with a reduced majority of about 66 seats. I think this is good for the UK because it gives us a more diverse representation in Parliament.

The other main talking point of the general election was the number of seats won by the Liberal Democrats. They had their best election since the 1920s. In my opinion one of the worst results of the election was the election of the somewhat controversial MP George Galloway. He is known to be a personal friend of the former dictator, Saddam Hussein.

On a more local scale, in Northern Ireland, the DUP won 50% of the seats up for grabs. This is a big disappointment to those in support of the Good Friday agreement as the DUP are an anti-agreement party. The general election overall turnout was quite low overall with one of the highest turnouts in Northern Ireland.

Tony Blair has now been admitted to hospital with a slipped disc. This shows the pressure which comes with the title Prime Minister. He has also had some minor heart scares in the past. This job would not be for me because of the high level of stress and decision-making which comes with this title. I now think that in the not so distant future Gordon Brown, the now Chancellor of the Exchequer, will become the new leader of the Labour Party.

**Stuart Hughes (13)**
Friends' School, Lisburn

# Grandma

I let my mind wander back to when Grandma was with us. She wasn't the ordinary grandma, she was unique, different and stood out from my friends' grandmas. I guess that it is probably because she didn't sit in an armchair all day with a cup of tea and her knitting on her lap, she lived life to the full, just like anyone should have the freedom to do so. The more I reflect on those days, Grandma did my French homework, sang me 'Twinkle, Twinkle Little Star' or made my dinner, the more I cry and the more I think how lucky I was, but I can't stop wishing she would be here helping me to choose the right foundation for my skin tone and help me work out what the circumference of a circle is.

I could look up to Grandma, unlike my parents, who spent most of their time at work or down the pub. It was as if she was God. I hung on to her like I was a little child, although I was eleven when she left me. Even though I had almost everything a little girl my age would have begged her parents for, I felt there was something else that was missing that I just had to have, but the only person who gave it to me was Grandma. Now that Grandma is gone I feel lonely and isolated from the feeling that she expressed towards me and that feeling was love.

**Laura Johnston (13)**
Friends' School, Lisburn

# A Day In The Life Of A Friends' School Pupil

I awoke very early in the morning, at about 7am. I got dressed, in my many green clothes, and made my way downstairs for breakfast. I ate, brushed my teeth, picked up my very heavy schoolbag and left to get the bus.

On my way down, my friend phoned me to tell me that all the buses had left. *Great*, I thought, *I'll be left on my own at the bus stop in the freezing cold and I'll be late for school.* I arrived at the stop and my dad, who took me down, drove off and left me in the cold. It started to rain and, best of all, I'd forgotten my umbrella.

I arrived in school, soaked to the skin and signed into the late room. I made my way across the school to my first lesson, Spanish. I met up with my friend who reminded me of a test that I'd forgotten about completely.

I emerged from Spanish, 35 minutes later, clutching my test paper, that was bearing the numbers 3/10. I proceeded to French, where my teacher seemed to delight in giving me, and my fellow classmates, a ton of home and classwork.

The rest of the day passed by very slowly. I had successfully been given homework by all of my teachers, who never listened when you tried to explain the homework timetable to them.

I got the school bus home, finished homework and went to sleep at around midnight, ready for another fun-filled day!

**Shelley Henderson  (12)**
**Friends' School, Lisburn**

# A Day In The Life Of A World War II Soldier

I jolted awake, sunlight streaming in through the tent canvas. Blinking I got up and went outside. My squadron were squatting round a fire roasting sausages. We were camped in a crumbling ruin of a Normandy castle. Fetching some breakfast I wandered around for a while taking in the beauty. I returned to my tent and picked up my equipment: a rifle, knife, cooking utensils and a medikit. The sergeant came around yelling, 'Get up and packed, we move off at noon, we gotta make Paris by Monday.' Groaning, everyone gathered their belongings and piled them in the truck.

The sergeant jogged over to me, 'Listen, this here's dangerous country, Nazis everywhere, so we'll need a guard for each jeep.' He looked at me imploringly.

Grudgingly, I agreed and fetched my rifle. 'I'll go in the scout jeep!' I shouted after him. He nodded without looking back and swung himself into a truck.

My squadron piled into the 10 cars, trucks and jeeps, squashed in like sardines. We had lost 3 men the day before and morale was low.

After 3 hours a jeep could be seen in the distance, as could a road block. I reached for my rifle and my car reversed to inform everyone else. Next, we formed a line of 6 and drove towards them very fast. A volley of bullets rained over them. As they fell, we advanced. We set up camp and ate a warm dinner to perk us up. I grabbed my blanket and nestled up against a tree and as I lay, I drifted off to sleep.

**Robyn Haskins (13)**
**Friends' School, Lisburn**

# Cat Versus Dog

Dogs are excitable and playful creatures, but cats think about things, so in a battle would enthusiastic tactics beat well-thought-out tactics?

Max, a cat and Pepsi, a dog, tested this.

The cat, being one year old had been defeated in battles against other cats, he was determined to defeat a dog. His victim was Pepsi. Pepsi was a border collie and is around six years old, she loves to run about so Max knew that he couldn't out run her so he watched her daily routine for a couple of days.

Pepsi would start with having a run but then she got tied up for the school day. Her owners would return and untie her.

After she was untied Pepsi would go and sniff smells, she would sniff smells for ages. Max took advantage of this. He too had a routine, he was always let outside of the house when his owners returned. Max waited at Pepsi's first stop, the playhouse.

He took his position and was ready to strike when suddenly he heard someone call for Pepsi. His plan was ruined because he didn't know that his youngest owner, a young girl had to go out because of a dress fitting. He would have to wait for another day to try his plan, but he thought to himself for a while and finally miaowed, 'One day us cats will force all dogs to look up to us and I will be the leader of that war!'

**Clara Conn  (12)**
Friends' School, Lisburn

# A Trip To The Circus

It was the night before the day we were to go to the circus and our whole house was trembling with excitement. It was my dad's idea, well it wasn't really an idea, he won the tickets in a raffle and thought he would make the most of them and take us to the circus. Ever since he had won the tickets I have been saving up and now have a grand total of five pounds to spend at the circus.

I decided to go to bed and I twisted and turned in there for about an hour before actually going to sleep. I had wonderful dreams in which clowns came into the audience and asked me to join them. I juggled with the clowns and then climbed up the ladder, preparing to entertain the crowd with my amazing acrobatic skills. I swung on the rope and slipped. I began to fall towards the net hopelessly.

'Wake up son!' my dad shouted as I suddenly woke up from that dream that was turning into a nightmare. 'We're going to be late!' he shouted to me again. I didn't want to be late so I dragged myself out of bed and then put my clothes on as quick as I possibly could. Ten minutes later we were all ready and me, my mum and my dad all got into the car ready to go to the circus.

When we got to the circus we found out it was closed and went home disappointed. In the end this was worst than my nightmare.

**Shane Brennan (12)**
**Friends' School, Lisburn**

# Burglars!

One cold wintry night, old Joe Black and his wife Meg decided to lock up the house and go to bed. The curtains were pulled and Joe slacked down the fire in the hope of keeping some warmth in the house until the morning. Before long they were both snug in bed with the light out. Meg waited to hear Joe begin to snore as he usually did, but she was so tired that she fell asleep almost as soon as her head touched the pillow.

It seemed like the early morning when Meg was awakened by a noise. What was it? Was it Joe snoring again? No, the room was quiet … this noise was coming from downstairs. Burglars! Well, nobody was going to disturb Meg Black at this hour of the morning and get away with it! Wide awake now, Meg reached for her dressing gown and felt her way in the dark to the landing. She'd better not turn the light on in case the burglar saw it. Walking as lightly as she could, she slowly crept downstairs. Halfway down she stopped and listened. Yes, the noises were still there. No voices, just thumps and soft bangs. She was feeling really frightened now, so she grabbed an umbrella from the stand in the hall and stood outside the door into the kitchen. They were in there those burglars! Meg could feel her heart thumping in her chest. She was petrified as gently she edged the door open. They were opening her cupboards! Taking her things! How dare they! Angry now, she suddenly opened the door wide and switched on the kitchen light. She shouted something at the figure which turned to face her and her eyes blinked to try to get used to the sudden bright light …

'Hello love! Fancy a cup of tea?'

**Sophie Brackenridge (12)**
**Friends' School, Lisburn**

# Trip To The Circus

One day, I went on a family trip to the circus. It was great seeing the acrobats swinging on trapezes, twisting and turning around, still looking exceptionally calm even though they were hanging from fifty-odd feet in the air. They were dressed in leotards of many different colours and dancing with ballet shoes on, in a beautiful and graceful manner.

The lions, tigers and monkeys were frantically running and jumping around the ring, creating roars of laughter from the audience. The lions roared and the tigers growled and they looked like they were about to pounce on an unlucky couple in the front row. The safety guards came in and so thankfully, the elderly couple in the front row were safe.

The ringleader was dressed in a slick black suit, whipping and slashing his whip, shouting and singing out in a loud voice. Then the clowns came out, cart wheeling, tumble turning and spinning around the ring, and there was great applause. They were dressed in bright green overalls with red noses, orange faces and purple wigs. They were cycling around on unicycles, waving and shouting out jokes while doing so.

The seats were tiered and so my family and I had a perfect view. The circus tent was decorated brilliantly and there were balloons everywhere, banners saying, 'Welcome to Tim Tom's Circus' and people going around with baskets of sweets and surprises to sell.

When the circus was over, the entertainers received a well earned standing ovation. An evening to remember!

**Lindsay Crockett (12)**
**Friends' School, Lisburn**

# My Dog

For my story I'm writing about my dog, Tess. I got Tess when she was about 6 weeks old, and she is now 5 months old. Tess was my Christmas present, but a very late one as I didn't get her until February.

The night I got her was a Friday and I was at my friend's house. Me and my friend, Rachel, were going to go out bowling with our youth club, but then my mum rang me and told me about the pups. I didn't really know what to do, but in the end we decided to go and see the pups.

When we got there my mum, dad, brother, me and Rachel, all piled out of the car and went into their house. As I walked into their living room I saw a basket on the floor with the tiniest pup I ever saw, in it. We stayed for a bit and in the end I chose the smallest pup!

When I got home I started thinking of names and even looked in the babies name book to help. Finally I decided on the name 'Tess' and when I looked that up in the name book it meant, 'fourth child', which was quite lucky, since there was already 3 children in the family and she would be the fourth!

I really love Tess and I'm so glad I got her, since I have wanted a dog for years.

**Helen Bell (12)**
Friends' School, Lisburn

# My Dream

My dream was to have a dog of my own. Every birthday and Christmas I made the same request, but I was always disappointed. The day my dream came true was Christmas 2001 when my papa gave me a big red box. I lifted the lid to find the most beautiful puppy I had ever seen. I was absolutely ecstatic. He was a white Jack Russell with a brown patch over one of his eyes. The minute I saw his face I loved him. I called him Toby.

Some time later my sister was dressed as a cat. She started playing with Toby when he grabbed her by the nose and bit it very hard. My mum was furious!

A few weeks later my sister had a friend over and Toby bit her. The last straw was when my friend was over and Toby bit her. That was it, Mum said we had to get rid of him.

I was heartbroken. I couldn't imagine our house without Toby, he was part of the family. Mum and Dad talked for a long time about where Toby would go.

My uncle who lived in Eniskillen, always loved Toby and said that he would take him. I was so glad he wouldn't be put down.

Toby went to live with him and is really happy. I was sad I wouldn't see Toby as much as I would like to, but every holiday I go and visit Toby, he remembers me.

**Sarah Aiken (12)**
**Friends' School, Lisburn**

# There Are Children Starving In Africa

Thomas sat staring at his plate. He really had tried to eat the broccoli, well if he was honest he had at least thought about it. The problem was that it looked like a miniature tree and it smelt rotten. He had tried hiding it under some potato, but his nan was wise to this and was insisting that he finish his dinner. His parents weren't saying much, they never did argue with Nan when they stayed with her. Nan was normally great fun and in fact Thomas had just had the best Christmas he could ever remember in his six years. Vegetables though, were a sore point with Nan, in fact finishing your meal was essential or else she would start, 'There are children starving in Africa who would be glad of that dinner.'

Thomas had heard this millions of times and even his dad said it. As Thomas sat pushing and prodding at his dinner, a news item on TV caught his attention.

The tsunami disaster on Boxing Day had been news now for several days, but it was the image of a small boy looking lost and hungry that Thomas noticed. He knew that his nan had been gathering clothes to send out there so he quickly got a handkerchief out of his pocket and filled it with the dinner he didn't want.

'Forget the kids in Africa, the ones in Indonesia need this,' he said to himself as he slipped it into the box of clothes.

**Victoria Coome  (12)**
**Friends' School, Lisburn**

# The Golden Scale

A huge majestic dragon of an ancient era, sat high and proud on an outcrop of malice stone which pointed high into the air; as if trying to touch the sky with its pointed spires. The beast looked magnificent apart from the bare white patch of skin he was sporting on his chest like a crest. It was for this he now searched, above the sea of trees. He took to the sky with only a few strokes of his huge curtain-like wings and glided off in search of the thief that stole his scales.

Thomas Baker was such a thief and with the scales in his pocket and his quest for passage into manhood nearly complete, was feeling rather good about him himself. That was until he heard a huge flapping sound above his head and a flash of gold erupted above the treetops. The dragon flicked out his tongue, trying to smell the man that had robbed him of his most precious gold. Thomas quickened his pace and sprinted away into the undergrowth.

That night he returned to camp to the singing and dancing of his return home. The festivities continued late into the night with the exchange of wine and the finest ale and good meats. It was in this moment the dragon stole his chance from the villagers and landed silently behind a few houses. As the head of the village threw magic dust of some type into the fire, the dragon moved behind the smoke while all of the attention was on him. The giant golden head loomed out of the smoke and a tongue of fire from its mouth incinerated villagers. Thomas dropped the scales and ran into the trees. He returned the next day to the smell of burnt flesh. He searched and searched until he found his mother's mangled corpse. He took the hunting knife from his belt, slit his hands and swore, 'On my own blood I swear to kill the creature that took my mother's life.' He raised his sword to the heavens and ran into the forest.

**Mark Campbell  (12)**
**Friends' School, Lisburn**

# That Winter Boy!

A lot of people like to jet off to the sun. I wouldn't like to do that. I'd like to jet off to the cold. I'm a winter boy, born in January and happy as a snowman when the nights are dark and the wind is howling. As I stand in the bus queue with huddled figures saying, 'Isn't it cold?' with a downwards cadence to their voices, I say, 'Isn't it cold?' with an upwards cadence to my voice.

I like the way the wind slaps me in the chops when I step out of the house to get the chilly milk; I like the way I have to watch my step when I'm walking to the Post Office because it might be icy; I like the way the sky opens up and snow pours out of the clouds like dandruff from a scratched head. In a previous life I must have been a Finn or a Laplander or an Inuit standing over my father's ice hole hoping for a glimpse of something fishy.

As global warming takes hold I'm sure that more people will appreciate the winter for the jewel it is. As the ice caps melt and Malton is by the sea all year and nobody in Britain ever wears a coat from March to November, the idea of winter will become a sought-after, trendy thing. Channel 4, rather than showing endless films of bright young things leaping about in Ibiza, will show endless things of bright, blue young things hopping about to keep warm in suddenly-desirable Siberia. People will stand in bus queues sweating, saying, 'Isn't it hot?' with a downward cadence to their voices and when the bus comes and they rattle off to work in steaming offices they'll dream of the holiday they've got booked in the British Antarctic Territory; the snorkel, parka and thermals already packed, the snow shoes standing beside the case like tennis rackets, the hot water bottles bulging in the overnight bag. People will show off frostbite rather than suntan. They'll show off about the fact that on holiday you can see their breath, even at midday. They'll prepare for the holiday by opening and closing the fridge door and wafting the cold around them, dreaming of the midnight sun.

Enjoy the winter while you can. It's all too short and summer's just around the corner with its endless heat and long warm nights with the sunlight pervading everywhere. I'm a winter boy.

**Andrew Carson (12)**
**Friends' School, Lisburn**

# The Dragon's Lair

Narvîk entered cautiously and stuck to the cavern walls and shadows like a fly on flypaper. At the end of the cave lay a great dragon. It was a magnificent brute with its huge body stretched out over the bed of treasure it was lying on. Its scales were gold, green and silver and reflected the feeble light like water. The amount of gems must have amounted to 500,000 gold galleons!

Narvîk crept closer to the sleeping dragon. As he edged nearer he spotted the bones and debris left by past dragon hunters. He wasn't going to meet the same terrible fate as them because he was Narvîk the Dragon Thief!

He was close enough now to touch the scales, but he couldn't see because of the huge amounts of smoke billowing out through the nostrils of the monstrous creature. He managed to work his way round the slumbering hulk. Narvîk couldn't believe his luck! He had penetrated the fortress of the legendary Gothen the Malicious.

He started to pick up the treasure that the dragon had so jealously guarded for his lifetime. Now he was just about to lose it to an ordinary Homo sapien! But what was this? The treasure started to burn his very hands with incredible ferocity. He couldn't contain the shout of pain so out came a horrifying scream, *'Aarrghh! Roar!'*

The dragon, woken from its sleep, roared with mixed delight and anger, lunged for the fresh meat and incinerated the rest of the body, then ate it whole with the man's scream echoing off the walls.

**Mark Campbell (12)**
**Friends' School, Lisburn**

# The Magic Paints

One day a young boy called Harry was looking in the attic of his grandfather's house when he found an old set of paints. In the paints there were eight colours, blue, yellow, green, red, orange, black, brown and white. He decided to paint a picture with the paints and he got a table, a paintbrush and some water together.

He began to think about what he would paint and decided to paint a picture of a football. He started to paint the picture and just as he had finished, a football appeared from the page. He was very shocked but once he got used to the football, he started to play with it. After a while he got fed up with the football and decided to paint something else. He thought for a while and started to paint a PlayStation. Again just as before, when he had finished the picture, the PlayStation appeared. He played for ages and then got bored and painted something else. This time he painted five-hundred pound notes and just as before, when he had finished the painting, they appeared from the paper.

He thought about what to buy and decided to buy a brand-new sports car. When he got it he remembered that he was only twelve and couldn't drive but that didn't matter because he could get anything he wanted. After a while he decided to paint something else and then it came to him, he was going to paint Cadbury World and just like the others, when he finished the painting it appeared.

Suddenly there was a noise, a strange ringing noise that wouldn't stop. He opened his eyes and looked at the alarm and realised it was all a dream!

**Andrew Brown  (12)**
Friends' School, Lisburn

# The Jungle Experience

As I walked through the treacherous paths of the Amazon jungle, sweat dripped from my brow in the humid heat. My heart stopped in my chest, just as my feet stopped in my tracks as I noticed, lying beside me on a rock, a lion. My first instinct was to run, but my legs were frozen, paralysed.

I thought it was sleeping as it hadn't noticed me. Slowly and cautiously I started to back away. My mind was racing, trying to think of a plan to escape alive. *If I keep silent and back away, then I can get back to my search for the red bellied tree snake,* I thought. I didn't want to think about what could happen if the lion noticed me. I continued to back away, making sure not to tread on any twigs that might wake the lion.

I heard the song of tropical birds in the background but they sounded miles away against the thumping of my heart. The lion's back was moving with every breath it took. I continued edging away. I was getting further and further away. I had escaped. I began to walk normally again. I hadn't realised it but my breath had been held for the whole time. I sat down to get my breath back, along with the feeling in my body. I was numb and trembling all over. I gathered my thoughts and returned to my mission through the Amazon to find the red bellied tree snake.

**Rachel Annett (12)**
**Friends' School, Lisburn**

# Robbie's Party

*Smash!* Johnny threw a rock at Mr Wilson's car window and the alarm went off.

'Quick,' said Simon, 'let's beat it!'

They ran back to their street and went inside and locked their doors. They could hear the police cars driving past and their sirens waking up the neighbourhood. It was seven o'clock in the morning and the boys had decided the day before to break Mr Wilson's car window. He had confiscated their football because they were playing too near his car.

Johnny was seventeen and Simon was the same age, only a few months older. They both lived in the same city, on the same street, opposite each other's houses. They had known each other for their whole lives. They lived in Belfast in a pretty rough neighbourhood. Crime and vandalism were common so they had to be tough.

The next day it was Tuesday. They both had school so they got up early and walked the whole way there. They were late as usual. They took their seats at the back and started texting their girlfriends who were in the same school but in a different class.

'Johnny!' screamed the teacher, 'put your phone away and you too Simon!'

Simon put his phone away but Johnny did not. In fact he just looked up at the teacher and continued with his phone.

The teacher shouted, 'I won't tell you again, Johnny, put your phone away now!'

Johnny ignored him again. He got sent to the principal's office. Johnny shrugged and slowly left the class. He didn't care much for his studies but Simon wanted at least to make his parents proud.

The principal was a strict man who always wore a black suit, which made him look sharp. With his greasy black hair, no one could guess he was the principal of Belfast High.

Johnny came in with his white tracksuit and silver chain round his neck. He had on his lucky grey cap.

'Now,' started the principal, 'I have heard that you have been cheeky to Mr Wilson again,' he paused and looked Johnny in the eye. 'This has been going on for quite some time now and I am sick of it!' The principal was mad.

'But Sir,' Johnny interrupted, 'I wasn't being cheeky! I was just taking a break!'

The principal grinned, 'A break? You haven't been doing any work at all! Johnny I'm giving you till Friday afternoon to catch up on all your studies and all your failed tests or I'll have to suspend you.'

Johnny looked up as if he was going to burst into an uncontrollable rage, but instead he just left the classroom and stormed out of the school.

That night, Johnny did a bit of homework and then he went outside to call for Simon. 'You comin' out?' asked Johnny.

'Yeah sure give me a second!' said Simon as he hurried to put his coat on. 'So are you going to Robbie's party tonight?' asked Simon.

'Well I've got a lot of homework to do but I'll stay for about an hour.'

With that they both went inside and got ready for the party.

It was ten o'clock and Johnny and Simon set off in their car to Robbie's house. Johnny was driving.

When they got there, they met up with Robbie, talked a bit and had a few beers. The music was loud and the neighbours kept complaining.

'This is a good party, Rob!' shouted Johnny.

'Cheers Johnny!' he shouted back. They were all partying with their girlfriends and they all got pretty drunk.

At about two o'clock they decided to go home.

'Johnny are you sure you can drive?' asked Simon cautiously.

'Yeah I'm fine Simon!'

They all got in the car, all four of them. Johnny, Simon and their two girlfriends Jess and Samantha. Johnny started the car but didn't put on his seat belt; neither did any of the other passengers. They turned up the music and cruised along at about 60mph.

'I think you should slow down!' shouted Jess (Johnny's girlfriend).

'No it's alright Jess. The faster I drive, the quicker we'll get there!'

They were all enjoying the music and the mood. Johnny couldn't see much on the road but all of a sudden he saw two large flashing lights. He couldn't tell what they were. All of his friends were shouting, 'Look out Johnny!' He was too drunk to realise what was going on.

The car smashed into the approaching lorry and flipped over. The last thing he heard was the screaming of his friends and then he went to sleep.

An hour later, police and medical help were there. All they could see was bloody corpses. They took all four to hospital but no one survived. All of their parents were notified and came straight down. They were horrified. It was the worst night of their lives.

A few days later, all four were buried. Johnny, Simon, Jess and Samantha. Their lives were over and their parents were in shock and pain. All because of a stupid little kid who had too much to drink, which took away four lives and ruined four families.

**Usama Wain (14)**
Friends' School, Lisburn

# To The Top

James is just a normal African-American living in Florida apart from one thing, he could ride a motorbike before he could walk. His papa, Big James, never was very good at motorbikes, but he was quite obsessed with them. He wanted his son to be very good at it. He lived his dream through his son. This is James Stewart's road to glory.

It was James' first race, a local race in Florida. He was very nervous. He got ready and went to the starting line. The 30-second board went sideways and they were off. James had never had this feeling before. The adrenaline was amazing. Before he knew it he had a 15 second lead but just as soon as he got it, he threw it away in a corner. He got up into 4th position, he felt mad and started riding out of his limits. He tried to clear a 75 foot double. This was a bad mistake. He came up short and his bike broke in two.

He woke up 30 minutes later in an ambulance but nothing could stop him from racing again and winning.

13 years later and James is 19 years old and about to make his professional debut in the 250cc class. He will race alongside the best motocross racers in the world.

This is the most nervous he's ever been in his life.

One hour later and he's about to race alongside 39 other bikes on the way to the first corner. The 30-second board goes sideways, the gate drops and they're off …

**Stephen Smyth (13)**
Friends' School, Lisburn

# A Day In The Life Of An Alien

Hi, my name is Alisha the alien and I live on Mars. Here is what I get up to in my ordinary day!

I wake up around 6 to the sound of the horn. Our mum wakes us up by pressing a button which sends a loud noise around the house. I hate it!

I get up and like any ordinary alien, I spend 20 minutes picking my outfit for the day. Unfortunately I have Unischool to go to, which is the name of the school we all go to. There is only one Unischool on Mars and the population isn't that big.

At Unischool we are learning about humans. I think they are strange and really don't think they exist. Our virtual-teacher told us that some humans claimed to visit the moon but no one believes it.

Today's lesson, continued from yesterday, was about humans and how they live compared to us. It is kind of weird the way they think we don't exist and then accuse us of those strange patterns they get in something called crop fields. We do have strange symbols to symbolise our kind but no one from Mars has ever been to Earth.

After Unischool I go home and spend some time with my friends. We play zoom-ball and pod-ball and we love to play crater, screen, slicers. It's like each player has to randomly choose one of those things using their pods and see who chooses the strongest weapon. All my friends are good friends and we are planning to go to the moon for our summer vacation.

After I spend some time with my friends I go back to the ship and rest and prepare for another day to come.

**Kirsty Stretton (13)**
**Friends' School, Lisburn**

# The Loch Ness Monster

Those pesky tourists, why can't they just leave me alone. All I want is some peace but *no,* they have to stand around squealing, pointing those stupid cameras and shouting, 'Where is he, why can't we see him?'

I have to get away from all this, I can't stay here any longer so I'm off to explore. I don't know why I haven't done this before. Staying in one place is *sooo* boring. It would be OK if those pesky tourists would go away, but they won't leave so I will.

Wow, there's so much stuff down here that I've never seen before, rusty bicycles, old tin cans, loads of plants and other stuff too. It's so much quieter down here as well, not like where I used to live, all you could hear were those pesky tourists.

I can see something, it's a bright light, it looks a bit like a … ooh it's a tunnel. Finally I can get away from this place and lead a happy and quieter life.

I've been swimming for a while and finally … wait, where am I? I'll ask … wait, who will I ask? Look there's something over there, it's a … wow, it's just like me.

'Hey and welcome to Loch Linnhe, the loch where all the monsters meet up,' says this other loch monster.

Wow this place is great, there are loch monsters just like me. We can do anything we want without those pesky tourists trying to take pictures of us.

It's great, those stupid tourists stand around waiting to see me when I'm really up in Loch Linnhe having fun. I miss home sometimes so I go home every so often just to annoy those tourists.

**Frances Thompson (13)**
**Friends' School, Lisburn**

# A Day In The Life Of ...

Carmen stormed out of the room; she had just had an argument with her mother. She headed for her bedroom so that she could write a letter to her friend, Anna, but she didn't even get to the staircase. She had bumped into someone in the hall. She looked up, frowning.

In front of her stood a boy almost her age. He was slightly taller than her with dark hair and eyes. 'What?' he asked.

She realised she was still frowning and tried to loosen the muscles in her forehead. 'Nothing, I'm Carmen,' she replied.

'Hi, I'm Brian,' he said.

'I'm sorry I have to go,' Carmen said after her father called for her. She was sure he was playing peacemaker between his wife and daughter again. She started to walk towards the sitting room but turned around to wave at Brian. When she turned around Brian was gone. At first she thought this was strange but then she guessed he was a fast runner.

An hour-and-a-half later, Carmen came out of the sitting room and went in search of Brian. When she couldn't find him she went back to her room, to write to Anna. She pulled out some paper and began to write. As she got up to switch on a lamp she noticed someone standing in the doorway. She switched on the lamp to get a better view.

'Hi Brian,' Carmen whispered.

He smiled back at her.

After what seemed like hours of talking, Brian got up to leave. Carmen said goodbye then stared at Brian as he walked right through the wall ...

**Rachel Walker  (13)**
**Friends' School, Lisburn**

# A Day In The Life Of Me

I wake up at 7.30am, after sleeping in an extra half hour, and quickly rush to get dressed. I go downstairs and take a banana and a drink. I then brush my teeth and put my lunch in my bag.

I rush out the door and walk quickly to the bus stop. As I turn the corner I see the bus moving away from the bus stop. I think to myself, *Great, I have to wait until 8.30 for the next bus to come,* but no, it is the nice bus driver and he kindly stops the bus for me. I quickly run over the grass, at the same time trying to get my bus pass out of my pocket.

I get into school at about 8.40am and get my books from my locker for the day ahead. I go to collect and talk to my friends and say, 'Here,' to my name as the register is called. I then go to my first class, already receiving homework and waiting for probably a lot more to come.

Then comes the last two periods of the day. It is games. We have to do two laps of Wallace Park and do cross country. It is pouring down with rain. I am in a T-shirt and tracksuit bottoms, freezing! When we have finished running, we have to walk back up to school. I get changed. I run to catch my bus outside school. I'll have to wait until the morning to know what will happen the next day.

**Aoife Brown  (13)**
Friends' School, Lisburn

# A Day In The Life Of ...

I started my day in a dark, dry place. I was compounded with my kind in an organised stack. They weighed down on my head. Suddenly, a shaft of light burst upon us. I and three of my friends were removed for *the work*. We had unpleasant substances laid upon our bodies, only to have them removed with pronged implements.

Sometimes the substances are sticky, sometimes slippy, sometimes solid, sometimes liquid, sometimes hot, sometimes cold, but always unpleasant.

We got shoved into *the finisher*. This sprayed boiling water, mixed with an acidic material all over us, including the pronged implements mentioned earlier. We have no hard feelings, it is just part of *the work*. We were left there for a while, before we were shoved in our barracks.

We stayed there until the next time we were called. One of our larger members was chosen as *the deliverer*. He would hold the unpleasant substances that would be placed upon us.

He was being transported to the place of *work* with the substances on him when he made a break for freedom. He fell the tremendous distance. When he impacted the ground, the unpleasantness sprayed everywhere. Unfortunately, so did he.

His remains were put in the land of the unwanted, along with the thing he sought to destroy. This was a fantastic victory for our kind. The dead soldier was both mourned and celebrated. Even so, in the back of my mind I knew the enemy had a back-up plan and for our next *work* assignment, everything would be back to normal.

It is hard being a plate.

**Timothy Bruce (13)**
**Friends' School, Lisburn**

# The Magic Shilling

Patrick O'Dea was the laziest man in all of Kerry! The very mention of work made him feel ill. Patrick dreamt of finding a leprechaun and his pot of gold. *Oh to be rich,* he thought.

One day as he walked by the shore of Lake Caragh, he spied a little man, he was wearing a green jacket and a red cap, with a set of tiny cobbler's tools. Surely it was a leprechaun.

Patrick grabbed the leprechaun tightly to make sure he didn't escape and demanded a wish. The leprechaun admitted defeat. He thought, *this man is far too rough and needs to be taught a lesson, so I'll make a fool of him,* so he said, 'Would you let me go if I gave you a magic purse? You put one shilling in and draw it out but when you put your hand back in there is another shilling!'

Patrick agreed and let the leprechaun go.

That night Patrick went to his local tavern. He bought everyone three rounds of drinks and a good meal. The bartender though was wary because he knew Patrick had never worked in his life so he asked for his money. Patrick put his hand into his purse and took out the shilling. When he put his hand in again there was nothing! The leprechaun had tricked him. The bartender took him by the ear and made him work until he had paid his debt.

That day Patrick learnt never to trust a leprechaun.

**Michael Corr (13)**
**Friends' School, Lisburn**

# Home Free

'Mayme!' The strained whisper had come from Jacob, hurrying me into the old barn in front of us, which seemed comforting compared to the sinister shapes of the trees in the blackness of night.

I recalled this as if it were yesterday. I began to think, as I sat in my house in Philadelphia, where I had lived ever since Jacob and I had come to this city, after obtaining our freedom. We had escaped that night, from Master McSimmons' plantation.

I was right in thinking that he would come after us. He came all right, with his dogs and guns. We knew that if we got caught, we would get a severe beating and would be picking cotton in the fields for months. Even the big strong men dreaded the cotton harvest times. Picking cotton was backbreaking work, pulling the puffy balls of cotton from their stalks into your bag and moving on to the next plant. The sun beat down on your back and with the sweat running into your eyes, you were urged to go faster by the overseer, who usually wielded a whip.

I clearly remembered the old farmer who had so kindly taken us in, given us food and that night, sent us on our way with the underground railway. Jacob and I stuck together and we reached Philadelphia on 12th November that same year. I remember standing in that great city, in my first house, this very house I'm sitting in now, thinking that I was home. I was free!

**Emma Boles** (13)
**Friends' School, Lisburn**

# Banshee, True Or Not True?

All those who believe in the myth of the banshee that travels around Ireland, will not be surprised to hear that there has been yet another mysterious death, the seventh this week.

Sinead Connor, 21, was in her house just outside the small village of Cong in Co Mayo, alone last night.

She was on the phone with her friend when she heard someone crying. She told her friend to hold on a moment, then went and searched the house and the garden. After finding no one anywhere in sight, she settled on the thought that she must have imagined it and carried on with her conversation on the phone. Then just when they were saying their goodbyes, Sinead screamed and the phone went dead. Her friend phoned her back and after no answer, decided to go round to see if she was alright. There was no answer at the door so she let herself in with her own key and found Sinead lying dead on the living room floor.

After a full post-mortem the doctors said there was no obvious reason for Sinead's death. So the cause of her death is still a mystery.

Could this be the work of the banshee? All the evidence points towards it but many are still saying no.

For all those who haven't heard of the banshee, it is supposed to be a ghost of an elderly woman who appears to people just before they, or someone in their community, dies and is sometimes said to be the cause of death. The people do not see her, but hear her crying. So maybe she is not a sign to fear, but a sign of comfort, mourning for the person who is about to pass on.

**Julie Allan  (13)**
Friends' School, Lisburn

# No Privacy In My New Home

'There is no privacy in my new home'.

These were the words of a Wallace Avenue resident whose house is now overlooked by a two-storey high building. 'The building was supposed to be a one-storey shed at the corner of the fire station, but somehow it has found itself as a two-storey building at the back of my house'.

A few of the Wallace Avenue residents met with the planning service and told them what the problems were.

The planning board said, 'We will get on to it as soon as possible and change the windows in the building to frosted glass, so that no one can see into the property'.

The planning service said that they had discussed a two-storey high building and told the residents that it was to be situated at the position it is in now.

This had taken place in February 2005 and therefore the residents had plenty of time to object to the plans. The fire service said that they had got full planning permission and built it to the regulations of what they had applied for, they also said that they would change the windows as soon as they could and were sorry for any inconvenience caused.

**Collin Cleland (13)**
**Friends' School, Lisburn**

# The Werewolf

A teenage boy was stumbling through a large, pitch-black forest. There was a dense snowstorm with bitter icy winds; his whole body shook with cold. There was a break in the clouds just long enough for him to see a full moon. He yelled and collapsed in a heap on the rock-hard ground. He gave a groan and his face contorted with pain as his body started mutating.

A young girl was alone in her house. Her brother was out. She didn't know where he was. She heard a lone wolf howl and shuddered, remembering the events of the day. She had gone to the old witch in her village to ask what she could do to get rid of the werewolf that was plaguing her. to this the old woman replied, 'You must take this silver bullet. Then you must find the creature and shoot it, but you must tell no one, not even your brother!'

It had sounded so easy, but now with the eeriness of the night it looked impossible. She put her hand under her pillow and felt the cold, comforting steel of the gun.

As the howls became more frequent she crept downstairs. She flung open the door and fired at the werewolf's neck, it hit! The werewolf fell with a thud to the ground. 15 minutes later there was a knock on the door, she opened it with trembling hands. Her brother fell inside. He had a bullet hole in his neck.

**Kyra Bothwell (13)**
**Friends' School, Lisburn**

# A Day In The Life Of A Dog

I rise from my deep, deep sleep with dreams of chasing cats and burying bones.

I hear my name being called in the distance. My master is looking for me. I get up and run as fast as I can to meet him. What will he bring me today, a bone or maybe a ball?

I meet him, he rubs my belly. Look, he has brought the lead. We are going for an early morning walk.

I hate this bit, I have to go in this noisy machine to get to the pond so we can go for a walk. I love chasing the ducks but my master tells me off and then he makes me walk in this disgusting place before we can go for a walk. It smells foul and my master tells me to go to the toilet. Then for the best bit. He throws sticks into the pond so I can get them. I jump in to the cool water and splash about till I find them. I could do this all day long but, too soon, he moves on.

I get home and have a snooze while my master eats. I can't wait till he finishes his lunch because then I get mine. I can smell it. It is here at last; my food, his scraps. Chomping through my food, I catch sight of a cat. I run through the fields not trying to hurt it. I just like chasing it. After I have finished with the cat, I collapse in a heap on the ground and bathe in the sunlight. Time passes quickly as I chase my tail and go exploring. Little do I know that darkness is creeping round the corner. Soon I'm asleep in my kennel.

**Amy Codd (13)**
**Friends' School, Lisburn**

# Teen Suicide Horror

Amelia Archer, 14, from Belfast, Northern Ireland attempted suicide yesterday, it was revealed this morning. Although she did not actually die, some very serious injuries were obtained as a result of what happened.

The troubled girl threw herself down a lift shaft from the 5th floor of a block of abandoned office buildings on the Donegall Road, Belfast and is currently undergoing treatment for major head injuries incurred by the fall. A source close to Amelia said she was going through a lot at the time of the incident. She was falling badly behind with schoolwork and had few friends.

'It just got too much for her. She needed to get away from it all.'

She is stable at the minute, but is being kept in hospital for observation. Once she is able, she will be attending intensive therapy and counselling to try to find the underlying cause of her actions on the day in question, and solve the problem so that such terrible events will not happen again in the future.

Amelia was very stressed and let it all build up inside her until she couldn't take it anymore.

Our thoughts are with Amelia and her family at this sad time and we wish her a full and speedy recovery.

**Laura Burns (12)**
**Friends' School, Lisburn**

# A Day In The Life Of A Piece Of Grass

One fine day I was swaying in the breeze along with my friends, dodging cows' hooves as they trampled with a large stride, when all of a sudden I was snatched by one of the cows. She chewed me and tore me into four different pieces and swallowed me down her oesophagus and through her alimentary canal into her four stomachs. I started to be pushed back up the cow's throat. The cow had regurgitated me and yet again she began to chew me as her cud. Could it get any worse? Well yes it did, once the cow had had enough of me, she swallowed me once again.

Down in the cow's stomach I was splashed with gastric juices. Then I was churned round in circles by muscular contractions made by the stomach. This made me feel dizzy! I, along with the other grass, was taken through the small intestine and large intestine where I was compacted into faeces which then became stored in the rectum. Following this, we were egested through the anus as what people call cowpat. Smelly gooey cowpat! Well, at least I was in the fresh air.

As I began to dry up I saw a little girl running through the grass. Over she came skipping with all her might when all of a sudden, she sat on me! Bullseye! I hit her right in the face but unfortunately I was squashed so really there was nowhere else my journey of life could take me.

**Amy Conn (13)**
Friends' School, Lisburn

# Hockey

Josh Haron's life was based around hockey. He held his first hockey stick when he was eight months old. He played for Ireland under 16s when he was twelve. An excellent goal scorer, Josh could dribble around players twice his size with ease. Now at fifteen years old, he played for Ireland under 21s and had attained over thirty caps for his country. Josh was a child wonder.

It was seven o'clock in the morning. This was no ordinary day. Josh was going to be the youngest person to ever play in an international final. The match was to start at eleven o'clock and was against Australia, a formidable opponent.

Josh and the team walked onto the pitch to a thunderous din of shouts and applause. A few quick handshakes and a toss of the coin and the match was ready to start, Australia with pass-off. A shrill whistle sounded and the ball moved like lightning towards the Australian left wing. The first half was almost over when Josh found a weak spot in the Australian defence and fed Totten, the Irish centre forward, the ball producing a swift goal.

The second half brought rougher play and three Irish players went off with injuries. Still Australia could not break the Irish defence.

At last the full-time whistle was blown. Irish fans erupted in delight and Josh was lifted high onto the shoulders of the Irish team while they screamed, 'We won! We won!' The International Cup was Ireland's.

**Marc Conlan (13)**
**Friends' School, Lisburn**

# Cheating Death

*(Maximus Larisidus, a Roman gladiator, is about to enter the Colosseum for his first combat.)*

I prayed to the gods while waiting in the tunnel, for I did not know what my fate would be. I was just a simple retiarius, clothed in just a white, short tunic and only equipped with the simplest of weapons, a net and a trident. Anyway, quitting then was just cowardly. I would survive, I had to. A horn sounded, and immediately the tunnel gates were yanked open.

'If you die, you die with honour,' our trainer yelled at us. That was true.

We entered the giant amphitheatre which had an electrifying atmosphere. Out came the sectors (our pursuers) and within seconds we had started.

My fellow retiarii looked as terrified as I was. I moved to the back of our group, but tried not to make it seem obvious. Although they had the same amount of men as us, they were heavily armed and protected.

Eventually  it was just me and some kind of samnite gladiator. He approached me. I remembered what I had been told to do at the Ludi, our training school. He lashed out at me, sword in hand, but I swung my net around his arm. With a counter attack, he swung his shield at me and it just skimmed my face. Using his sword though, he managed to cut my heel, and I fell to the ground in pain. It was over. He looked into the crowd. Silence. Then they gave the thumbs up and they began waving their handkerchiefs. I was saved!

**Thomas Wilkinson  (12)**
**Friends' School, Lisburn**

# A Day In The Life Of Mary Slessor

*(Mary Slessor was a young girl from Dundee. She had a very hard childhood working to feed her big family. Although she had a hard childhood, God opened her eyes and she went to Africa to be a missionary.)*

Getting up at five wasn't strange as back home I was usually up before it. It was probably the heat or the smell of fruit and flowers that was making me drowsy but I had to resist. I had a lot of work to do. I was going to the market to preach. On my way I overheard two women talking.

'It's been in the bush for two days now,' said one.

'I know we can hear it crying but it will not last long,' remarked the other.

I stopped them and demanded to know what they were talking about. What they told me made my blood run cold.

'A mother died giving birth!' said one.

'So her baby was put out in the bush to die too, if we don't, bad luck will come,' continued the other.

I ran off to the place where the women had spoken of and heard the unmistakable sound of crying. Following the sound I found a baby girl, tiny, pale and delicate and covered in pockmarks.

Unsure whether she would live or not, as she would fit my description of someone who had gone through torture and had completely broken, I still took her in. I fed her and put her to bed as I thanked God for helping me save a life.

**Caroline Rodgers (12)**
**Friends' School, Lisburn**

# Pupils Exclaim, 'Down With Jamie's Dinners!'

One school in Manchester, where Jamie Oliver worked his magic by improving lunchtime meals, has had a mass of five hundred pupils protesting against the greens!

At 12.30pm today, lunchtime at Maryford Comprehensive School, pupils aged twelve to sixteen marched out of the school gates onto the road because of the healthy meals they were receiving.

Some were holding banners that said, 'Bring back the burgers' or 'Keep the ketchup' while all of the young teenagers were chanting, 'Down with healthy dinners.'

Jamie gave his reaction to today's events at a press conference in London this afternoon. 'I only tried to help these kids live longer and feel better about themselves in the long term.' Mr Oliver stated, 'At this rate they won't live to see their thirtieth birthdays! Obesity is a major growing problem and something needs to be done to stop it.'

Health Secretary, Patricia Hewitt, who has only just started the job after the recent Cabinet reshuffle, visited the school after she heard about the protest to speak to the headmaster, Jeremy Builds.

When she came out of the building thirty minutes later, she had this to say, 'The police have got the situation under control. We will try to negotiate with the children to find a compromise in the school menu.'

It is thought that now one in twenty-five children is obese. Hopefully these young teenagers will realise this and look to a brighter future with healthier food for school meals.

**Chloe Smyth (12)**
**Friends' School, Lisburn**

# A Day In The Life Of Hannah Brady

*Hannah was 13 when she was separated from her Jewish family during the Second World War. Unfortunately she was murdered along with her mother and father and many other Jewish people. Miraculously Hannah's brother, George, survived Auschwitz and the other cruelties of the war. Sadly he was the only member of his family who survived the ordeal.*

It was September of 1944 and Hannah was 13. George had already been in Auschwitz for four weeks and today Hannah was reading the list of names for the next trip to Auschwitz.

There it was, my name! It was going to be a reunion. Brother and sister together again. Together forever, we would never be apart. I had to get ready because I wanted to look nice for George. My friend Margot, she was like a big sister really, helped me get ready. I washed my hair and Margot brushed it to make it neat. I really did want George to think I was looking after myself and I was.

When the whistle blew for people to get on the train for Auschwitz, I must have been the first one there, I was so excited. The train journey was very long and people were sick! But I was fine. When the train finally came to a stop, I could hardly wait. We were all led to a large building and ordered in. Then the doors slammed loudly behind us. That's where I am now.

**Sophie Wilson  (12)**
**Friends' School, Lisburn**

# A Gathering Light

*(This is a write on or a continuation of the book 'A Gathering Light' by Jennifer Donnelly. This is about a girl called Mattie Gokey who lives in the year 1906. At the end of the book she leaves her family in the country to study at University in New York. I pick up the story when she is sitting in the train carriage heading for New York.)*

I ignore the temptation that's gnawing at me, trying to get me to turn around and run and leap off the train. As the train leaves the platform, I settle myself and take deep breaths to calm down. The carriage is stuffy and the man opposite me is beginning to sweat.

'You want that window open, Miss?' asks the man.

'Please! Thank you, Sir, it's very warm in here.'

I watch the man closely as he pushes and pulls the window upwards until a light breeze hits my face. The sweet smell of North Woods hits my nostrils and I close my eyes and picture my family reading my letter, the letter I never expected to write. Now even as I think about it, the tears begin to well up in my eyes.

I've left my family all alone now. I think of Lou, she would be the one who would storm out. She is the one who would blow her top and try to get drunk again. Then there is Abby, she would calmly reassure Pa and Beth. She would speak directly to Beth but really she would be speaking to Pa. She would do the same thing as I did when Lawton left, pretend it wasn't happening. In a sense she would become me, but as I sit here, I wonder how long it will be before she is sitting on a train heading away from the family she once loved. The family that I shall love forever.

**Lynne Smylie  (14)**
**Friends' School, Lisburn**

# A Day In The Life Of A Six-Month Old Baby

7.30am    It's about time Mum and Dad woke up! I've been lying staring at the ceiling for ages. It's got to be Sunday; the day nobody does anything! I'll make myself comfortable then - I guess I'll be here for a while! Better close my eyes - if this mobile spins around one more time I think I'm going to be sick!

8.00am    Here they are at last, and now they're whispering baby talk. I hate that - it makes me feel unintelligent! Oh if I could talk, I'd make them see how awful it is to hear that sickly babble all day, every day! Ah, milk! It's about time; I'm dying of thirst.

10.30am   I really wish I could walk - crawling is so slow and awkward, and all I can see is legs, feet and stubbly ankles! I know exactly how tortoises must feel!

1pm       Lunchtime at last, I hope it's something new; my food is so bland and boring! No such luck - healthy-eating puréed carrots again. Why can't I have curries and pizzas like grown-ups?

7pm       I've spent the afternoon being cuddled and prodded by relatives. It's so uncomfortable lying in people's arms for ages! I've given up crying though - it just makes them fuss even more and they give me a horrible, tasteless dummy and put me in my cot because they think I'm tired - I just want to do something new and exciting!

Finally   It's bedtime. At least tomorrow's Monday - parent and baby group - civilised conversations!

**Judith Smyth  (14)**
**Friends' School, Lisburn**

# Drunken Boast

*(A young Viking raider, Skeggi, makes a boast that he can kill the dreaded beast that haunts the lower mountains. The story starts with him hunting the beast.)*

The wind blasted down the mountain pass, on to the face of the burly figure making his way up the mountain. The figure pulled his helmet off to rub some warmth back into his frozen face. He sighed, pulled on his helmet and set off again.

His name was Skeggi and he was born in a remote village near here. Skeggi was tall, strong and violent like most of his people. The reason he was slogging his way up the mountain was because of a drunken boast. Skeggi's thoughts turned back to the night …

*It had been a successful raid. They were all richer. So, they went to the tavern to celebrate as usual. Skeggi had been particularly successful and, as a result, had become particularly drunk. So when the candles burned low and the old storytellers came out, Skeggi had wagered his loot he could slay the beast.*

Howling brought Skeggi back to the present. He spun round slowly as he identified the source of the sound. It was a huge wolf, about four feet tall at the shoulder, with crazed hungry eyes. Skeggi raised his axe, gave a war cry, and leapt at the beast. His axe crushed down into its spine, but its claws cut deeply into him. As it lay in its death throes, he hastened to find its lair where treasures were rumoured to be. As he rounded the corner, he stopped. Here was the real beast. He was in trouble.

**Adam Tinson  (14)**
Friends' School, Lisburn

# The Race

I had to get up early this morning. I had done this hundreds of times before, just another race, just another day.

The qualifying had already taken the life of a fellow competitor. He was crushed inside his car. I wondered what were his last feelings, joy at a full life, or fear of dying young and not seeing family or friends again? I don't know. I have very mixed emotions about this. I had a bad dream and woke up at three o'clock in the morning in a cold sweat; there were tears from my eyes and a strong pain from my neck. Was this a sign? Or was it the way I had been sleeping? I couldn't get to sleep after that.

It is now seven o'clock and I am being driven to the circuit, San Remo. Ah, the memories, my third race and first win. I love this circuit.

I walk to the pits and get my helmet and other protective body gear, I carry them to the toilets and begin to get changed. I notice a rather large bruise on the side of my neck, it hurts to touch. I don't remember getting this. Is this a sign? Or am I just getting more and more depressed and paranoid about the death of my friend, James? He was one of the best drivers around and a close friend.

I tell the team manager that I don't want to race, but he says, 'We are leading the championship with Sauber not far behind, stop being so superstitious, you'll be fine. Now get in that car and race.'

The word fine is hanging in my head. I am confused now, what is fine after all? Fine. Ha! I am in pole position for the race though.

The warm up lap is over, the race is now on. Twenty laps on and I am driving well. I am going over a bump. My car bottoms out and I lose control and I barrel over and over. My neck goes crunch. It all goes black.

**Conor Auld  (14)**
**Friends' School, Lisburn**

# Hope - The Diary Of A Disabled Person

I woke, as always, as Mum ripped the curtains open, letting the light stream into the room. Flecks of dust danced, illuminated by the morning sun. They looked so free drifting to and fro, occasionally somersaulting and spiralling. I longed to reach out, catch them, catch a little of their freedom for myself. My hand jerked upwards, out of my control, causing them to scatter, chaotically twirling away from my clumsy grasp, out of my reach.

Everything in my life seemed to be 'out of my reach'. The simplest of everyday tasks - walking, talking and even holding a spoon - proved too difficult for me to achieve. If I could I would cry, do something to ease my intense and ever-strengthening feelings of frustration. Why was I doomed to be trapped for the whole of my life in this useless husk of a body? Why couldn't I gain the movement that everyone else took for granted, but I craved so dearly? Wherever I went, people stared, young children pointed, mothers looked away.

Sometimes people would talk to me, but they did like they were talking to a pet. They didn't know there was a person crying out for help inside of me. They didn't understand that I did know what they were saying to me.

I had heard some conversations about something that had gone wrong with my brain when I was being born. Mum always cried when I was brought into the conversation. Why should she cry? I was the misunderstood, motionless one. My life was worse than death. I was sure of it.

But then there still was hope, hope that someone would find the person locked inside my body, screaming to get out. I would have died if hope didn't give me a reason to live.

**Lauren Watson (13)**
Friends' School, Lisburn

# The Dragon Gem

It was a clear, bright morning. Not a sound was to be heard. This was a perfect morning for hunting. So Leohaz left his small town of Fawnhill to go hunting for deer in the Skigh forest. When he reached the forest, he sat down on the grassy floor and made a circle around him with a stick. He then placed a large slice of meat in the centre of the circle and then walked into a bush to hide until his prey came. Soon after he had hidden in the bush a rustling noise came from a bush opposite him. He suspected it was a deer picking up the scent of the meat, or maybe it was a rabbit or a otholope. An otholope is a mystical beast which is very rare but very tasty. Whatever it was Leohaz was very hungry. Just then a gunshot went off where the bush had rustled. An otholope leapt out of the bush. It had a severe wound on one of its legs and was bleeding. Then, after it a man jumped out holding a gun. The man then shot again wounding another one of the otholope's legs. It fell to the ground in pain. The man searched the animal. He then swore and walked away. Leohaz crept out of the bush. He walked over to the otholope. It had died. Leohaz saw something in its mouth. He picked it out. It was a gem. He held it up. It started to glow very brightly. Suddenly it exploded, shattering gem particles everywhere. Leohaz saw a huge dragon emerge from the particles. Leohaz then woke up. It was a dream. He looked at his hand. It hurt. He saw green crystals engraved in his hand. His back also hurt. He looked in the mirror. He had wings. He also had scales, sharp teeth and a tail. He was a dragon. He fell to his knees and cried.

**Andrew Wylie (13)**
**Friends' School, Lisburn**

# The Extremely Unlucky Mountain Climber

Alan Willton made his way to the local mountaineering shop and asked the shop assistant what he would need to start climbing.

'First of all you will need a safety harness, oh very essential, and you'll need ... ' and dragged off into a very long list.

Alan came out of the shop £3,000 poorer and carrying seventeen massive bags of equipment out to his car. He dropped one of his ice picks into an open drain and had his safety harness stolen by a rabid pack of dogs.

Having been completely unaware of this, Alan drove to the most convenient mountain in his local area, where he pulled out his mountaineering equipment and crushed his foot. He then proceeded to read the climbing guide upside down, and climbed the mountain the wrong way up. However, a mysterious gust of wind came and blew him off. He then climbed the mountain properly as if nothing had happened.

Halfway up the mountain, Alan got his arm stuck in a crevasse. Then a giant mutated squirrel climbed out of a cave and gnawed off Alan's feet, ignoring the screams of pain. It made a strange, high-pitched noise and from the nooks and crannies of hell, clambered out the squirrel's many fierce minions. They stole the ice pick and left him hanging by his arm, when his tendons in his arm gave way and he fell through the roof of a very conveniently placed coffee shop, and impaled his eye on an umbrella.

**Gary Uprichard (13)**
Friends' School, Lisburn

# Hell

Jamie had always hated that place. Nobody understood him. His mum said he was silly, but she didn't understand. He tried to tell his dad, but he just got an empty bottle thrown at him.

His dad was always drinking, he had started when he lost his job, it had changed him - happy and friendly, to a violent slob.

He still had to go. He walked to school, or rather ran. As he left the house he met Johnny, waiting for him. Jamie knew what would come next. Johnny sidled up and the next thing Jamie knew he was on the ground. They all just appeared - Justin, Big Dave, Sam and Jake. They kicked at him and tore his clothes. He saw red stains on his shirt. He could see no mercy in their cruel faces. He was crying, the biggest took a swing at his head. Everything went black.

He didn't know what time it was when he came round because his watch was clogged with mud. He hurried on to school. When he got there people were staring and pointing, some worried, most laughing.

Mr Johnson told him to go and get cleaned up and that he should stand up for himself; fight back. Jamie didn't come back for a while. Mr Johnson sent people out to look for him. They found him hanging from a tree. He was pale and bloody and obviously dead. Nobody had noticed him, nobody had cared, but now they do, now that it was too late.

**Ralph Walker (13)**
**Friends' School, Lisburn**

# A Short Story On Being Stranded On An Island

I was on the boat and I noticed a wave blasting towards me. I tried my best to stay on-board but the force of the wave made us capsize and I couldn't hold on. I looked around me and noticed an island nearby. I swam ashore and onto the sandy beach. I looked up and all I could see was trees and I could hear all the wildlife rattling in the grass and squeaking in the trees. I was very frightened and I was all alone. I wondered if there was someone on the island who could help, so I walked through the island dodging the many vines and branches that lay on the ground.

Suddenly I heard chanting. I crouched down and peered in through the bushes and saw a tribe. I was wondering whether to go in and see if they could help me. I decided to go in and when I did they all crowded round me and they were surprisingly happy to see me. I told them about what had happened and they all helped me by feeding me and then rowing me over to a nearby island where I could get home from. I thanked them so much for all their help and said goodbye.

**Hannah Wilson (12)**
Friends' School, Lisburn

# The Final Countdown

General Zion was ex-army and extremely strong and agile. As soon as he had sensed my presence he had jumped into combat position immediately. He was obviously a black belt in karate like me, but much more advanced in the moves. I wasn't thinking and lunged out with a karate kick but he was too fast, grabbing my leg and flipping me onto my back. He wasn't even out of breath. I couldn't get up but with us being in a building site there were plenty of other things to use apart from strength and agility.

So when Zion launched a kick at my head, I picked up one of the nails that was lying nearby and wedged it into Zion's leg. He howled out in pain and fell to the ground. I used this time to recover from my pain and to put three powerful punches into Zion's head.

Zion was getting up again. I turned frantically looking for something that could serve as a weapon to finish Zion off. I was too late because despite his injuries, Zion had managed to produce a foot-sweep, which made me stumble and trip over a piece of wire on the ground bringing me to the ground. It was all over. Zion had found a metal bar and knowing that I was going to die, the last moments of my life were spent thinking that this was such a horrible way to die. But now I say, 'Is there a better way to die than to die fighting?'

**Jonny Steele  (13)**
Friends' School, Lisburn

# Cerberus' Treasure

Persias shivered as he crept through the forest land, home to the River Styx, the river of death. In the thick mist he could easily imagine unnatural things lurking and he kept his hand on his sword. He moved cautiously, listening for the sound of river.

Persias was a veteran of the Trojan wars, fighting for ten years, and seeing his home destroyed. When the long and bloody war was over, he was left homeless, but Persias had a plan to make fortunes. In the dying days of the Trojan wars, Persias' friend Quaelus had been struck down by an arrow. With his dying breath Quaelus had told Persias how to find the Moon Sapphire, a brilliant stone as big as one's hand. 'Find Cerberus. Answer his challenge. Get the sun key and open the rock. Go friend Persias ... '

Two years later Persias stood at the source of the ominous river. He called out, 'Come Cerberus, for I seek your aid.'

A ghastly wail emitted from the black crack in the mountainside, before a sinister voice echoed around the canyon. 'What seek you, human? Speak or I shall reap you.'

Persias called out, 'I seek the Moon Sapphire.'

'Then you will have to best me!' roared the voice. Cerberus appeared. He was twice the size of a horse, five times as wide. His mane was of blue flame and he had three heads. Persias was terrified and fled. It was definitely better to live another day.

**Marcus Tinson (13)**
**Friends' School, Lisburn**

# A Day In The Life Of A Forensic Investigator

*Beep, beep, beep, beep!*

Joey Jordisson hit the button to turn off the alarm. He glanced at the time, 'Aw hell, I'm late for work again.' He quickly put on a pair of jeans, a T-shirt and his black MDPD: forensics jacket. He ran outside, jumping into his Land Rover Discovery and sped to work. When he got to the crime lab his supervisor was waiting for him.

'Mark, listen, I'm sorry I'm ... '

'Don't bother, just get your butt down to route 917, an officer's been killed,' cut in Mark.

'Will do,' Joey said, jumping into his Land Rover.

When he got to the scene he saw the squad car at the side of the road and the body beside it. It was a man, mid-30s, brown hair. His head had been brutally beaten with a blunt object. Lying beside him was a blood-covered crowbar, 'Looks like we've got the murder weapon,' said Joey. He collected a red fibre off it from where the murderer's sleeve had snagged. Out of the corner of his eye he saw a colourful object. It was a coke can lying at the side of the road. He picked it up and dusted it for fingerprints. He collected the prints and put them in his case. At the lab he ran the prints and the fibre through the computer. The prints had no match but the fibre he collected was only used to make sweaters for one university.

Joey went to the university to look about. In one of the ICT suites he found a can of the same brand of coke. He dusted it for prints and lifted a set identical to the ones on the can at the crime scene. Checking the computer records, Joey found out that the last person to use the computer was Craig Thomas, a forensics student at the university.

Joey knocked on the front door of the house. A man in his early 20s wearing one of the university sweaters answered it. 'Craig Thomas?' Joey asked.

'Yes, what's wrong?' asked Craig.

'We have evidence of you being at a murder scene, would you like to tell us how it got there?' asked Joey.

'Alright, I'm no good at lying, I'll tell you the truth. As you probably know, I'm a student of forensics at the university and I want to write a book on an actual case to get extra credit. I couldn't find one that was unsolved to think of a theory on so I decided to make my own. I stood at the side of the road, flagged the officer down. When he pulled over and got out, I hit him with the crowbar and ran back to my car and drove away. I was so pumped with adrenaline I forgot to lift the crowbar,' confessed Craig.

'Craig Thomas, I'm placing you under arrest for the murder of Officer John Deacon. Officer Clarke, read him his rights.' said Joey.

'I thought it would have been the perfect crime, no motive, an alibi, what went wrong?' said Craig.

'You forgot to take into account one thing, when you break the law, the law will find you, and use all its power to send you to jail for a very long time,' said Joey. 'You'll have a long time to think about that. 25 to life to be precise.'

**Christopher Weir (12)**
Friends' School, Lisburn

# A Day In The Life Of Kerry

My name is Kerry. I'm different from you, but the same. I look like you but every day is a struggle to breathe. I have cystic fibrosis. My lungs are clogged up and I need constant medication and physiotherapy.

I woke up this morning coughing as I always do. I can cough for up to an hour or more. I just feel sick. I have physio twice a day and my mum's coming in to do it now.

I'm 15 but I'm so helpless. I'm like a baby. In the morning I'm always worse than in the afternoon. But I still cough. I just want to wake up, wake up and breathe. I look in the mirror. I'm so pale and my hair is sticking to my face with sweat.

I have my lunch but I can never eat very much. I call some friends over and we go out for a meal. I always feel so awkward because I eat as much as a two-year-old. They look at me and I can tell that they're thinking, *what a waste of food.*

I finish my meal and it's around 10.30. I just want to go to bed but I have to go home and get bashed about for my physio. I want to live a normal life. I know I will live a short life and I may be gone in the next 5 years but I've got to live in hope.

**Becky Whittaker  (13)**
**Friends' School, Lisburn**

# End Of The World Is Near!

Recent tests and studies have shown that by the year 2146, the world will be at its end. Professor John Choom of Oxford University has told us this and has been proved right by the head of NASA, John Chestnut. 'The tests have shown that there will be a comet hitting the Earth's crust at precisely 9,687mph causing a huge explosion, breaking the world into pieces'.

This had caused NASA to build a new space shuttle to put living places on Mars and the moon, and they are hoping that this will be ready by late 2007.

The studies have shown that the comet is 20 light years away and will come into contact with three other planets as well, before reaching Earth. This is going to cost, as NASA will have to send up a lot of shuttles, so the government have been planning to put up taxes. We have Dr James Wicking of the Geologists' Board here to tell us his opinion: 'I have been checking documents to see if this is true or not, and all evidence clearly points that this is going to happen. We are doing all we can to stop this incident. We are planning to put a shuttle into space with four astronauts to blow the comet up, but for further details, keep posted on the news and the internet'.

Well that's all we know for now, but we will have more tomorrow.

**Steven Woods (13)**
Friends' School, Lisburn

# To The Future

One night in a deep, dark laboratory, there was a mad scientist called Max, who was on the track to discovering time travel. He had worked out all the calculations and physics of it and all he had to do now was build it.

He spent three days building this man-made wonder of the world. Finally he had finished, but being the mad scientist that he was, he knew not to ruin it, so he drew a picture and put it in, then turned time back 30 seconds. Of course, there was nothing on it because it was only drawn 20 seconds ago, so he knew it was a success.

Then he decided to put it to the big test and he sent himself forward in time by 1,000 years. There was a big flash and while travelling, he had a huge illusion of colours and clocks. Then there was another big flash. He was in the future and he had a second to look around before a robot rushed up to him.

'Beep bop bo beep,' said the robot, then a giant hand came out of the robot and put Max on a conveyor belt.

As he went down the conveyer, he was pulled out of his shoes and was put into a pair of high tech red shoes. Then a giant was just about to step on him, so he went back home.

He noticed he was still wearing the shoes, 'A souvenir of something that will never be,' said Max.

**Matthew Morris  (12)**
**Friends' School, Lisburn**

# A Day In The Life Of Cristiano Ronaldo

Hi!

My name is Cristiano Ronaldo, I play for a top football club called Manchester United. Its home ground is Old Trafford.

I was born in February 1985 on the island of Madeira. I played footie day and night, and always wanted to play for my country and become famous, and that's how I got where I am today!

Today was an important day for me, and emotional too! Here is what happened ...

I had been very nervous. Last night I got butterflies in my stomach because today was the FA Cup Final. I couldn't sleep for ages, so I slept in a bit! At about 9.15am, I got a phone call from my friend, Wayne Rooney, who plays for Man Utd. He was wondering what time we had to be at the Millennium Stadium. I realised it was 11am, so I didn't talk to Rooney for long.

I was staying in a hotel, so I had missed breakfast, but I thought I could get some on the way to the stadium. I rushed into the shower and washed myself. By this time it was 9.45am. Then I got dressed in a tracksuit, did my hair, which took ages, then began to clean my boots. When they were clean, I ran down the stairs and jumped into my BMW convertible. I went to the shop nearby and bought an apple for breakfast. I was spotted by some fans, so I quickly signed autographs and then headed for the stadium

We had a light lunch of pasta, got ready and went onto the pitch. I was really scared, but when we started playing it was OK. I tried my best against Arsenal, but we were beaten on penalties. I was very sad and began to cry, but I knew that I'd tried my best, so I was fine after a while.

I hope you have enjoyed hearing about my day!

**Olivia Pierce (12)**
**Friends' School, Lisburn**

# My Diary, By Jonny Wilkinson

*(This is an extract from Jonny Wilkinson's diary two days after he had his neck operation after he suffered injury in the Rugby World Cup Final)*

*5th December*

The doctors say that my neck is healing well and that the worst is over and I'm on the way back to rugby.

'Hero to Zero!' another back page headline from The Sun. 'Wilko's Wrecked!' Why do they keep beating me down? I wish I could just be out with the lads celebrating on the parade!

The nurses keep poking, prodding and pinching me like a voodoo doll. Everyone keeps saying, 'So how does it feel?' or 'You're my hero'. I don't care. I just want to go out and train with the lads as normal. Nothing is normal now!

I'm lying in a hospital with wires, tubes and my self-esteem running out of me. Christie came to visit yesterday. I didn't say much, but I was really glad to see her. Everyone at home is preparing for Christmas and I should be out by then. It is so irritating knowing no one can feel my agony inside. They claim that I won England the World Cup. I didn't, I just dropped a goal at the right time. All of us worked very hard to get this far and now we've won the ultimate prize. I hate the way they say that I won it … England won it!

Johnno, Josh and Clive are coming in to see me later. They have arranged to get me a picture in a gold frame of the drop goal I scored. I'm grateful, but I just want to go home and relax!

**Mark Williams  (14)**
**Friends' School, Lisburn**

# Melanie And The Magical Cat

There was a girl called Melanie and she lived in Africa. She lived with her dad and brother Aaron.

One day, Melanie and her brother Aaron were in the jungle looking for acorns, when they heard a crackle from behind them. They both turned round to see what it was. There was a small tabby cat with bright blue eyes. Melanie went and picked it up and brought it home.

At home, her dad didn't allow animals, so Melanie ran upstairs.

Her dad shouted up, 'Melanie, can you tidy your room please?'

All of a sudden, Melanie got a shock. She looked down at the kitten; it was glowing, then it became tabby again. Melanie looked round: her room was tidy! She thought the cat was strange, it had magic powers. She could use it in school and at home, cool!

The next couple of weeks, Melanie used the cat until one day nothing happened. The cat lost the powers it had to help Melanie because she had helped it and its powers had run out.

The next day, Melanie woke up, the cat was on the floor. It was glowing, when suddenly it turned blue, green, red, then vanished. Melanie didn't see it for two days. When it came back, it was thin and sick and could barely walk.

Melanie took it to the vet. There was nothing he could do. The kitten died, and until this day, Melanie has been helped by this cat. She's now 109!

**Sophie McCutcheon (12)**
Friends' School, Lisburn

# The Day Everything Went Wrong

'Help, help!' shouted Sam, as her house was burning away. 'Somebody, help me.'

In the background, Sam could hear her friends screaming as they tried to escape the horrific flames.

It was the night of Sam's birthday and she had some friends over for a party and sleepover. Little did she know everything was going to go wrong. The start of her bad luck was when she nearly drowned at the swimming pool. The next bad thing was when her best friend's clothes got stolen at the swimming pool. And now the storm.

During the night, a storm started outside, with thunder and lightning striking every ten seconds. The girls thought the storm would stop very soon, but that didn't happen. A strike of lightning hit the roof above Sam's room and set the house on fire.

'Jump through the window, girls,' shouted a voice outside.

Before Sam could look around, all her friends had escaped. She tried to move, but her legs wouldn't move, they were trapped underneath the rubble. 'Help, help, somebody help me,' she yelled. She didn't think anyone heard her because of the loudness of the roaring flame and the buzzing of the fire engine. She felt the pressure on her legs getting heavier and heavier. She didn't think she was going to stay alive.

'Is anybody in there?' shouted a voice outside her room

'Yes, please help me,' she replied.

'Just keep calm,' the man said.

Outside, everyone was worried about Sam and wondering where she was. Before they could do anything, the house went up in flames.

**Jenna McQueen  (13)**
Friends' School, Lisburn

# The Day Everything Went Wrong

This is the story of the day everything went wrong. It all started when my alarm didn't go off at the time it was meant to. It was supposed to go off at 7am, but instead went off at 7.20am. (I always thought it looked a bit dodgy!) When it did go off, I had to rush getting dressed and eating my breakfast. While I was eating my toast, a big blob of jam fell off the toast and onto my shirt. As I reached for a cloth to wipe it off, I swiped my glass of milk and spilt it all over my trousers. *Just what I need,* I thought to myself.

I glanced over at the clock: 7.43am. I had two minutes to get to the bus stop. As I headed out the door, I realised I'd forgotten to do my hair. *No time,* I thought, *I'm going to have to look like a prat for the day!*

I made it to the bus stop just as the bus was about to leave, but when I got to school, I realised I had forgotten my PE kit. Mr Smith was going to kill me! As I headed for the locker rooms to get my books for the day, I put my hand into my pocket to get my locker key out and realised I'd left my key sitting on the desk in my room. 'Great,' I said, 'no books for the day.'

Lunchtime arrived without any hassle, which was a relief, and I sprinted up the hill to be into the lunch hall early to get chips. As I turned the corner, I went flying through the air (not really, but it makes it sound good!) … some idiot had left their bag lying in the middle of the path! My wrist was aching really badly. I can't remember what happened next, I think I must have passed out with the pain. The next thing I knew, I was lying on the bed in Matron's room, holding my wrist. She looked at it and told me it was definitely fractured and possibly broken. Matron then phoned my dad, explained what happened and told him to come and pick me up from school.

He took me to casualty and they X-rayed my wrist. It turned out I had snapped it clean in half and that it would have to be in a cast for at least six weeks. All that over wanting to get chips first!

When I went to school two days later, I got a lecture from my year teacher about running to the lunch hall. I apologised and said I wouldn't do it again.

Well, that's the story of the day everything went wrong. I've learnt a more important thing from this … not to run to the lunch hall any more because, for six weeks I can go straight to the front of the queue anyway!

**Ben Maze  (13)**
Friends' School, Lisburn

# The Day Everything Went Wrong

On the 13th May 2001, my family and I went for a picnic in Glasgow. The picnic area was in a rural part of Glasgow. The weather was great; the birds were flying in the cool breeze.

When we arrived at the picnic area, the whole family helped to set out the picnic. We were just about to eat our food when the weather took a turn for the worse. The sun went in behind the grey clouds and the cool breeze became a strong wind, and then it started to rain. So we packed away the picnic and got in the car. I was thinking to myself how the day couldn't get any worse, when the car broke down. It had probably broken down in the worst place possible. There was no garage in sight and there was no signal on our mobile phones, so we got out the map, only to find that the nearest petrol station was five miles away. My dad and I walked five miles to find the petrol station, to find it was closed for lunch.

When the shop did open, fifteen minutes later, we told a man what had happened, so he gave us a lift in his van. When we got to the car, he filled the car up and we gave him £80. Then we went home and found the house's power had gone out.

**Ross McCaughey  (13)**
**Friends' School, Lisburn**

# Front Page

Last night I attended the MTV Awards. It was a glitzy night including acts from Britney Spears, Lemar, Black-Eyed Peas and lots of other top names.

While the stars were making their way down the famous red carpet, I was checking out some of the fabulous outfits and beautiful gowns. Christina Aguilera was looking stunning in a baby blue mini-dress by D&G, while one of the guests, Catherine Zeta-Jones, looked gorgeous as usual, in a bright red, long, flowing dress with real diamond sequins along the bottom, by Gucci. Jay-Z came along with his Destiny's Child babe, Beyonce Knowles, in matching outfits involving lots of bling!

The awards were well-deserved, some of them going to The Killers, winning best newcomer. Also, Gwen Stefani and Lemar bagged best male and female solo artists of the year awards. The Black-Eyed Peas took home the Best Fashion Award.

Movies like 'A Cinderella Story' and 'A Shark Tale' both stole top movie awards.

The performances were ones never to forget as McFly came whizzing on stage in their hippy, custom-made Beetle, singing 'Five Colours In Her Hair', picking up a member of the crowd to sing along with. Michael Jackson crooned 'Earth Song', which was very colourful and powerful. In the middle of the song, he got a bit of a fright as there was a bomb scare, but it was just a scare and no one was hurt.

All in all, it was an unforgettable night of glitz and glam and celebrities galore!

**Amie Johnston (12)**
**Friends' School, Lisburn**

# The Day Everything Went Wrong

I can still remember the day clearly. It was Friday the 13th. Although I wasn't superstitious, after that day, I'm not sure whether I am or not. Let me tell you about it …

I woke up at 5am and for a moment, I wondered if an elephant could have escaped from the circus and gone to sleep on my head (it felt like it), but it was 'only' a headache. I got out of bed to get an aspirin - and cracked my head on the shelf. Ow! I made it downstairs and got my aspirin and then went back to bed. My alarm went off three hours later, right beside my ear. *Rrrriinng, rrriinng.* I jumped up and banged my head on the shelf *again!* It felt like my head was exploding! Groaning, I realised that the aspirin hadn't worked and that I'd have to go to school feeling like a herd of rhinos had run in through one ear, danced a jig, and run out through the other.

I managed to get to school on time and the day passed without anything going wrong until the last period, which was swimming. We had got changed and were walking out the door, when I slipped on a wet patch on the floor and fell into the pool - fully dressed in my school uniform. So I had to walk home dripping wet, while enduring all the curious stares.

Finally, when I got home I realised that I had forgotten my key and would have to wait till 5.30, when my mum came home.

I think you'll agree that that was a very bad day.

**John McCulla  (13)**
**Friends' School, Lisburn**

# The Day That Everything Went Wrong!

It was a Wednesday night at around seven-thirty when it all started going wrong for me. My mum was driving me out to JJB so I could get a new football to play in school, but we were just passing the cinema when someone turned out of the exit. They drove straight across our lane, so my mum had to dodge them and she went flying across the road and we crashed into a tree on my mum's side of the car and I then got knocked out.

The next thing I remember was me lying in the hospital bed and a nurse talking to me, but I only remember her telling me that I had broken my whole right arm. Then she said my mum was worse. I then asked how bad and she replied, 'She has whiplash, a broken wrist, bruised face and a shattered pelvis.' She went on to tell me that I could go home that night, but my mum would have to stay in for over a week.

I went home and my dad said I could have the week off to recover. But I could not do any homework because of my arm. Out of the nine classes I had on Monday, I had five homework pieces due in for then. All my teachers shouted at me for not trying to do them. I tried to explain that I couldn't because of my arm, but they said I should have used my other arm. I had argued with my first teacher and he gave me a Saturday detention.

**Ross McGarel (13)**
Friends' School, Lisburn

# The Day Everything Went Wrong

It was morning. I woke up three hours late for work, as my expensive multi-tasking robot servant had malfunctioned the day before. I wasn't too pleased.

As I was getting myself dressed, somebody knocked on the door. I answered the door and there was a robot servant.

'Good afternoon, Sir, would you like some lunch?'

I was in a rush, so I just said, 'No thanks, I'm late for work.'

I ran out the door and started going down the stairs. It was the first time in many years that I had taken the stairs anywhere, but I was late for an important meeting. I never was a very big fan of business trips, you can see why. Everything seems fine, and then something always goes wrong unexpectedly.

I ran past the receptionist, out the turning doors and froze. My Mercedes McLaren business hover car was gone. I couldn't believe it. I thought fast and started running towards the metro station. I ran in, it scanned my octopus card at the barriers and went through to the platform area. I sat down on a bench. I was exhausted after all of that running.

Then all of a sudden, two metro platform security wardens came running towards me, one with his laser pistol aimed at me. I put my hands up. Just then, a sudden rush of horror went through me as I realised I had forgotten my briefcase, with Mr Dukem, my boss' terms and conditions for the negotiator. The other security warden put my hands behind my back and put a pair of laser handcuffs on me. They took me away from the platform, just as the metro I was going to get on arrived.

They took me to a highly-protected room, with security guards on both sides of the door and hallway. They sat me down on a seat and left the room. I sat there for what seemed to be forever.

I was about to fall asleep when the door swung open and three law enforcement officers, wearing bullet-proof vests and carrying laser assault rifles, entered the room. One of them got out his triviam electronic organiser and projected a hologram. It looked like a wanted poster. He studied the wanted criminal's face, then looked at mine.

'We've got the wrong guy. Let's go,' he said.

Before they left, they explained to me that there was a very dangerous criminal on the loose, and that one of the security wardens had mistaken me for him.

Well that was it. I was a lot later than I originally was. I decided to brace myself and call my boss. I turned on my multi-com device. Just as I did, I received a message from Mr Dukem. It read, 'Meeting today cancelled due to negotiator falling ill, received Monday 17/06/3042 at 7.30am'.

I just felt like crying. I went through all that for nothing …

**Nelson Lui  (13)**
Friends' School, Lisburn

# The Day Everything Went Wrong

Oh nooo! That's the tenth web today that has been dusted off by one of those giant fluffy things. On top of that, I haven't seen a fly all day!

Well now, I see myself as quite a generous spider, but really, on a day like this I can't 'Spin 4 a mate', 'Donate a fly', or contribute to any of those other charities. This is mainly because I have a very large family and for me, charity begins in the dark corner of the ceiling!

I have just come back from trying, yet again to catch a fly. Just one tiny one would be great, I'm not asking for a bluebottle or anything! However, while I was gone, things went from bad to worse.

First of all I got spotted by a, what humans call little and what I call absolutely enormous, girl in a pink frilly dress. Well, she started to scream when she saw me. Most humans do this, but I'm not that ugly, am I? I personally see myself as quite handsome! Anyway, this was obviously an 'Oh no! An icky spider, whatever shall we do?' girl. So I decided to get her back for being so horrible to me and started to run towards her. Then out came the big black shoe. It almost missed me, but cut off one of my legs! I've never been too scared of humans doing this as I was captain of the Shoe-Dodging 'A' Team back in my school days. I must make sure none of my former teammates hears about this!

So, after a long limp home, here I am lying down with seven legs and fifty hungry, whining children. Even though today was most certainly the day everything went wrong, I know that tomorrow will be worse - it's spring-cleaning day in the humans' household.

**Kerry Logan  (12)**
**Friends' School, Lisburn**

# A Day In The Life Of My Hamster

I poked my nose out of my nest of sawdust and saw that it was daybreak. I decided to do some exercise before my great escape, so I scurried over to my wheel and ran for about five minutes, then dashed to the water bottle for a drink.

I heard a rustling from my nest and Spike ran over. Spike is a creamy coloured hamster, about my size. He is lovable, cute, and unadventurous, unlike me; I'm always looking for an escape route.

Finally I had an escape route, a foolproof plan and I was ready to carry it out.

I gnawed at the bottom of my cage and I was almost through. Finally, I scrambled out of the hole I had made and scampered towards the door. Now came the hard part: the stairs. There was a drop of around 20 centimetres, and if I fell, I would break my leg. I slowly climbed the banister and slid down. When I got into the hall, I could almost smell victory. I was going to escape. I swiftly climbed the curtains and jumped out the open window, onto the grass.

Finally, I was free! Suddenly, a shadow was cast over me. A hand loomed overhead. I rose onto my hind legs and attacked, scratching and biting, but the hand was too strong. I was carried inside and locked inside a high security glass cage.

Well, it was going to be tough escaping this time, but soon I would have freedom!

**Matthew Rea**
**Friends' School, Lisburn**

# The Day Everything Went Wrong!

Mum had just told me that our next door neighbour was coming round to fix the PVC around the window in my bedroom, she expected it to be tidy when he arrived.

So, I tidied my room. Mr Next Door (I don't know his name!) arrived and was inspecting my windows with close scrutiny, when I heard a thump and turned around to find a bird (a starling to be precise) had flown into the window.

The chain of unfortunate events began in an instant. The glass window cracked and the glass shattered all over Mr Next Door. I think a piece may have stuck in his finger as he started jumping up and down with one hand wrapped around his index finger!

Anyway, Mum took him to hospital and we were surprised to learn that he needed an operation as he'd severed a major vein. We went home and Mr Next Door's wife collected him from casualty a few days later.

The next week, we received some shocking news ... the hospital had read the wrong chart and removed his appendix by mistake!

Next day, the phone rang. I thought it was for me, but surprise, surprise, it was Mrs Next Door informing us that Mr Next Door had become very ill. She thought it may have been the side effects of the operation, but took her husband to hospital anyway and, upon X-ray, they discovered that the scalpel blade had been left in his abdomen. Result ... septicaemia. Fatality!

Mr Next Door's family knew that his dying request was that his coffin should be crafted from the old beech tree in his garden. That very beech tree which housed the nest of the starling which flew into the windowpane.

Results: Mr Next Door dead; starling loses home ...

And all because I asked for my window to be repaired!

**Sophie McDermott (13)**
**Friends' School, Lisburn**

# Finnlay McCool

Finnlay McCool was a teenage giant from Antrim. Finnlay was the most stylish and trendy giant in all Ireland. He had blond, spiky hair and blue eyes. The freckles on Finnlay were the size of apples!

Finnlay loved shoes. His favourite make of shoes was the 'Funky Guyant' range. He always begged his parents to give him money to buy the newest pair.

One day, Finnlay was up the town to buy the latest pair of trainers, when a messenger came up to him. The messenger told Finnlay that a Scottish teenage giant called Angus II wanted to fight him. Finnlay laughed to himself, 'How's that guy going to get over here anyway?'

Angus wanted to beat Finnlay because Finnlay's dad had beat Angus' dad years and years ago.

When Finnlay got home with his new pair of shoes, he noticed something about his room. All of his lovely, stylish trainers were missing! *Where could they be?* he thought. *They wouldn't fit anywhere, not anywhere the humans own anyway, like in a dump.*

'Mum,' he yelled, 'where are all my shoes?'

'I thought that you had too many, so I threw them in the sea,' she explained. 'They wouldn't fit anywhere else. I made a game of it,' she chuckled to herself, 'I threw them further each time. I bet that I probably made a trail to Scotland!'

That night, Angus walked along the trail of shoes, all the way to Antrim. He rapped on the castle door and his mum answered it.

'Would Finnlay be in?' asked Angus.

'Yes,' she replied.

Finnlay went to the door. Angus went to hit Finnlay in the face, but Finnlay ducked and Angus fell. Finnlay kicked Angus in the face and Angus took a nosebleed, all over Finnlay's new shoes! Finnlay was furious and ran to smack him. Angus was terrified and ran all the way back to Scotland, throwing Finnlay's shoes back to the shore so that Finnlay wouldn't follow him!

Finnlay got his shoes back and was happy.

**Tori Mallon (12)**
**Friends' School, Lisburn**

# A Day In The Life Of Gwen Stefani

*(An extract)*

Her alarm clock sounded just as she was about to check the time. It was 5am, Saturday morning! Imagine having to get up at that time every morning, going to get your hair done, your nails, make-up, having a stylist poke around you. It may seem like Heaven to you, but for this poor wee superstar, it's Hell! Gwen sat down on the seat of a cramped dressing room in the MTV studio in London.

'Why do these stupid dressing rooms have to be so small?' said Gwen, with a slight croak in her voice because she had just sung for a recording of MTV Chart Show.

'Oh, will you stop complaining, Miss Stefani!' said her agent in a stroppy voice. 'You never stop,' he said again with a stroppy tone.

'Well it's hard not to, when you're as fed up as I am!' Gwen started.

She was interrupted by her agent's pager sounding.

'Oh, we have to hurry, your private jet is leaving in about half an hour to go to LA,' he said.

'Right then, we should go, and you wonder why I'm so fed up, dragging me halfway around the world every day to do pointless programmes!' Gwen said with a sigh.

They arrived at the airport, and as they were waiting in the lounge, a couple of Gwen's fans came swooping over …

**Emma Kennedy  (12)**
**Friends' School, Lisburn**

# Lurgan Take The Gold!

A brilliant end to a brilliant season for local hockey club, Lurgan Ladies.

The under 14 league finished with Lurgan A as winners, captained by Emma Thornbury. The strong Lurgan team won all 10 matches, beating off strong rivals Armagh, Portadown, Dromore, Lisnagarvey and Lurgan B team.

The Bs played very well, since playing 3rd years. They won 4, lost 3 and tied 3. One of the ties was with Armagh, meaning Armagh lost a point, securing a win for the A team.

On Thursday, May 21st, Emma lifted the cup. This was after a close match with Armagh (2-0). Lurgan won. The Bs played Dromore and tied 2-2.

At the end of the league, the table stood like this:
1 Lurgan A
2 Armagh
3 Lisnagarvey
4 Portadown
5 Dromore
6 Lurgan B

Coach Ivor Lennon says, 'I'm very proud of both my teams. The B team should be very proud of taking that vital point off Armagh. I hope the B team, who are now the A team, will win the title next year'.

The 1sts unluckily missed out in getting into Senior 1 for the 17th year in a row. Captain Kerry McColum is leaving this year to go to university, so can no longer play for Lurgan. Well done to all the girls and we hope to see them all again next year.

**Claire Jordan (12)**
**Friends' School, Lisburn**

# The Treasure Guard

It was a wet and windy day in the Kent garden of Mr and Mrs Kimrid. Their two children, Molly and Tom, were bored. They had used up all their paints and board games from Christmas ages ago, and now there was nothing to do. Molly decided that they should go outside and explore the field that was at the bottom of their garden, so they put on their boots and coats and ventured outside.

They had been walking through the field for about half an hour when Tom noticed a cave at the bottom of one of the hillocks. They climbed down into it and walked along until they found a small wooden door which had runes engraved into the surface of the rich brown wood.

When they entered, they found a huge mountain of gold and silver, surrounded by brightly lit-up, insect-like creatures, which were buzzing around it. As they looked around, they found that the cave was covered in gems and brightly-coloured rocks. When they turned around, they saw that the creatures had come together to form a young woman, who came towards them and told them that she protected the cave from evil and had been instructed to wait for a pure heart to look after the treasure. She then disappeared and left them standing alone in the cave.

That was ten years ago, and the children still go to the cave to make sure that it wasn't a dream.

**Alexandra Pengelly (13)**
Friends' School, Lisburn

# The Truth Behind Snow White!

Snow White was a lonely girl with a heart of gold and beauty beyond any man's wildest imagination. She was pale in face, with red-rose lips and her hair was as black as coal. She had always dreamt of her handsome prince, yet never her true love.

All men were intimidated by her true beauty, and found it hard to talk. Yet she tried so hard to find that man who was right for her.

So you've all heard the story of Snow White and the Seven Dwarves, but no one knows the truth.

Well, it says in the story that the evil witch, who was not as beautiful as Snow White, was jealous and went out of her way to kill her. But this is not so true.

Yes, she was a witch, but she was also Snow White's sister and was much more beautiful than her. And Snow White was the one that was jealous, as the witch was very happily married with two children.

Then it says the witch came to Snow White with poisonous apples, but this is not so. The witch came to Snow White's door to invite her to lunch with her family and was bearing a gift of a basket of apples. Snow White lunged for her chest with a cook's knife and then stabbed herself.

The dwarves later found her stabbed beside what they thought to be an evil witch.

From then on, the story is true and she found her love at last!

**Rebecca Palmer (12)**
Friends' School, Lisburn

# The Serpent Of Skye

When you ask someone about Scotland, the first thing that usually comes to their head is the Loch Ness Monster. Of course that isn't real, but most ignorant people believe it is. However, if you were to mention the Serpent of Skye to someone, they'd probably snigger and walk off. However, the serpent is far too true, as is known by four fishermen from the serpent's home place, the Isle of Skye. Its origins aren't too clear, but they can be slightly explained through this tale …

Angus, Michael, Thomas and Carter were out at a small fishing stream at 11.13pm on a dry, dim night. On this night the stream was left bare, with absolutely no life inside, and yet for some reason, shadows kept appearing under the water. Carter mentioned that he had seen something strange and at this exact point, he was devoured in a flash by the serpent. The serpent was so fast, Michael and Angus didn't see it, but Thomas saw it and the sight of the horrible monster sent him insane. The other two ran away as fast as they could, but then they got struck by the beast, at which point they blacked out and ended up in hospital.

Angus fell into an eternal coma, while Michael was able to tell half of the tale before dying of his wounds. Maybe this means there is more to this tale than you think …

**Alexander McReynolds (12)**
**Friends' School, Lisburn**

# Town Terrorised by ... A Hopragon?

Early this morning, chaos struck. A group of boys were sitting under a tree when a 'monster' appeared from behind them and roared ferociously. His fire-breathing sent three of the boys flying through a lorry, and the other two were burnt instantly.

The other three boys are seriously injured and warn everyone to *stay in their houses!* Most of you who got a bit startled by the small 'quake' yesterday, well this must've been the shake you felt. For those of you who saw this gigantic creature and want to know what it is, well we may know.

100 years ago, a 38-year-old scientist named Dr Martin, tried to prove that he could make the first horsesheepdragon, aka Hopragon. When Dr Martin shared his idea with his colleagues, they simply laughed, but that didn't stop him. He worked for years on an experiment he called 'The Perfect Being'. He kept arguing with his boss, saying that this will happen, but the boss was annoyed so he sacked Martin.

He didn't cancel his project though, he kept working at it and he finally made the egg. He waited for it to hatch. He watched it for weeks, months and years and finally gave up. He was so annoyed that it didn't hatch, that he dug a hole in the ground and buried the egg. This egg has finally hatched and until it is killed, everyone must *stay in their houses and don't leave until told!*

**Hayley McKay (11)**
Friends' School, Lisburn

# The Lost Life Of An Evacuee

I had to leave my best friends, my loving family and my home in Belfast, all in one day.

My mother came into my bedroom (that I share with my two older sisters and my three younger brothers) and told us all to pack our most prized possessions, put on smart clothes and meet her in the kitchen. She was trying to stay calm, but I saw the sparkling tear in her eye.

Our father kept himself locked up in his study, too scared to face us. I knew what was happening, I knew it was the day I'd been dreading. My younger brothers, Timothy, Benjamin and James, didn't know what was happening; they had been told repeatedly, but they saw it as an adventure!

I was quiet while packing my things, even when one of my siblings spoke to me. I kept my mouth shut. I was too overcome with sadness with the thought; I would maybe never see my mum or dad after today.

I walked solemnly to the train station. When it was time to depart, I hugged my mother for what seemed like forever. I never wanted to let go. She told me not to worry, and that I would see her after the war. It was all a blur after then.

I must have fallen asleep, maybe even for the last thirty years up at Portrush. I tried to find them, I tried my best but didn't. I am now 37.

**Sarah Mathewson  (12)**
**Friends' School, Lisburn**

# Finn Mac Cumhail

*(A Celtic legend)*

Demne's mother sat by the fireside. Tears like diamonds fell from her eyes and shattered on the rough blanket where her son lay. His tiny face gazed up at her.

A woman entered, her sword sparkling in the firelight.

'Fiachel ...' his mother whispered, 'take him ...' Her voice cracked. She held up the tiny baby. Fiachel reached out and grasped the child, and she was gone.

The deer lowered its head to drink, then turned its delicate head, sensing danger. The stone hit it once, and it was dead. Demne picked it up and returned to the cave. Bodbal and Fiachel glanced at him. They had been talking. Demne felt a sense of unease.

'Demne, you are fifteen, old enough to fend for yourself. You must go.' Bodbal stood and handed him a sword. 'Go to the poet, Finneces. Taste the Salmon of Knowledge, and discover the truth ... go, child.'

Finneces watched as Demnes reached out to turn the salmon on the fire. His hand slipped, touching the roasting salmon. He put his finger in his mouth, tasting the salmon ...

'Demnes,' Finneces hissed, 'you are Finn Mac Cumhail. Goll Mac Morna killed your father ... avenge your father, then you can rest.'

Goll Mac Morna towered above Finn, who was on the ground, weary and badly wounded. He struggled backwards, trying to get to his feet. Finn stood, blood oozing from his wounds. With the last of his strength, he plunged his sword deep into Goll. 'Father,' he murmured, 'I won ...'

**Victoria Mayers  (12)**
Friends' School, Lisburn

# The Day Everything Went Wrong

19th August 1999, the day we were all dreading. Granda had been sick for over a year now. We knew one day it was going to happen, but it doesn't ease the pain.

We had been at the hospital all night with Nanny and the rest of the family. The doctors had said that the end was near, so everyone was at the hospital, just waiting and talking about the good times they had shared together.

Granda knew everyone. Everywhere we went, he always seemed to know someone. Either from drumming competitions, or he had done some work for them. He would always stop and talk to someone he knew. We would stand there listening, wondering what he was talking about.

He always made me laugh and I loved spending time with him. When he left me, it broke my heart. I would stay up at night crying about that awful day that he died.

We all went back to Nanny's house from the hospital. It seemed like Granda really did know everyone, because it seemed that the whole world had come in and out of Nanny's house that day, each person as distraught as the next one.

Nanny kept a very brave face, smiling and making sure everyone had enough to eat and drink, almost as if it hadn't happened. A lot of people thought she would have fallen apart when Granda died, but she proved them wrong.

My cousins and I were sitting on the couch. Ashleigh was three years older than us; she was crying, we didn't know why. Granda was going to come back and things would go back to normal, so we laughed at her. But now that I've realised he's not coming back, I'm the one who's crying.

**Aimeé McCluskey  (12)**
Friends' School, Lisburn

# The Day Everything Went Wrong!

Everything was going OK, that was until we found out that we would be running the cross-country in the local park. As you can tell, this isn't one of my favourite things! Just to make things better, it started to rain. I went into the changing rooms, got into my PE kit and then did my stretches. When I came out, the rain was lashing down. I could tell this was going to be no typical day!

Of course, the usual sporty girls darted off. You know, the ones that come back without a hair out of place. Whilst I trundled off, wondering how long it would take me this time.

By the time I'd completed my first lap I was absolutely exhausted, as well as the rest of the not-so-sporty girls around me, though it was Hannah I was really worried about. You see, she has asthma and was looking really pale, as if she was about to faint. At that, she collapsed onto the ground. Everyone else ran on, not wanting to be last finished - what was I going to do?

I picked her up and made sure that she wasn't hurt or bleeding anywhere. Once I'd checked that, I found the nearest park bench, set her down and got one of the girls that had finished to get the teacher. When the teacher finally came over, we both helped Hannah back up to school and waited for the school nurse to come and check her out.

It was just another day everything went wrong!

**Leah McCall (13)**
**Friends' School, Lisburn**

# The Day Everything Went Wrong

August 6th, 1945. My fifteenth birthday and it is a glorious morning. I can't wait until my friends arrive and we can go to the Sumo wrestling contest. Even though the war with the Americans is still being waged in the Pacific and my father is fighting with the Imperial Japanese army, it is quiet here. There is no way the Americans will ever reach this country.

My mother gave me my present this morning and with it was a letter from my father. I can't wait until I am old enough to fight and defend my country. My father says he is proud of me, but he will be even prouder when I am fighting alongside him. He writes in his letter that the army is fighting fiercely against the American invaders, and describes the heroism of the kamikaze pilots. His letter makes my day and as I read the words again and again, I hear the sound of an aeroplane high above my house in Hiroshima. I look upwards and shade my eyes with my hand against the sharp glare of the sun, but it is too strong for me to see anything.

I hear a yell and I recognise Hoshi's voice and I run to meet him and see what present he has brought me.

I am blown off my feet and then I hear the roar of the blast, and then there is the blinding flash. I cannot see Hoshi and I scream out his name, but there is no reply.

**John McRitchie (13)**
**Friends' School, Lisburn**

# The Day Everything Went Wrong

It was a Tuesday afternoon when it all started. John had gone out of his class and was headed for the library when his dad called, 'Over here, sport.'

John spun round and he saw his dad. He calmly walked over to him and said, 'Hi, Dad.'

His dad said, 'Do you want to go for a walk, son?'

John said, 'Yeah, Dad,' a little too eagerly.

They started off on their walk and his dad said, 'Why don't you take a seat?'

He sat down and patted the place beside him with his hand, almost daring him to sit down. John sat down on the bench and they started chatting to each other like mates. John was about to get up, when his dad said, 'I think it is time to tell you why me and your mum split up. You're nineteen now and you should be told.'

John spurted out, 'You said that it was because you had just grown too far apart.'

His dad gave an eerie laugh. 'Ha, kids these days are so gullible. Say the moon is made out of cheese and they'll ask you what kind. We didn't split up because of each other. We split up because of you, Jonathan. You were so annoying and loud and you cried all the time. I hated you.'

*Hated you,* kept ringing in his ears.

His dad continued, 'Let's stop these weekend visits, because I don't get a kick out of them anymore.' His dad got up and was about to walk away when he turned, gave a look as if he wasn't worthy to be his son and said, 'I thought that my son would be smarter too.'

John dropped everything and just ran; ran until he could run no more.

**Stephen Johnston (13)**
Friends' School, Lisburn

# Liverpool Are On Their Way To Glory

*Liverpool are making history as they defeated Chelsea at Anfield on their way to the Champions League final.*

The atmosphere was amazing. It was the second leg and the first had ended 0-0. The winner would go to play against AC Milan in the final of the Champions League. It was just moments before the kick-off and the crowds were singing their team's anthem.

The whistle blew and the crowd cheered. Chelsea was the favourite to win, with Liverpool being the underdogs. Liverpool had just lost the ball and the fans signalled a free kick, but none was given. Lampard was already up to the centre line. There was a tackle by the Liverpool captain, Gerard, and they got the ball again. Gerard ran the pitch until he was about 50 yards out and crossed it to Baros, who chipped it over Peter Check and then got brought to the ground. Luis Garcia had received the ball and shot at the net. A Chelsea defender tried to clear it, but it was too late. He had cleared it just after it had crossed the line. The whistle blew and the Liverpool fans roared. They had gone into the lead only four minutes into the game. The first half came and went with many chances, but still no result for Chelsea. The second half was the same, and when the final whistle blew, Liverpool had won!

A match that no one will forget. 1-0!

**Jordan Owens (12)**
**Friends' School, Lisburn**

# Mad Doctor Matt!

There was once a doctor who was utterly insane. His name was Matt! He spent day and night in his converted kitchen working on a time machine. This was unknown to anyone but him, as he was very protective over his work.

He spent many days and nights on his machine until one fateful day he got it. 'Yes!' he screamed. 'My creation. It's mine, mine, yes, only mine!' he exclaimed in his high-pitched, crackly voice. 'It's time, time to use it. Yes my precious, it's time!'

So he set off to get his old watch, then revealed his creation. A watch, plain and simple with a dial and screen. He removed his watch strap and attached the new watch to it. Then slowly he raised his hand and strapped it onto his wrist. 'Moment of truth,' he muttered, and typed in 1965, the day he was born. There was a sudden flash and he was gone, from that time, place and room, vaporised.

Only a few seconds later he arrived in a street. There was a sign saying, 'Harling Street Hospital', the hospital he was born in. He went inside and sure enough, his mum was there, young as ever with a baby, him, in her arms. Time to go. He typed in minus 22 million years. Flash, and he was there in the magical age of dinosaurs. He looked around and to his terror, he saw a huge bulk of muscle. Just like that, he was eaten.

Matt shouldn't have meddled with time!

**Joe Murphy (12)**
**Friends' School, Lisburn**

# Season Review

*Chelsea Win Premiership.*

For the first time in 50 years, Chelsea FC won the Premier League and won by a considerable amount of points. A lot of thanks have to go to the owner of the club, Roman Abramovich, for giving the club hundreds of millions of pounds to buy players and to Jose Mourinho for guiding Chelsea to the title.

*Glazer Buys United.*

Malcolm Glazer has been trying to buy United now for nearly two years. He has now bought United for £3 a share.

He has beaten the barrier he needed to break to control all of United, which is 75%. He does not know anything about football and is not like Roman Abramovich, who watches every match and loves football. He is only after making money out of united and could put United £790 million into debt.

*Liverpool Get To The Final Of The Champions League.*

Liverpool FC has surprised Europe by getting into the Champions League final. A major thanks to this has been because of Steven Gerrard. He is the driving force of Liverpool FC, and if he leaves Liverpool and goes to Chelsea in the summer, it will be a major loss to the Liverpool team. They were on their way out of the tournament when Steven Gerrard scored a magnificent goal to put them into the quarter-final against Juventus and beat them, and then met moneybags Chelsea in the Champions League semi-final and overcame them with a disputed goal.

**Jonathon Patterson (12)**
Friends' School, Lisburn

# The Modern Hercules

Roger was up early and said, 'Mum, I feel sick.'

When his mum came, she told him he had to stay home and no playing games, as he had the twenty-four hour flu.

When he was watching television, the remote control fell under their very heavy sofa. Disaster, the baby shows were about to start and the remote was missing. Roger stood up and suddenly felt weird. A tingling sensation passed through his hands, then his arms and finally his entire body. As soon as it had started, it was over.

Roger continued and lifted the sofa with one hand, while picking up the remote with the other hand. He walked over and stopped mid-stride. He looked over and saw the sofa in one hand; he dropped the sofa in shock.

He remembered a book he had read about a man who was super strong. He thought it was Hercules, but he was not sure.

He knew what to do. He went to all the material shops in the town and bought lots of red lycra. When Roger got home, he made a costume. It was very bad. After several attempts he got it right, but he did have to buy more material.

The next day, Roger put on the superhero costume and went to save lots of people.

'Help, help. He stole my handbag.'

'I will help you,' Roger said.

In a few seconds there was a tangled heap of a mugger and a rope and a stick.

**Gareth Nelson  (12)**
**Friends' School, Lisburn**

# A Day In The Life Of A Farmer

Farmer Sam woke up at twelve midnight and got groggily up to check on the sheep. He walked down to the shed. There was a sheep in the corner having trouble lambing. Sam put on his yellow lambing suit and went to the sheep. He caught hold of the two front legs that were appearing, and helped the sheep to lamb.

After checking that the lamb was OK, he went back to bed because he would have to get up three more times in the night, before having to milk the cows at five.

At 5am, he got up for the fifth time that night and went into the kitchen. His wife, Maggie, had cooked porridge and made a pot of tea for them both.

After breakfast Paul, the farmhand, arrived to help milk the forty cows. They always milked the cows by hand and not by the new machines that most farmers used now. By 11 o'clock, all the cows had been milked and fed, and the two sheepdogs, the farm cats and all the chickens had been fed and let out too.

The farmer invited Paul inside and had another cup of tea, and then sat down exhausted.

Maggie wanted to go shopping, so Sam left Paul to look after the animals and took her into town. While Maggie went shopping, he bought some more chicken feed. They went home again and Sam pottered about doing odd jobs.

So after a very busy day, Sam fell into bed at seven and slept like a log.

**Laura Montgomery  (12)**
**Friends' School, Lisburn**

# The Day Everything Went Wrong

Yesterday was the day everything went wrong. It all started as soon as I woke up. I pressed the snooze button on my alarm clock and turned over to go back to sleep, when I noticed out of the corner of my eye, the time was 7.45! I knew there wasn't enough time for a shower or breakfast, so I just washed, packed my bag and got my uniform on.

Luckily, my dad could give me a lift down to the bus stop. He dropped me off at the end of the road, but the bus was leaving. I ran as fast as I could, but my bag spilt out my books, lunch and PE kit. I thought nothing else could go wrong, but then it started raining out of the heavens. I sat under a tree and tried to keep as dry as possible. I was not a happy bunny.

I got into school soaked to the skin, with a runny nose. I just made it for the end of collect, and I was soon off to sit through another brilliant assembly. *(Cough, cough.)* First period came and I had packed books for Wednesday, and not for Tuesday. In nearly every class I got lines, or a detention. I knew this had to be the worst day of my life.

Finally, the end of school and this time I caught the bus. It didn't take long to get home, but I received a message from my mum walking up home saying she wouldn't be home until 5pm, and if she was any later, to make my own tea. But there was only one problem. I had forgotten my keys, so I sat outside in my partially wet uniform for an hour and a half.

I have a few tips on how to make sure you don't end up like me … never press the snooze button, always look at what you're packing, make sure your bag is well shut, and remember your house keys.

**David McGuigan (13)**
Friends' School, Lisburn

# A Day In The Life Of Eden Wilson

I would like to spend a day of my life being Eden. Eden is my baby cousin. She is only 11 months old. Her birthday is on the 12th of June. I would like to go back to Eden's age, because I love the way they get amused so easily. I would also like to go back to that age, because you get to have a lot of fun. Eden has only just started to crawl, and she has lots of toys.

If I went back to her age I would not be going to school, which would be bad because I would not have all the friends I have now, but the good thing would be that I would get to sleep most of the day. Everyone has good memories of when they were babies, but when you grow up, you remember the bad memories more than the good ones.

When you are young, everyone thinks you are cute. Your family has lots of people over and that gives you a lot of company.

She watches baby programmes and gets to hang about with her nanny, Vera, and my other cousin, Leah, all day. Leah is only two, and Eden and her get along very well.

When we go to Coco's and everywhere else, she gets to play in the ball pit, but I can't because I am too old.

How I would love to go back to that age! If I went back to that age, I would have so much fun.

**Rachel Petticrew (12)**
**Friends' School, Lisburn**

# A Day In the Life Of Zantoo!

I lay in my bed, my foot in pain as usual, bit I knew I had no choice but to go to the well to get our daily water, so I got off the ground and started walking with my two jars for the water.

My name is Zantoo and I'm twelve. I live in the Sudan with my two-year-old sister, Tecla, and my sick mother, Fillbea. my father died when I was young, so I'm the man of the house.

It takes me three hours to get to the well, and at the minute, it's 3.30am, so I should be back at about 10am because of the queues to the well!

I do this every morning to get the water we need for the rest of the day, to cook, wash, drink and clean. The water contains germs, but we want to live. When I get back we shall all wash with half a jar of water, then drink it for breakfast, because the rice is only for night-time. Then I walk for another hour to go to our land with our very little rice, and I water and harvest it.

Sometimes I sit on the grass and think of me, rich, in a brick-wall house, but then I get back to the real world.

For tea, we have rice or water, then we snuggle up on the floor like a happy family, and sleep.

**Kathryn Mercer (11)**
**Friends' School, Lisburn**

# Happy Slapping

'Happy slapping' is a craze in which groups of teenagers armed with camera phones slap or mug unsuspecting children or passers-by while capturing the attacks on 3g technology.

According to the police and anti-bullying organisations, this began as a craze on the UK Garage Music scene before catching on in school playgrounds across Britain. It's now a nationwide phenomenon. Police have investigated at least 200 incidents in the last six months. Most go unreported. The gangs have become more sophisticated, seeking victims in parks or public areas, where their crimes are unlikely to be captured on CCTV.

There have been cases where victims have been knocked out and some have even been brought into hospital. The craze appears to be becoming more violent as the attackers try to outdo each other.

'You see someone just sitting there, they look like they're dumb. You just run up to them and slap them and run off. It's funny', said Johnny Wilson, 16, from Belfast.

It is known for attacks to happen in the victim's own homes. Attackers are also using public places and public transport.

Bluetooth makes it easy for these kids to share their videos with others. Schools are finding it hard to cope with. They have tried banning mobile phones in the hope that it will stop attacks.

Now with half of 7 to 10-year-olds owning mobile phones, parents and authorities are hoping the new craze stops before the violence evolves into something even worse.

**Emily Wallace (14)**
Friends' School, Lisburn

# A Night To Remember

It was a dark night. I had put on an extra jumper because it was so cold. It had snowed earlier that night and it had settled. As I walked across the crispy field, the snow crunching beneath my feet, I saw a dim light in the sky. *It must be just an aeroplane,* I thought but the light was getting brighter. It was coming closer and then in my sight was a spaceship!

It was very dark although it had lights shining off their light. It was coming closer to the ground. I ran to the nearest tree and hid. I was so scared. *This is a dream,* I thought to myself. I pinched myself. The pain shot through my body. There was really a spaceship about to land!

As it touched the ground I held my breath. *Maybe they have seen me,* I thought, hoping they hadn't. The entrance opened and out shot a bridge descending down to the ground. Then I heard footsteps and out came an alien! It looked like it was wearing a spacesuit. Its flesh was a purple colour and the bones were very easy to see. It had a long protruding neck holding a round head. I felt amazed that I was seeing this. He took a glass jar out of his pocket and scooped some snow into it. He screwed the lid back on and tapped. It became frosted. Then he walked back into the spaceship. The doors shut behind him and the ship took off. I just stood there stunned. Something had happened that night that I could never have dreamed of. I began to return home.

*That was a night to remember!* I thought.

**Nicole Burnett (12)**
Friends' School, Lisburn

# Conspiracies Of The Bermuda

'Come on John!'

'Yeah what's up?'

'Well you're just flying over Brazil now, you'll soon be back to England. About a day to go, how do you feel?'

'Okay, didn't get much sleep, turbulence, you know?'

'Yeah you gotta hate it.'

John Smith was going for the world record of flying solo around the world. He was four days into his flight and had stopped for fuel twice. He had left England and flown east over Asia. Now he was over South America heading for what was known as the Bermuda Triangle. He had been warned about it before from HQ as he called them, but he said it was just another conspiracy theory. He got another radio message from HQ and they said that he could take a different route. John told them that he wanted to get the shortest route and get the record time. So he kept flying and was close to the area when suddenly his plane started to dip and had seemed to have lost power.

'What the!' John knew he was going to be killed by the impact of his plane hitting the water so he pressed the eject button and landed on an island. He lay there for a few minutes to let the events sink in. He suddenly felt dizzy and then fainted. He woke up and there looking into his face was something that he'll never forget.

**Christopher Young (13)**
**Friends' School, Lisburn**

# The Myth Of Avorax Aduntis

A long, long, long time ago, precisely 5,000,000 years ago in Greek times there was a dragon that lived near the city Asvorax, home of the great emperor of Greece. It was a very, very rich city, the houses were made of gold and each one was three storeys high. The Emperor's house was made much more expensive. It had five storeys, the walls were made of gold and he controlled 30 acres of the land in Asvorax, his name was Avorax Aduntis, the very well-named dragon slayer. He had been through every city in Greece to fight in dragon slaying competitions. This was easy until it came to the Dragon Vorgak who lived above Asvorax in the Smokey Mountains. Avorax was scared but he was trying not to show it. Vorgak's cave was big, filled with gold and all sorts of treasures. No one could get them unless they were brave enough like Avorax. Everyone believed he could slay this dragon. Vorgak kept on terrorising the people of Asvorax. Every day he would sweep down and breathe fire on the people of Asvorax. They were getting angry. Finally Avorax lifted up his sword, his helmet and his armour. When he did this he climbed the dark and treacherous path to the Smokey Mountains where the dragon lay waiting. He fought the dragon and he won. The people of Asvorax had a parade for him and celebrated this great victory over the dragon. This is the myth of Avorax Aduntis.

**Jack Redpath (12)**
Friends' School, Lisburn

# A Day In The Life Of David Beckham

Today I went to my team training at Real Madrid. We got warmed up and then we passed the ball around the whole team. The coach pulled me off to one side. He told me that I should take a few penalty kicks because he said he was watching Euro 2004 and wasn't too happy about my penalties. He set the ball in front of me and told Casillias to get in goal. I shot the ball at the net five times and scored four times. The coach said, 'That's better. But let's hope you do just as well in the match this afternoon against Liverpool.'

I didn't like the way he commented on my performance but I really wanted to play. It was an hour before the match and I was getting ready. I took a few more penalty shots and then I stretched my muscles. All the fans crowded into the stadium screaming and shouting, 'Come on Real Madrid!' I jogged onto the pitch, waiting in anticipation for the match to start. Then the referee blew his whistle for the start of the match.

In the end we won by three goals to nil. The coach was proud of me because I scored a penalty, after Owen being tackled. The whole team went running into the changing rooms, shouting and cheering. When I got out of the stadium the family and I went to a restaurant and then we headed home to our luxury villa in Spain. I then played a short game of football with my children and then went to bed, awaiting a long training session tomorrow morning.

**David Seeds (12)**
Friends' School, Lisburn

# A Day In The Life Of A Puppy

I wake up every morning at seven. The reason that I wake at seven is because that's when my master gets up. He takes about fifteen minutes to get dressed, have his breakfast and brush his teeth.

After he finishes all that he will come and feed me. The food that he feeds me is special food for a dog like me. Every morning my master leaves at ten-past eight.

When he leaves the house, that's when the fun starts. All the others come round and we eat my owner's food. We have a great time.

All my friends call me Blobby because I'm fatter than them, but my owner calls me Bappy.

My owner's name is Josh. Sometimes when I am eating I fall asleep and lie there for ages. After I wake up I go for a walk to burn off the calories. When I am on my walk I chase lots of cats. When I have chased enough cats I go home and sleep in Josh's bed. When I wake up I watch TV.

Josh usually gets home at five, so he eats his dinner and we go and play with a Frisbee and a tennis ball. After I am finished playing I go in and have a sleep for the night in my kennel.

**Josh McMullan (12)**
**Friends' School, Lisburn**

# A Night Of Awards

Last night the British Soap Awards were announced. The actors and actresses arrived in their glad rags. I was there and interviewed a few from EastEnders.

'It has been a great year for EastEnders and for Kat', said Jessie Wallace who plays Kat Moon. 'Kat has had a lot of dirty scenes and a really good storyline'.

When asked who he thought would get the sexiest female, Shane Richie said, 'I don't really know but I think Jessie has a good chance'.

Javine and Steve, the winner of X-Factor, were there to present the award along with Katie Price and Peter Andre.

June Brown, the actress who plays Dot Branning in EastEnders, got the lifetime achievement award after 20 years of acting. Barbara Windsor was there to present her with it.

After two and a half hours of glitz and glam the winner of best soap 2004-2005 was announced. All of the soaps were in the running.

When the award was announced there was a cry of delight from the cast. The winner was Coronation Street! The cast rushed onto the stage with delight to collect their awards. This was a great achievement for everyone in Corrie.

I'm sure that there were a few after parties and even more sore heads this morning.

I'm sure that the thousands of viewers that watched it on TV thought the entertainment was great because it certainly was live.

I hope that Coronation Street have a good year and I'm already looking forward to next year's awards.

**Kathryn Magill (12)**
**Friends' School, Lisburn**

# A Day In The Life Of ... A Piece Of Sand

Hi, I'm a piece of sand. My name is Sandy and I am fifteen years old. My mum is a big beach and my dad is a sand dune.

Every day some little feet and some big feet walk over me. Sometimes it tickles and I laugh and laugh. Other times people stomp on me and it is sore.

I really like it when children and sometimes even their parents build sandcastles with me. Then the big, bad children come along and kick me and hit me and knock me down. It really hurts and I cry but no one seems to care. Maybe they don't hear me.

When I am older, I wonder if I will be a beach like my mum or a cool dune like my dad. I might not even live here anymore. The wind might blow me away to another place.

I have a girlfriend and she is 14 years old. She has blonde hair and we have been going out for two years now. Every day I see her and we eat ice cream and play tag or other games for ages. Her name is Sandra. Sandra's favourite flavour of ice cream is strawberry with strawberry sauce.

I hope that if I do get blown away by the wind that I will get blown onto a golden beach.

I love being sand because you don't have to do anything. I can sunbathe all the time and I have a permanent, golden tan.

This is the life!

**Rebecca Lister (11)**
Friends' School, Lisburn

# A Day In The Life Of A Giant Beef-Berry Pie

Once upon a time there was a pie, but this was no ordinary pie, this was a *giant beef-berry pie* and his name was Pieman.

One morning Pieman woke up and thought of his loving parents. (His dad was a beef pie and his mum was a blackberry pie). So he went downstairs to greet them but much to his surprise they weren't there. 'That's strange, they should be here, I thought they never slept,' he muttered to himself. So Pieman went and looked all around the restaurant (as that was where they lived) but couldn't find them anywhere.

Pieman went outside to look for them but instead found a shrivelled up, wrinkly, old dead chicken. But the strange thing about this chicken was that it was headless. So Pieman went off to investigate, first to find his mum and dad and then to find out why there were dead, headless chickens lying about the place. So Pieman set off to work.

First he looked in the ice cream parlour as his parents loved ice cream, but there was nothing there, then he searched all the restaurants in Foodsville but still nothing. He searched all over town when he suddenly thought, *Maybe the chickens and my parents disappearing have a connection.* He tried to think about where to find chickens and then remembered, 'A farm!'

He set off to the biggest farm in town to find out what was happening. He finally got there and to his shock there were headless chickens everywhere, with laser beams coming out of their fingers. They were about to cut his parents into pieces but, 'Noooo!' Pieman came and belly flopped and killed them all.

So Pieman saved the day, 'All in a day's work!' he said as he dozed off into a deep sleep.

**David McCrossan (12)**
**Friends' School, Lisburn**

# A Day In The Life Of Paris Hilton

I woke up this morning at around 7am. It was just in time for my photo shoot. Today I was getting lots of photos taken with my sister, Nikki, for a new magazine cover.

It was a really sunny day which was good because the photos were being taken outside.

At about 7.30am I was taken down to a dressing room to see what clothes I would be wearing and what make-up I would have. Soon after my hairdresser came in and showed me a few hair designs so that I could choose which way I wanted my hair. I had to try on about twelve outfits until I found some that I really liked.

After I got all of that sorted it was 9am. Just then I went out to get breakfast and to meet up with Nikki, my sister. I was really late and Nikki had been waiting there for about thirty minutes!

The pictures were being taken in a fancy big hotel in New York. When we arrived at the hotel we went out to where the photos were being taken. There were lots of cameras and photographers.

We had half an hour to get changed and get our hair and make-up done, but half an hour wasn't enough. It took nearly two hours but no one got too cross at us!

They started to take the photos at 12am. Every now and then we had to stop for a break or to be shown which way to pose or to get our hair and make-up fixed up.

We had lots of photos taken and were getting very tired.

It was 4pm when we finally got to leave. My sister and I decided to go shopping in New York for some new clothes then we went out for dinner.

When we got back to our hotel we were staying in we got changed into our pyjamas and watched a movie. Then we went to sleep because we had had a very busy day!

**Laura Killough (12)**
**Friends' School, Lisburn**

# The Story Of The Leprechaun

I woke up this morning, happy as ever, had the usual fried rainbow and roasted gold for breakfast. I then got dressed in my little green outfit with the brown boots and not forgetting the small green hat. I met up with my friends, Claire the unicorn, Emma the fairy and Amie the girl that thinks she's Pinocchio. We went into the small village of Cadbury where we went into Dairy Milk for lunch. We all ordered the same thing, melted Dairy Milk with toffee sauce. It was tasty.

After lunch we went to the city of Galaxy. We walked about the shops, looked in New Look for new shoes for Claire, then a new wooden nose for Amie, then finally a new fairy dress for Emma. Time went very quickly in the city of Galaxy. We swiftly moved on to the town of Milky Way where we got our tea. For tea I had a giant Milky Way Crispy Roll, Claire had nothing because she said she was on a diet, Emma had a Milky Way with a glass of milk and Amie had a small Milky Way salad.

We started to head home because it was getting late. I headed home to my house at the end of the rainbow. We took the long walk home and eventually we got there. I then went to my house as did Claire, Emma and Amie. Finally I got to sleep after a long day.

**Stuart Lightbody (12)**
**Friends' School, Lisburn**

# Monkey Business In San Maree!

It was a sweet morning in San Maree with birds chirping and the sun shining, Mother Nature at her best, but for me, it was even sweeter.

I had been saving up for a long time and all the money had been added up so finally I could get the one and only Texas football shirt.

I was walking down to the shop with my bulging wallet and suddenly a monkey popped out and sat there on its big, blue bottom eating a chocolate truffle!

Now, in San Maree we don't get very many monkeys, in fact, none until now! Even stranger though was the weird blue cream in the truffle's centre.

Recently I had been learning about food colouring in school and that blue stuff didn't look like any old food colouring, it looked like 'Trigaflash' colouring. 'Trigaflash' you ask? Well it's only the most deadly chemical in the entire world!

This troubled me for some time after that so I decided to look into both the truffles and the Trigaflash and after some sleepless nights I found out a few things; Trigaflash kills *humans* instantly and, maybe not so important, the mayor loves truffles!

I may have been a small boy but I wasn't stupid! 1 and 1 make 2! I had to tell the mayor.

At once I ran down to the town hall where the mayor was in the middle of a photo shoot, one problem, the shoot was to advertise the truffles! After one bite he immediately collapsed!

The monkeys were never seen again.

**Rory McIvor  (12)**
**Friends' School, Lisburn**

# A Simple Living

It was 9am at the airport in Los Angeles. I walked towards the exit holding a black, leather briefcase. I deliberately stepped to the side knocking into a guy holding an identical briefcase.

'Oh sorry mate, you all right?' he asked in an Australian accent. The man worked for Phoenix, my hirer.

'Oh yeah, I'm fine,' I replied. 'Good day,' I said as I picked up his briefcase as he did mine.

When I'd left the airport there was a black Ford Mustang GT waiting for me. I took the keys that the Australian had slipped into my pocket and unlocked the car. It seemed as if it hadn't been driven yet. Inside, the seats were very comfortable and everything was immaculate.

I opened the briefcase and found a file containing the details of the two people that I was going to 'clean'. It showed photographs, names, addresses and where they worked.

I glanced at my watch - it read 9.30am. It was time to roll. I started the Mustang's engine and drove off towards Pasadena.

When I reached my client's (who was called Marco Donovan) apartment in Pasadena it was 12.30pm. I opened the second case that was in my briefcase. It held a gun that was a foot long with the silencer attached. It didn't weigh too much, nice and light, perfect.

I opened the door, holding the weapon inside my jacket. When I got to the elevator the sign read, *Closed For Maintenance.*

I cursed under my breath, now I had to go up to the forty-eighth floor, to the penthouse.

While walking up the staircase, I loaded my gun. There were fifteen bullets in the magazine.

About half an hour later, when I had reached the penthouse the door was already open, as though it had been busted open forcefully. I walked into the room silently and cautiously.

There was Marco in his armchair. He was dead, and by the marks around his neck he had been strangled to death. Suddenly, behind me I heard a floorboard creak.

I spun round and fired a single shot through the air towards where about I'd heard it. No, I had missed. The guy was a small Chinese dude about five foot two. He ran for the steps and jumped onto the banister. The guy flew down at about thirty miles per hour!

I ran after him as fast as I could, but when I reached the ground floor he was nowhere to be seen! The security guard, as I hadn't realised before was dead too.

I walked carefully outside and looked around. There was nothing to be *seen!* I spun round to make sure I wasn't being crept upon. Suddenly two legs came out of nowhere and grabbed me by the neck. I dropped my gun as I gasped for air. The little man screamed and hurled me away from the gun.

He then somersaulted onto the ground and picked up my gun. 'Oh no!' I cried out. He smiled and shot me in the chest. I keeled over and spat up blood over the ground. *This is it,* I told myself.

The Chinese guy shot twice more to the left of my torso and finally a last bullet went through my heart. I fell to the ground and shut my eyes. The last thought that went through my brain was the only memory of my mother who died when I was little.

Now it was my time to join her.

**Lee Livingstone (12)**
**Friends' School, Lisburn**

# A Day In The Life Of A VCR

The night had come and I was turned off for a sleep. Thank goodness! I had been playing videos all day. First 'Stuart Little' then at the end 'The Blair Witch Project'. From comedy to horror and thriller to romance I had a hard day.

It was the morning again. I knew this because every morning I would greet 'Postman Pat'.

This episode only lasted twenty minutes and then I played 'Balamory'. It was time for the kids to go to school so yet again I was switched off for a nap.

That nap lasted longer than I thought. It was now time for the family's traditional Friday night marathon. This is the time of the day that I hated. Hours and hours of endless movies. Oh I wish that I could have a break. Then suddenly something went wrong. The TV went all fuzzy and the video stopped playing.

The next day somebody knocked at the door. In came an old man carrying a box with polystyrene in it. Suddenly it was all dark and I was in the box. About ten minutes later everything was bouncing around. It was quite a while before we got to wherever we were going.

When we finally got there I was carried into a big factory full of VCRs. Where was I? I didn't know but all I knew was it was a new adventure and one I would make the most of.

**Kirsty-Louise Knox  (11)**
**Friends' School, Lisburn**

# The Day Everything Went Wrong

It was my brother's birthday. All of his friends were coming to his party and there was also some of my friends coming. For his birthday we had ordered a bouncy castle to come for all of his mates to play on but as it happened the phone rang. Mum went running for it and it was the man that was bringing the bouncy castle, he said that he couldn't come. For starters that wasn't the first thing that went wrong, Mum had burnt most of the food for the party. I thought in my head that this was going to be a good day but already two things had gone wrong.

As things kept going wrong that day, outside was beautiful - it was sunny, there was a little wind and the grass still had a little dew left on it but I thought I may as well make the most of this lovely day. As all the party guests started to arrive the rain started to fall from the sky. We were all brought inside. Jack, my brother's friend, was running around like a mad man. I knew there was going to be something broken. I was right, he had run out into the hall and he tripped. He had sent the new vase flying. As this happened I tallied up that this was the third thing to go wrong that day.

The rain had now stopped and we all went outside again. Everything was going alright again but I wondered how long this would last for.

**Duncan Malcolm (13)**
Friends' School, Lisburn

# The Day Everything Went Wrong

It started like any other day. I got up, got dressed, got breakfast and set off for school. From then on everything just got worse and worse and worse.

For a start, rain began to pour out of the heavens, when I left my house. Then once I finally got onto the bus for school, the clouds cleared, the rain stopped and the sun shone clearly in the sky.

I made it to school almost without any more problems but trust my luck to get a white splotch on my blazer. I couldn't figure out what it was until I looked up. A bird's nest was staring me in the face. After removing the bird mess I went off to my first class but not today. Oh no, today was the day I was to get my results of a test back. The teacher handed me my paper and *smack bam*, right in the middle of the page was 15% in huge red writing. Then below it was a note telling me I was in detention after school today.

Later more eventful things happened; the vending machine ate my money, I got dumped by my girl, I dropped my lunch, I tore my trousers and I forgot my books for French and got 250 lines. School was over and I went to detention. It wasn't so bad. We were allowed to do what we wanted. I thought perhaps my luck had perked up but *oh no*. When I walked out of detention I went to cross the road but trust my luck, I was paid a visit by a car bumper at 30mph.

The 'perfect' end to a 'perfect' day. A night in the ER. Well on the bright side, it could have been worse. I could be next door in the cemetery.

**Craig Lewsley  (13)**
Friends' School, Lisburn

# The Day Everything Went Wrong

When I woke up this morning I just knew it would be one of those days. You know, the ones where everything goes wrong. It started off badly, I got up and went for a shower but, in the middle of my shower the water went off! Luckily, I had gotten the shampoo out of my hair but not much else. As I made my way downstairs I realised that I was late today. I ate my breakfast in a hurry and ran to get the bus for school.

I reached the bus stop just as the bus was leaving. I thought the bus driver might have stopped for me but he didn't. I settled down to wait for the next bus that was in 20 minutes.

It would have been at this point in the movies when it would start to rain. Luckily, things weren't that bad yet, but there was a chilly wind blowing. I hunkered down to wait.

I arrived at school 25 minutes late. That meant that I didn't have time to get my books out of my locker. Could anything else go wrong? Apparently they could. I got punishment after punishment from teachers for not having the right books, apart from geography, which I had books for because we'd had homework that night. Class after class I tried to explain myself, 'They were in my locker and I was late into school,' I'd say, but it wouldn't make any difference.

Eventually the last bell rang. On the bus home I was half expecting the bus to break down. It had been that sort of day.

**Nicola Laverick (13)**
Friends' School, Lisburn

# The Day Everything Went Wrong!

After a whole day of unpacking boxes and adding finishing touches to my brand new, glam apartment, I decided I deserved a glass of wine and a read of the Evening News.

I was just flicking through the paper when one particular advertisement caught my eye, 'Uptown guy looking for downtown girl, non-smoker, GSOH'. At the time it seemed like a good idea, a night out would do me good and this was the perfect opportunity …

So I telephoned the number and arranged a date, Monday the 8th of June at the Pizza Place on Belfast Main Street at 7pm, we were both to carry a rolled up newspaper for identification purposes.

Well that was the day that everything went wrong. I woke up at 9am … great, late for work. It was a mad rush trying to get to the office and after a good telling off from my boss, you know the usual, 'You are always late, and this is your last chance.' He kindly informed me that I had a second nose growing and walked off laughing. How humiliating, I don't know how I missed the huge spot on my nose. However, I struggled through the day, work, work and more work until I was finally released and allowed to go home.

After sitting in traffic for about an hour I arrived back home and rushed in, had a shower, dried my hair which turned out ever so frizzy and tried to deflate my forever growing spot. Then while ironing my outfit I heard an announcement on the radio that said, 'Kerri Jones, hi from Leo Magee and good luck on your blind date'. That was me they were talking about, fantastic! Now everyone would know I was a desperate old sod who had to resort to reading the lonely hearts column in the paper. I got so carried away that I forgot about the iron and burnt a hole in my new dress!

Brilliant, I had frizzy hair, a spotty face and jeans and T-shirt to wear; I just hoped this man wasn't too fussy. By this stage I was cutting it fine for time, so I took the car. No problems there, thank goodness. When I arrived I saw a gorgeous guy standing by the entrance, with a newspaper tucked under his arm and I thought my luck must have changed. So I walked up to him and said, 'Hi I'm Kerri Jones; I'm here for the blind date.'

He looked at me oddly and asked, 'Do I look desperate?'

'Only joking,' I said unconvincingly and slithered off into the pizzeria.

Frantically I scanned the restaurant, there was a sea of happy couples, and then I spotted him. I'll paint you a picture ... greasy blond hair, pimples, Harry Potter glasses, enormous teeth, anorak and a rolled up newspaper clutched in his sweaty paw. I just couldn't take any more ... beam me up Spotty ... oh, I mean Scotty!

**Emma Megoran  (13)**
Friends' School, Lisburn

# The Day Everything Went Wrong

'Quickly Hannah! You're late for school!' These were the words that I awakened to on the day when everything went wrong.

There had been a power cut during the night and neither my alarm clock nor my dad's alarm clock went off. I scurried out of bed and jumped into the shower only to realise that there was no hot water. I had a cold shower and afterwards put my uniform on as my teeth chattered with the cold. I grabbed my toast along with my bag and ran to the car.

'Come on, Dad! Can't you go any faster?' I asked, gulping down my toast.

'No honey, there are roadworks and the light is red,' came the reply.

When the light eventually turned green, we drove off, only to hear a soft whirring noise. One of the tyres had a puncture.

When I finally arrived at school it was 9.40am. The lesson had started 25 minutes earlier! I walked into class and tripped over someone's PE bag. The whole class burst into laughter. I quickly got up and explained to the teacher what had happened. He excused me and I sat down.

The rest of my day at school was fine - apart, that is, from breaking my friend's tennis racquet at lunch, setting my teacher's hair alight in Home Economics and losing the school hamster.

It was almost time for bed and I couldn't wait to go to sleep in case anything else went wrong, because let's just say I'd had an ... adventurous day. I drifted off to sleep thinking, *Hopefully tomorrow won't be as ... well ... chaotic. Because, really, the only thing I did wrong was to get up in the first place!*

**Hannah Kearney  (13)**
Friends' School, Lisburn

# The Day Everything Went Wrong

What a day! I can hardly begin to tell you what happened.

It all started when I got up out of bed this morning. I was having a lovely dream about lying on a sunny beach in Florida when I heard a voice from downstairs shouting, 'Caroline, get up or you'll be late for school!' I sprang out of bed and realised it was 8.30 - *help!* I rushed out of the room, slid on the floor and *bang!* I had fallen to the ground flat on my face and my arm was throbbing - not a great start to the day!

Anyway, I got ready and ran downstairs. When I got to the kitchen, I was greeted by my mum with, 'April fools! It's Saturday!' I sank into the chair exhausted.

My arm was still throbbing, so I decided to watch TV but, you've guessed it, there was a power cut. I got really bored so I went into town for a while, my arm feeling slightly better. I found a top I really liked and went to buy it, but I accidentally left my bag in the changing rooms. When I went back to get it, it wasn't there. Someone had stolen it. All my valuables - gone.

I ended up walking home and rang my mates to try to cheer up. We decided to go ice skating. I was having a great time skating with my friends and, for the first half hour, hadn't fallen down once! I was commenting on this to Sarah but I spoke too soon when, out of nowhere, a speed skater came zooming round a corner and knocked me flying!

Well, maybe I skated into him but no matter, I found myself lying in the middle of the ice rink with everyone staring at me. My leg felt slightly strange and, to my horror, when I looked up I saw a bone sticking out. *Argh!* I'm sure I was heard at the other end of the world!

After I screamed, my memory went blank until I woke up about an hour ago. My mum told me that an ambulance came and drove me to the hospital where they operated on my leg to try and fix it.

So here I am with my leg in traction, lying in a hospital bed. They tell me I'll be here for twelve weeks at least. So much for my holiday in Florida. I was meant to be leaving next week!

**Caroline Lloyd (13)**
**Friends' School, Lisburn**

# The Way Through Hellview

As we packed our VW camper for our road trip, the weather was starting to get rapidly worse, from just a drizzle to a major thunderstorm, but still we continued on our journey.

Deron was first to drive and after a couple of hours we called into a small diner for something to eat and to stay at a motel. It wasn't that nice but what do you expect from a cheap place like that? Next day we got an early start and we planned to stay at a place called Hellview. We laughed the name off and drove on.

About five hours of solid driving later we pulled into a cloudy town signposted 'Hellview'. Driving through everyone seemed to scatter inside to their houses and the shutters shut. All but one was inside. An old man on his front porch sitting in an old and creaky rocking chair cradling a double-barrelled shotgun.

As we approached him he cocked his gun and stood up, we stopped and negotiated with him and he agreed to talk to us.

We asked him for directions and he replied, 'At the fork turn left where there's a store but on the right stay free from sight, the only way to ever leave is over flooded by the storm. They've deleted all the tourists at the bottom of the lake,' said the man. Hearing this we decided we didn't really want to be one of those tourists at the bottom of the lake so we returned to our car and headed to the fork in the road. We turned left and sped away down the dusty track where we were met by the 96 villagers from Hellview. We put our foot down and smashed into them. They were all over the car, clawing at the windows, after a while they all fell off and we returned home to have beers and a BBQ.

**Oliver Armstrong  (13)**
**Friends' School, Lisburn**

# The New York Times

*Alien invasion on the Big Apple!*

Terror swept the city last night when four large UFOs landed in the Big Apple. These four large pod-shaped spacecrafts were nothing like we had ever seen in Star Wars before. They were larger, more dangerous and most importantly, real.

You are probably thinking, *What on Earth? This is surely a hoax.* But sadly, I can tell you that this is not. The site has been surrounded and evacuation plans have been put to use for a one mile radius.

What are these aliens planning? Are they just trying to make it in the Big Apple like everyone else, or do they have plans for mass destruction?

I have just been talking to Dr Workscintscoff and he says, 'I do not know what these aliens are planning, or if they are planning anything at all, but we are taking extreme precautions and setting a one mile barrier around the site, this is all we can do for now.'

It is all incredibly reassuring don't you think? When your nation's brains don't know what to do, you are being evacuated when there may be no danger and none of the scientists will go within 200ft of these aliens.

Is this an act of 'the force?' A hoax, or maybe our nightmares have finally been realised? One thing is for sure, we're definitely not dreaming. These aliens may blow us up at any second. No one knows. Or, any minute now the pranksters may come out of their papier maché spaceship and say, 'Got ya!' I think not.

Could this be the end of the Big Apple?

**Jenny Barr (13)**
Friends' School, Lisburn

# New Cure For Diabetes

Scientists in the Oxford University experiments lab have tried to find the cure for diabetes for many years now, but after much deliberation we can confirm a breakthrough. The new medicine to cure diabetes is called Dytroxillin and the brilliant scientist, Doctor Howard Robinson, created it. So far the new Dytroxillin tablet has only been tried on rats but all scientists are positive that it will be effective in the treatment of humans.

Dytroxillin tablets are made from the fluid in the seed heads of lupin plants. The seed heads are cut open and their fluid is extracted. It is then heated at 176.34°C and added to chrominal acid. The fluid expands and turns white before it is cooled and formed into Dytroxillin tablets. Each seed head forms half a tablet. As lupin plants are quite common in the UK it will be an easy medicine to produce and will not take up many resources.

Prime Minister Tony Blair granted Doctor Robinson £2 million for the research of diabetes, when he heard of the invention of Dytroxillin. As he explained to the public before he got elected for a third term, he wants to take care of the health service and improve it.

This scientific breakthrough is so important because over two million people living in the UK have diabetes and have to suffer from its effects every day.

The Dytroxillin tablets work by rhythmically controlling the body's blood sugar level. Three tablets will have to be taken every day on a six month course until there is enough of the Dytroxillin in the system to start controlling the blood sugar levels in the body automatically and to teach the brain to manage the blood's sugar levels on its own.

**Steven Allen  (12)**
**Friends' School, Lisburn**

# Pandora's Box

Once there was a wealthy man called George. He married a beautiful brunette woman called Pandora.

When George went shopping he saw a very expensive shop and went inside and with his amazement, he saw a wonderful box. It was encrusted with diamonds, sapphires, rubies and emeralds. With his money he bought the box. It wasn't until after he had bought it that he found out what was in it. He took it home in an attempt to think of what to do with it.

When George came home he told his wife never ever to open the box. Pandora promised that she wouldn't but with each passing day she became more curious about the box and what was in it. One day in the middle of the night while George was asleep, she opened it.

Suddenly all the evils in the world came rushing out like disease, famine and crime. George woke up and shouted at his wife for what she had done and it was her fault that people were dying.

When George had left the room in disgust, Pandora heard a voice saying, 'What about me?' She searched the room and followed the voice. The sound came from the box, she slowly opened it and then a pretty butterfly came out with the word *hope* across its body and flew away.

Then Pandora knew everything would be alright.

**Hannah Downie (13)**
Friends' School, Lisburn

# Are Aliens Winning The FA Cup?

In an exclusive interview with this paper, Patrick Vieira has admitted that numerous signings that have been made by the Arsenal manager, Arsene Wenger, in previous seasons have actually come from other planets. This means that the Arsenal team are the first aliens to lift the FA Cup.

According to Patrick, one of the newest Arsenal signings, Robin van Persie, who supposedly came from Feyenoord, was actually from Pluto and after Arsene Wenger signed him in 1998 he boarded a rocket for England. He has only just arrived after his long journey. Other names mentioned are Thierry Henry, who came from Mars and Robert Pires, who came from Uranus. Most shocking of all must be Jens Lehmann who comes from Seduran, which is a planet outside our solar system. On that planet they have super fast reactions. That explains how he saved the penalty in the FA Cup final.

Also at the end, Patrick, who himself comes from Mars told of how he and others were forced to come.

'I was working in a field one day and then I saw the Arsenal management team coming over the horizon with their ray guns. I was forced to get up and leave.' Have your say about this on page 18.

**Jonathan Bell (13)**
Friends' School, Lisburn

# Daniel's National Quest

Daniel is a national hero for stopping a terrorist crashing a plane into the White House. But now, his boss is going to give him a call ...

'Seek and destroy!' rang out from Daniel's mobile (as he dozed in front of Desperate Housewives). This brought him to his senses and he rushed to find his Nokia 3175i in his 'slightly' untidy penthouse. 'Hello, Daniel speaking.'

'Daniel!' was the sharp, stern reply, 'don't use your real name on an unsecure line. I've told you not to, can't you remember anything?'

'Sorry Jeremy, now what's the 411 on the 911?'

'Phone me on the landline and I'll tell you.'

Daniel cut off the call and redialled on the secure line.

'Well,' Jeremy said uneasily, 'we have received a video message from a purple three-headed beast.'

Daniel interrupted. 'You're talking about a rare beast called a hydra!'

'Well, all our scientists say it isn't a projected image,' was Jeremy's reply, 'so we want you and your team to destroy this mythical beast.'

'Right?' Daniel laughed in reply.

'You don't seem to take my order seriously,' said Jeremy.

'We'll get to it right away and keep you informed,' replied Daniel. He called to his flatmates, Adam (Heavy Weapons), Sarah (Hacker) and Rachel (Kung-Fu Fighter) and they headed for his brand new sky blue Peugeot 206. They raced off along the highway knowing that this challenge to find the beast was going to be the biggest test ever of their skills and friendship.

**Jonathan Swain  (12)**
Friends' School, Lisburn

# Obesity, Is It Killing Us?

So many people in America are seriously overweight. The main problem is all the fatty junk food they eat. There are KFC, McDonald's and Burger King.

One girl is so overweight that she has refused to leave her house and now has a carer. This is the case for so many people in America. Jamie Oliver has said that he will be going out to see if he can change the minds of so many young kids so they don't become obese when they are older.

In America, they ask you if you want to super size your meal. The majority of people say yes and that's how they become obese. Other countries don't have the same problem as America. The areas most affected by obesity are New York, Los Angeles and California. Their doctors have recommended exercise, but often that doesn't work. Therefore, people opt for the method of removing the fat by having a tummy tuck, which is expensive and painful.

The people who eat these foods eat them morning, noon and night. I reckon they should cut it down to 1-2 a week. That way there will be less obese people in the world. Alternatively, even eating fruit and vegetables.

Buy a pupil for less at Friends' School, Lisburn. Contact Mrs Dickson the Principal for more details.

First customer through the door of Claire's Accessories will get free whatever they choose from their wide selection. Monday 23rd May.

*Wanted* Plate smasher required for the circus. It's a smashing opportunity. Come to the Island Arts Centre on Monday 23rd May.

*Lion spotted walking out of Belfast Zoo!*
On the morning of 18th May a group of Youths spotted a lion walking out of Belfast Zoo. The kids ran to the nearest police station to let the zookeepers know that the lion was loose. Later on the lion was caught and is now safely back in its cage.

**Shauneen Toland (12)**
**Friends' School, Lisburn**

# A Missing Paragraph From Noughts And Crosses

*(By Malorie Blackman)*

Lennette left the house with all the shouting behind her. She walked swiftly down the road. Her pace quickening with every step she took, then suddenly she stopped in her tracks and glanced behind her. She winced at the sight of her own house.

As she started to walk again she wailed, 'I'm not a nought I'm not, I'm not.' She buried her head in her hands and quickened her pace. Then she shouted again, 'I won't believe what my family say, I'm a cross. Just look at my skin, it's black not white, it's so clear that it's black.' I then heard her mutter, 'I know what I have to do. I'll walk out in front of the next car, no the next bus, a car is too risky, I might not die. Then it will look like I am trying to commit suicide instead of just being an accident. I'll make it look like I am daydreaming, it will be more convincing that way.

Her pace then slowed way down. I wondered how long it would be before the next bus came along and killed her. We passed a bus stop. I tried to stop and check the time. If I had, I would have lost sight of her. All I was focused on right now was trying to catch up with her, which was pretty hard seeing as her pace had quickened again and I hadn't noticed, so I was nearly running to get near her …

**Nicole Quinn (12)**
Friends' School, Lisburn

# Badminton Comes Third

Badminton is rapidly becoming more popular with the youth community in Britain. This is partly thanks to the world number one mixed doubles pairing of Nathan Robertson and Gail Emms. The sudden increase in popularity is thanks to their incredible display in Athens 2004, in which the pair lost in the final to a very resilient Chinese pairing of Zhang Jun and Gao Ling.

Nathan and Gail defied all odds as the United Kingdom wasn't expecting any medals to come their way in badminton, with Nathan and Gail not having a realistic chance.

The government hasn't shown much interest in badminton in the past, it's all been football and rugby.

This year, the government has funded a total of £9.2 million into the EBA, to make its overall funding to £16.6 million. This makes Badminton Britain's third most popular sport behind rugby, second and football, first.

Nathan lives and trains in Europe's top badminton country, Denmark, whilst Gail lives in England but often travels to Denmark to train with Nathan.

**Ruaraidh Sim (11)**
Friends' School, Lisburn

# Snow Passage

Ahin Harakas woke with the terrifying scream of his mother. He was only seven when the butchering of his mother took place, but it's been etched into his mind ever since. He won't forgive the man that did it, for it was his mother who understood him, even though he was different. He was an albino and everyone cast him aside as a freak, a weirdo, but not his mother, she understood.

Ahin, a large albino man, is now searching for the man that killed his mother, and this search brings him right back home, the place where he dreads the most.

As he enters the kitchen of his old home he decides to get a drink, but as he goes to the fridge, he sees a small piece of card under the fridge. It is an ID card: 'Robert Hopkins, Seattle / Epaj Harakas, Nepal'

'Father?' mutters Ahin. 'No! He didn't kill her!' As he screams a man appears at the door.

'Ahin … you don't understand … I can't have a freak in our family!' explains his father.

'You killed her!' screams Ahin as he reaches for something to hurt the man at the door with, he grabs a knife and dives at his father. He slices a gash in his neck and as his father bleeds profusely, Ahin turns the knife on himself and it is all over …

**Blair Treacy (13)**
Friends' School, Lisburn

# The Legend Of The Giants' Causeway

Five thousand years ago where Portrush meets the Irish Sea, is where aliens were living. They had inhabited the Earth and lived inside the Giants' Causeway, which stretched the whole way to Scotland. The aliens lived here because it was large and hollow and if they saw light they would blow up and turn into individual blocks of stone.

The aliens lived in the Giants' Causeway ever since they had come to Earth 129 years before. The large, blue seahorse-like animals had come in many small spaceships, but most of the white dome-shaped ships had crashed, and some even sank into the sea.

The aliens spent their days sleeping and only woke up and got up at night, when they mainly searched for food. The aliens liked to feast on small bugs such as spiders and woodlice. After the aliens had found their food, they mostly sat up sharing memories of their home planet and telling legends that had been passed down through generations.

One day when all the aliens were asleep the causeway where they all lived started to crack open. The split in the roof was noticed by the aliens the next day, but they didn't do anything about it as it was very small. Over a period of time the small crack progressed into a large split into the east side of the roof.

The split went the whole way across the roof until it finally split into two parts. The bright light that was shining from the sun awoke the aliens and as they got up they saw their home sinking into the sea. Many looked down to see it go, but some looked up and realised they were directly below the sun. They panicked and tried to run, but before they got very far they burst into flames.

The aliens burned for the rest of the day, until the sun went down and they hardened into rocks.

**Lauren Walker  (13)**
Friends' School, Lisburn

# Invasion Of Earth

It was one of the hottest days in the year in America. You could even see the tarmac bubbling and melting in the heat. People were in their swimming pools and running through their sprinklers.

A giant shadow was cast upon the city of LA. All attention was directed towards the sky. There was a spaceship in the sky. It was circular with a shiny, metallic colour. On the top and bottom of it were two pyramid shaped gems.

There was an eerie green glow that came out of the bottom gem. A great beam came out of the lower pyramid. When the beam hit the ground nothing happened. One of the people went to investigate this strange beam. He touched it and a surge of electricity travelled through his body. He was knocked off his feet into a swimming pool.

Then there was another bright glow and aliens came out of the beam. The aliens looked like robotic skeletons, they were gold in colour. They rushed out in numbers of well over 5,000. They carried big guns with a green crystal in the barrel of them and started shooting and on contact the beam from the gun would melt anything.

The area had to be evacuated and the army was informed. News travelled across the world quickly and soon all of its armies were there.

Soldiers were sent in, but they were no match for the alien's sophisticated weapons and were gone in an instant. Tanks drove in and destroyed a few aliens, but for every alien destroyed another five were beamed down from the spaceship. The tanks soon suffered the same fate as the soldiers.

The leaders of the world came to the conclusion of firing a nuclear bomb. The bomb was fired in less than five minutes and took less than a minute to reach its target. About a third of the aliens were wiped out on impact and the explosion dealt with the rest. In one huge mushroom cloud of smoke the aliens were defeated.

**Chin Mun Soong (13)**
Friends' School, Lisburn

# Who Is Peter Pan?

A few days ago we heard reports of a young boy flying in mid air outside a nursery window.

We have been hearing names which belong to this boy such as Peter Pan.

Our reporter went to the Darling House where people have claimed to have seen the boy fly through the air.

They described him as a young boy dressed in ragged green clothes and wearing a hat with a red feather sticking out of it.

We interviewed Miss Rowland who claimed to have seen this boy. 'Going home after a long day's work, I noticed a shadow along the ground. I could not make out where the person was at first until a child came up to me and said 'Look Miss, Peter Pan's up there.' He pointed to a window. There a boy around thirteen was 'hovering' outside a nursery window. With shock I screamed and the young boy disappeared'.

We have heard that his name is Peter Pan, but we do not know anything else about him. Where does he come from? Why is he here? What is he? How does he fly? We interviewed Wendy, the eldest of the Darling children, to find out what she knows about the boy.

*'Do you know anything about this character Peter Pan?'* 'Peter Pan? Of course I do. He is called 'the boy who never grows up'. He lives far, far away upon the North Star on an island called Neverland. There are fairies, mermaids, pirates and Indians! Young children live there called 'The Lost Boys'. They don't have a mother to look after them'.

*'Fairies and mermaids, there's no such thing!'* 'Everything is magic out there. Everything is real. There are strange characters in Neverland, a crocodile that stalks a pirate called Hook and a fairy called Tinkerbell who supplies fairy dust to help children fly'.

We have heard Wendy's words, but how do we know this is all true? Find out in tomorrow's edition!

**Ellen Morrison (12)**
**Friends' School, Lisburn**

# A Day In The Life Of A Beggar

I am a beggar, living on the streets, in shop doorways. I sit holding out my scruffy hat, longing for someone to throw their change into it. Many people walk past, scowling their faces, perhaps at the smell or maybe just my presence. I may be homeless but no less a person, though very few people look at it from my point of view.

Every day is the same for me. Most days I sit on the side of a street, against a wall watching everyone around me having a life, spending their money but not even sparing a pound for me. Many days I have been without food, sometimes surprising myself on how long I can go without feeling faint. On more fortunate days, I find an old sandwich or half-drunk cup of tea that someone has just set down, which can make a meal for me.

When the night draws near, I hope that there won't be any rain if I can't get under a bridge or in a shop doorway. On Friday and Saturday nights there are drunk people that often stagger past me. It gets quite scary at times because they sometimes randomly start fights with complete strangers. Thankfully they have ignored me but it's at times like that when I wish that I had a home to go back to like them. Even though they are drunk and starting fights, they are so much more fortunate than me.

**Hannah Clarke (13)**
Friends' School, Lisburn

# Loch Ness Monster

*Nessie: found and saved*

In the past few weeks the Loch Ness monster has been spotted numerous times on the edges of the loch. Apparently she is only seen between five o'clock and seven o'clock in the morning.

One eyewitness said that the creature came to his neighbour's farm at around six o'clock and consumed a field full of corn. Another said that her orchard was bare when she got up yesterday morning. Many eyewitnesses have been questioned about this amazing event.

Mrs Prachett has lived near the loch all her life and has never experienced anything like this before. She was one of the first people to see the mythical creature approaching land.

Early this morning Nessie was found struggling on the edges of the loch. Local men and women, with the help of naval patrol boats, eventually pulled the monster back into the water.

After Nessie was released back into the water, she was greeted by what seemed to be two mini Loch Ness monsters. Scientists believe that these must be her offspring.

A team of scubadivers have been sent to the depths of Loch Ness, to check for more of these creatures.

How many more Loch Ness monsters are there creeping in the depths of the Scottish loch?

**Kerri Mulholland (13)**
Friends' School, Lisburn

# The Oakgrove Horror

The door creaked open as Ciaran, Sam and I walked slowly into the sports hall looking for our PE kits so that we could play in the Gaelic match. It was dark, very eerie and everything creaked and squeaked. There in the corner were our PE kits. We made a dash for them but suddenly out of the floor an 8ft tall hooded thing came up. When it saw us it reached behind its back and pulled out the biggest axe that I had ever seen. It swung for us but we ran out of the sports hall and down the corridor. I, being the slowest of the group, quickly fell behind until there was a large gap between us. Then up between the gap came the thing. I quickly tried to stop, tripped and slid right through its legs down the corridor and right into the back of Ciaran and Sam. I opened my eyes and found myself locked in the changing rooms with Ciaran and Sam.

We never did get out, not till this day (14th October 2065) but nobody has ever been able to get in either.

We've tried everything like running at it, barging at it, pulling at it even trying to climb out of the window. Hell, we even broke a door of one of the showers and started to hit the door with it but it just wouldn't budge.

Ciaran died a few years after that at an old age of 72, then I went at 81 and finally Sam went at 83.

The thing that locked us in the changing room carried on haunting the school till the end of time without anyone else ever finding it.

**Adam Donaghy (11)**
**Oakgrove Integrated College, Londonderry**

# Fuzzy-Wuzzy's Woeful Tale

Fuzzy-Wuzzy's career had hit rock bottom. His life as a TV bear had come to a premature end along with his hair.

He had been the biggest children's television star since Paddington had fallen foul of the country's immigration laws (luckily, enough jars of marmalade had been replenished all round to give a satisfactory end for his fans).

He was widely renowned by parents as the only children's idol who hadn't had connections with criminal activity. Even Barney had been charged with crimes relating to misleading the public (no matter how hard you sing, it's never going to rain lemon drops and gum drops).

But then it happened.

The thing that had driven Rupert the Bear from charming child star to owning that sleazy bar off Kings Street (It's Happy Nite . . . Every Nite!).

The thing that every TV bear dreaded.

He began to moult.

He knew it was over when the toupee he had been wearing just wasn't cutting it any more.

The tabloids had a field day.

'Fuzzy-Wuzzy was a bear!'

'Fuzzy-Wuzzy had no hair!'

'Fuzzy-Wuzzy wasn't fuzzy . . . was he?'

Only a week after he had been fired, they were spilling out everything from affairs to terrorist connections.

His name is being officially changed to 'Fuzzy Has Been' at a hearing next week. Nothing but memories left.

That and £10,000,000 in forged notes. Fuzzy smiled. Just because the media were rats doesn't mean they were wrong.

**Emer Curley (12)**
**Oakgrove Integrated College, Londonderry**

# Something Strange

As Julie-Ann looked through the window she noticed something strange across the street, 'What was that?' she asked herself. She didn't want to go out because she felt strange, she waited for about half an hour. As she looked out again, she saw it again, except it walked across the street. This time she really did start to worry. She thought it was a burglar or something. Without going out to the door she tried to alert the neighbours who were looking out of the window, but nobody else could see what she could see. She started to think that it was all in her head and that she was dreaming. She went to bed that night thinking of all the different things that it could be, she was thinking so hard that she drifted off to sleep.

The next morning she woke up and had forgotten all about it. She went to school, then to her after school club. She came home that day and did her homework, then watched TV and as she was getting ready to go to bed she felt a sudden chill run down her spine, it was there again, she started to get really scared! This was the third time in two days that she had seen it. Her baby-sitter was in the house with her so she went to the door and looking through the window she was shocked and amazed to discover it was …

**Laura Phillips  (13)**
**Oakgrove Integrated College, Londonderry**

# The Last Celt

The wind was high; Taary knew this was time. Taary was wearing a long flowing blue dress, her long black hair waving naturally in the violent wind. She held the dark brown, finest oak bow in her hand. Taary stood at the edge of a grassy cliff, looking over the ocean; she could hear the waves, smell the sea, sense the blood and murder of the past on the beach below her.

Ireland was fine. But now that the English were moving in, building their plantation, life's only worth was a bit of metal, everything depended on it. It was a silly idea, Taary and her mother often cried when thinking of their beloved father, husband, being sent away for not paying their silly tax. But soon Taary cried alone, as her mother too had been taken.

A tear slipped down Taary's cheek; it spoiled the effect of black hair, white skin and proud face. She pulled an arrow from the folds in her dress. Sharp. Taary crouched down, every bone in her body aching. She took aim. It was now or never. She struggled pulling the bowstrings towards her; the thought of this man in pain was thrilling. The man fell, his sleek steed was scared; it ran, with the evil king's feet in the stirrups. He was dragged through the water, washing him of his sins.

Taary froze, but she soon found the need to run when she heard the voice of a man and woman behind her laughing ...

**Jamie-Lee Fulton (13)**
Oakgrove Integrated College, Londonderry

# Our School Outing

The date was the 13th of May 2000 and the venue was Benone Beach. It was a day I will always remember.

The policemen took us on a trip to Benone Beach. It was a laugh. We had to take a packed lunch with us. We played games. The games were called tug-of-war and egg throwing. We played tug-of-war first. We were split up into two teams, one was the girls and the other was boys. I think the boys won! Anyway, after that we played egg throwing. The aim of the game was to throw the egg as quick as you could to the person next to you, and you have to be fast as well because you might get splatted with the egg! I think Robert and Emer got splatted!

After that we had our lunch. I had sandwiches, a yoghurt, an apple, a bottle of juice and a packet of crisps.

When we were finished eating we were allowed to play about in the sand and have a swim in the water.

About half an hour later we had to come out of the water and get ready to go home. When we were on the bus, on our way home, everybody had started to sing songs. Then eventually we got home!

I liked this trip because it was the best trip ever in primary school!

**Amanda Doherty (13)**
**Oakgrove Integrated College, Londonderry**

# The Man

It all began on a stormy Sunday night. The wind was blowing and the lightning was striking through the black sky. Suddenly there was a loud knock on the front door; I was a little freaked out because half of the neighbourhood was on holiday apart from Mr and Mrs Jackson, the Dohertys and Mrs Lemon.

I got up from the chair with the fire poker in my hand and eventually headed for the front door. I looked out through the peep hole and there was a man who I had never seen before standing at my front door. I ran to the phone to call my mum's cell, but the line was off and that's when the horror began.

I ran around the house closing the blinds and locking the windows. I had to check the front and back doors but as I approached the back door there was a shadow. The handle began to turn. I said quietly to myself that I was going to make it through this. The door began to shake. I ran upstairs trying to escape the creature that was in my house. He began calling my name, 'Lisa! Lisa!' I realised who it was. My ever forgetful father. Dad had broken the lock on the back door to get in. He apologised for frightening me. Then we had ice cream and went to bed.

**Christopher Devenney  (13)**
**Oakgrove Integrated College, Londonderry**

# Faith In The Stars

Faith drifted through the stars amongst the silver-skinned spéirbhean. Sometimes she would briefly touch one of their shimmering bodies and energy would course through her veins like an electric shock.

*This is where I belong,* she thought, staring out at the twinkling stars. On Earth she was shunned like a piece of garbage, mocked for her clothes and beliefs by her unforgiving, scrutinising peers but here, here she was a goddess.

One of the sky women called to her and Faith shivered with delight. 'Come play Earth child, come play with us in the great abyss!'

The group flew over the clouds awakening their sisters with calls of mischief and play. A dozen other beautiful spéirbhean joined the group stretching their long, graceful limbs after a deep sleep. They glided like birds over the sky, twisting and swooping in synchronised motions. What a thrill it was to fly! Oh, to be a sky woman how wondrous would that be?

Faith screamed with exhilaration as she felt her humanity stripped from her like a snake shedding its skin. Seeing this, the spéirbhean circled Faith with cries of love and acceptance.

'You are one of us now Earth child!' they whispered as, without a backward glance at the world that had forsaken Faith, they flew away into the stars.

**Emma Arbuckle  (13)**
**Oakgrove Integrated College, Londonderry**

# Land Of Dreams!

Once upon a time there were three children: Amelia who was 13, Westen who was 6 and Jodie who was 4. They all looked alike. They lived with their wicked aunt and uncle, Mr and Mrs Angry, because their mum and dad were supposed to have died in a car crash.

They missed them very much. One day, they went out to the jungle of a garden and Westen fell into the pond. Amelia ran after and jumped in to rescue him. Suddenly, she found a door in the pond floor. What was behind it ... ?

They all jumped in and went through the door and there was a slide that looked as if it went on for miles.

At the end of the slide there was a land. Amelia in surprise said, 'This is the Land of Dreams!' It was made of chocolate and had a small village made of marshmallows.

'It's amazing,' suddenly shouted Westen. There was everything you could ever want.

People were asking who they were and where did they come from. There were children playing in gardens full of beautiful flowers. Suddenly Jodie and Westen ran, *'Mummy, Daddy!'* they shouted.

'Don't be so stupid,' Amelia whispered to herself. She turned around there they were. They cried with happiness and hugged and kissed. 'Where were you?' Amelia asked.

'We were here but there was no way of getting back,' they said. 'Stay with us. There is everything here. Fairies as well.'

'Of course,' they shouted in excitement.

And they lived happily ever after.

**Dervla O'Connell (12)**
**Oakgrove Integrated College, Londonderry**

# The Rare Princess

Once upon a time in a land far away, there lived a princess. Her name was Princess Isabella. Princess Isabella was not like any other princess, she played rugby and she was also 8 feet tall.

Princess Isabella lived with her father in a castle at the top of the hill at Fantasy Island. Every morning Princess Isabella would make her and her dad some breakfast. Princess Isabella's dad was not so well so he had to stay in bed. This was a disease that had just hit Fantasy Island about a month before. Her dad would stay in bed all day and wait for his daughter (Princess Isabella) to make him his breakfast. Princess Isabella drove a monster truck. This monster truck of hers had only three wheels. Every Sunday, Princess Isabella would drive her truck to rugby training.

After rugby training Princess Isabella would come back to her castle and get some lunch for her and her dad. But one day Princess Isabella was at her rugby training and her dad was in bed at the castle. Then three strange men came to the castle door. The men knocked and knocked but no answer. The three men decided to go around the back of the castle. The men soon realised that the back door of the castle was open so they went inside the castle. The three men found lots of the princess' jewellery. The men quickly got the jewellery and ran away with it. They got into their van and drove away as fast as they could.

When the princess came home she noticed that her jewellery had gone and she rang the police straight away. The princess hoped all day that the police would phone and tell her that they found the jewellery. But no, they didn't ring that day. But they rang the next day and said that they caught the men and they would now send the jewellery back to her. The princess got her jewellery back and her dad lived happily ever after.

**David Gourley (12)**
**Oakgrove Integrated College, Londonderry**

# The Great Adventure

Mr Bing and Josey were six years old. They were trying to get to the other side of the world to get a golden bar. The Evil was sending men to kill them as he was going for the golden bar. It was like a race. The golden bar was worth millions. They needed it for the poor people.

They set off. They were in Ireland and they were going to Australia. They were in a Toyota Supra. The Evil had a boat and a few cars so he had the advantage. A car pulled up behind them when they were halfway through England. *Bang!* A bullet hit Josey in the arm.

A minute later Josey shot the man in the head. He was killed instantly. They used a boat and crossed to America. 'Straight for Australia,' the Evil shouted. Josey and Mr Bing were behind. The Evil had only three more miles. Mr Bing and Josey had ten miles. But they had a faster boat so they were catching up.

'At last, Australia,' cheered Mr Bing. Just as the Evil reached there, both pulled out their swords and fought two against one. This was not fair. Then two of the Evil's bodyguards came out. The fight was on. One bodyguard was down but just then the Evil killed Mr Bing. Then Josey took a rage. The last bodyguard fell.

Then Josey was almost dead. He fought with all his might. At last *splash!* Mr Evil fell. He got the golden bar and gave it to the poor.

**Philip Sheerin  (12)**
**Oakgrove Integrated College, Londonderry**

# Jose Madozy

Once upon a time, that never happened, there was a man called Jose Madozy. Jose lived in his mobile home, 'Castle Luxury', with his friend Pete, a six-foot tall bright orange kangaroo that couldn't jump. He also had a horse, White Lightning, who was really a small brown donkey that would only go backwards.

Jose lived in the Land of Dreams That Never Come True. It was not a nice place to live, as it was completely covered in blue sand, purple rocks and had a green river running through it.

There was also a large yellow lake, which contained luminous red fish that tasted like chicken.

Everyone lived in the only town, Applesbury; it was called this because they used to grow oranges there.

Jose had an enemy, Big Bad Black Bob (who was actually very small and quite pale). Bob wanted to take over the kingdom and make everyone work for him making stuffed teddy bears that he could sell to the elephants. Bob's only friend was his dog Fang who was a small brown terrier with no teeth.

Bob made a gun of sand that fired rocks and went to Jose's home to shoot him. Jose saw Bob coming, jumped onto White Lightning's back facing the wrong way and rode out through the front door. Bob was so confused when he saw this that he shot himself. Everyone was glad that Jose had saved their town so they made him king.

Everyone lived sadly ever after!

**Sean McElroy (12)**
Oakgrove Integrated College, Londonderry

# The Fairies

Once upon a time, in a hidden rainforest in America, there lived a small group of flower fairies.

On this day everyone was busy. It was the night of the flower ball. Rose was the oldest child in her family and at the age of sixteen she needed to find a husband. Rose lived with her mum, Tulip, her dad, Weed and her sister Buttercup.

Rose was very happy she had a reason to go out shopping and spend money! Everyone was very busy doing things to get ready for the ball and Buttercup felt very left out, she had no one to talk to and went off for a walk. As she walked along she thought that no one would even notice that she had gone.

Buttercup was gone an hour before anyone came along. 'Buttercup, Buttercup what are you doing?' Running along the road was her aunt Primrose.

'Nothing,' replied Buttercup.

'Everyone is so busy and have no time to talk or to play with me.'

'Oh, so you are just going to sit there and do nothing. Well in that case you can come and help me.'

So Buttercup went off to help her aunt. Later on Buttercup went home, got changed and they went to the ball.

At the ball Rose met a boy called Thorn. Two years later Rose and Thorn got married.

As for Buttercup she is now sixteen and is getting ready to go to the ball.

**Caroline Thompson (12)**
**Oakgrove Integrated College, Londonderry**

# The Magic School Bus!

One day Miss Daydream said, 'We are going on an extraordinary trip to Wonder Zoo where monkeys juggle and lions squeak and elephants laugh and nothing seems as it should; come on people, what are you waiting for, Christmas?' The children got up and followed Miss Daydream and stared at her as if she lived in Fairy World.

The playground was cold and the children had goosebumps everywhere. Miss Daydream pulled a bus out of her pocket which was yellow and had the school crest on it. She set it on the ground and it grew to the size of a normal bus. The children hopped in, the bus spun round and round.

The bus came to a stop, as the children came off the bus, Miss Daydream gave them tickets. They went inside a red and white striped tent which had a ring as big as a pool. Everything Miss Daydream said and more. The horses drove motorbikes and mice sang! But soon it came to an end. They waved goodbye and went on the bus. With a whizz they went.

Next thing they were at school. They had to write about their trip. Then they heard a knock, it was the circus, they had come to school. They set up and put on a show. There was a fox car that looked like a fox and a parrot which put on an act which made the children laugh out loud. Then the animals made Miss Daydream join in. What a laugh that was.

**Natasha Buchanan  (11)**
Oakgrove Integrated College, Londonderry

# War Trench

Another flash of gunfire erupted over my head. The icy raindrops stabbed my face; the mud smeared my hands and clothes. The smell of decaying bodies was unbearable. As I wiped water from my face I couldn't tell which were raindrops and which were tears. Lice infested my head.

The raging war had lasted for two years now, much longer than anticipated. The American troops were giving us hell and their infantry, weapons and armour were a lot more advanced and sophisticated than ours! *'Hit the deck,'* someone shouted. I dived behind a mud pylon. Silence, then … *boom.*

My body was blown back into the mud. Huge chunks of debris and muck landed on my chest. No longer was I shielded by the mud pylon. I was open to enemy gunfire. I was isolated upon no-man's-land. I lay there, watching the bullets plummet in every direction. I *had* to save myself. Before turning up on the day of recruitment, I vowed I would live to see the end of the war. I vowed I would come out alive!

My life flashed before me as my fingers scraped through the mud, dragging my tired, limp body back to the trench. With every handful of mud I drew, I had another flash of my home in Montreal - my wife - my children. With every slice of energy I had left, my body rolled down the mud bank into the trench - I had lived to see another day!

**Martin Wilson  (16)**
**Oakgrove Integrated College, Londonderry**

# The Operation

As I lay on the hard cold bed waiting for the surgeon I started worrying, *what if he does something wrong?*

Then the door opened with a squeak. In came a short, plump doctor with a strange look on his face.

'Hello, my name is Doctor Smith. I will be doing your operation. Nurse!' he called.

I started to panic as I drew close to the surgery doors. With a thud, my bed burst through the doors.

They stopped in the middle of the room. The surgeon put his gloves on with a snap.

'Hold still while you get some general anaesthetic.'

As he pushed in the syringe I felt the cold liquid run through my veins. I started to doze off. Everything went blurry.

I woke up two hours later to find myself in a big room with three other people. I started to worry. What had happened?

I was scared. I had never been this scared before. Then it started to kick in, the sore throat, the tiredness from the anaesthetic. I realised where I was. I was in recovery when the nurse noticed I was awake. She came over and said, 'Are you OK?'

I forced out a, 'Yes.' I fell back to sleep. I woke up with my mum right beside me.

She said, 'Are you ready to go?' I thought it was a bit early but I was glad to be home.

**Tyler Stothard  (14)**
**Oakgrove Integrated College, Londonderry**

# The Girl

Moss was in the middle of telling me about a cannibal he'd defeated in the Amazon jungle (he was trying to distract me into making a mistake!) when the door to my office burst open and the most beautiful girl I'd ever seen entered, screaming, her eyes wild with terror, 'Help me!' she screamed, 'It's after me! It's going to eat me! It …'

Before she could say any more she fainted and I had to jump forward quickly to catch her before she hit the floor. Her name was Louise and she was lovely. She had a beautiful face, long hair and slim hands. Her feet were big - I've always fancied girls with big feet.

'Who do you think she is?' the blue rat who lives in my head asked. He was shivering, the way he always does at the start of a dangerous case.

'I don't know,' I said.

'I don't trust her,' Moss Downey grunted.

'Shut up!' I snapped, wiping her hair from her face, gazing at her closed eyelids and her gently parted lips as she breathed lightly, still asleep. (I knew her name because I'd read it on the label inside her jacket when I'd taken it off and hung it up.)

Eventually Louise awoke.

'Where am I?' she gasped, staring around my office frightened.

'It's OK,' I told her. 'You're safe with me. I'm Martin Kerrigan.' She smiled when she heard that.

'Thank heavens!' she cried, 'I was coming here when the monster attacked.'

**Martin Kerrigan  (14)**
**Oakgrove Integrated College, Londonderry**

# The Chocolate Touch!

Once upon a time in a country called Canada, a young boy, aged twelve, went to a school called Bon Bon's, which were his favourite sweets, but more than anything the boy loved chocolate. His name was Kevin Choco.

One day, Kevin went to the shopping mall with all his friends. He spent all his money on a box of chocolates, but his friends spent theirs on proper food.

That evening, Kevin went home, ran up the stairs (so his mum would not see the chocolates!) and hid them under his pillow.

Kevin went to his bed early that night so he could eat his chocolates. When he woke up, his bed was made of chocolate, so he went downstairs and gave his mum a hug to see what happened but she turned into chocolate. Kevin's dad took him to the doctor's.

The doctor said to him he had the chocolate touch and there was no cure except not to eat chocolate ever again. They went home and after two days it finally went away.

But Kevin loved chocolate that much and his friends were teasing him with it. He ate it again and again. He had forgotten all about the chocolate touch.

That night, he had a dream. He knew that the dream meant that if he did not stop eating chocolate then the chocolate touch would come back and he did not want that because if you get the chocolate touch a second time, then you have it forever, so he never touched it again and he lived happily ever after.

**Caoimhe Doherty (12)**
**Oakgrove Integrated College, Londonderry**

# Magic Martha And Fire

Once upon a time, there was a little girl who was twelve years old and her name was Magic Martha. Magic Martha lived in a place called Dream Land where she was brought up by her mother Marietta and her father Manderin.

One day, Magic Martha woke up to find a dragon outside her window. The dragon was a Horntail Snorlack. Magic Martha wondered whether her mother bought it for her or if it had escaped from somewhere. When Magic Martha went downstairs for breakfast, her mother was already waiting for her.

Magic Martha asked her mother about the dragon. 'Mother what is that dragon doing in the garden?' she asked.

'I bought it for you,' she replied.

Martha was so amazed, she thanked her mother and she went out to see the dragon. An hour later, she came in for a drink and she told her mother that she was going to call it Fire.

One day news came out that in a far away land there was a wicked fairy who was going to try and take over Fairyland.

Magic Martha knew where this land was even though she had not been there before because her mother and father had told her about it. That night Magic Martha and Fire flew over to Fairyland.

When she got there it was the most beautiful place she had ever been to. In the distance, Magic Martha saw a very tall castle which was the wicked fairy's and there she saw the wicked fairy and her husband. As soon as the wicked fairy saw Magic Martha she tried to put a spell on her just like her husband but the dragon breathed fire over the spell and the spell bounced back and hit the wicked fairy and she hit the floor.

Magic Martha flew up to the window and climbed into it. She put a spell on the wicked fairy and her husband and they regretted what they had done and became good again and they lived happily ever after.

**William Douglas (12)**
Oakgrove Integrated College, Londonderry

# The Adventures Of Link

'You're all ready to go, Link,' informed Navi the fairy.

'Thank you, I'll be on my way now,' replied Link, exiting the treehouse as he set off to save the Kingdom of Hyrule.

As Link climbed down the ladder Navi shouted out to him, 'Wait, the Great Deku Tree might want to speak with you first.'

'OK, I'm going,' he said impatiently.

'Hello, Great Deku Tree, did you want to see me?' Link said with an honourable tone.

'Yes I did young one, I have a very important mission for you, as you know I am old and I won't be around much longer so before I go, listen to what I have to say. In the Castle of Hyrule there has been a dark presence there for quite some time now and you have to stop it.'

'Me? Why me?' interrupted Link.

'Because you're different from the other Kokiri children, now come and open this treasure chest and get your sword and shield, you will need it for your journey and goodbye forever Link,' said the Great Deku Tree, as he turned white and shrivelled up. Then a seedling popped out of the ground and he would be called the Great Deku Tree's Sprout.

As Link was crossing Hyrule field he came to Hyrule Castle but the gate was closed so Link used his hook shot to hook on to the wood and climbed over it and then he heard a voice.

'I had a feeling you would come Link, ha ha ha,' chuckled Ganondorf the evil king, 'please kid, you can't beat me, you might as well give up now.'

'No, I'll never give up.'

'OK kid, your funeral.'

It was an epic sword fight and halfway through the battle Ganondorf threw a lightning bolt at Link and Link hit it back to Ganondorf, he fell to the ground and then Link pulled out his bow and arrow and on the end of the arrow was a big bright light and he struck Ganondorf with it and then Ganondorf and all evil vanished from the face of the planet.

**Luke O'Kane (12)**
Oakgrove Integrated College, Londonderry

# The Little White Box

I remember the day as if it was yesterday. It all happened fifteen years ago. Late in the night, the sapphire sky was staring down on everyone in the town sleeping. The waking sun stretched into its horizon. The haranguing wind howled and the twisted branches knocked, incessantly and vociferously on my window. With the sudden knock of one of the branches I was awoken from my deep sleep.

The room was coldly dim, except for a small glowing night light, a star fallen from the sapphire sky. Dressed in my favourite baby pink nightdress I sauntered over to my bedroom door. I pressed my ear against the door, but it was quiet, not a sound. Twisting the globed door handle, I gently opened it. I delicately scampered to my mother and father's room.

The cover was straightly made, the bed was untouched. Warily I crept down the slushy, carpeted stairs glancing from side to side. Suddenly there was a tumultuous crash. I fleeted back up the stairs until I heard a familiar voice. It was my granny with colourless hair and her skin like leather. I was stagnant in the middle of the stairs. Granny was carrying a piece of glinting broken glass which must have caused the ear-splitting sound.

**Catherine McKinney  (14)**
St Catherine's College, Armagh

# Blackberry Pies

I toddled along the riverbank listening to the tranquil flow and freedom of the stream. The lush tickly grasses ran their way up my long legs. It was one of those nippy November evenings and the whole village was in hibernation. The trees swayed and danced as the callous wind exposed their naked flesh to the cruelness of that autumn's evening. The remaining flowers were hurled about, nothing but pieces of string. The icy rain tore through me revealing my freezing body. My gigantic basket flooded with scrumptious marbly blackberries and russet raspberries. Steadily I staggered on the gargantuan, rust-patterned carpet of leaves, each step gradually weighed down my unyielding hand to the messy, muddy path.

Nearing home, incense smoke spat out from the warmth of my chimney breast. The vivid burgundy front door became clearer and clearer as I fought off the mist and dragged my bulky blackberry basket up to the front tarnished step, 'I'm home,' I bellowed, greeted with the smell of delectable home-baked pasty. The warmth of the kitchen surged over me like the ruthless wind. The sweet sugary smell led me to the palatable pasty perched on the cooling tray, 'One bite, who will notice?' Mind made up, I picked a piece stuffed it into myself; all the flavours, all the steam, all the hot stickiness filled my mouth with indulgent pleasure. Suddenly, I heard the familiar sound of the creaking staircase so I quickly gathered up the crumbs and pretended to be washing the blackberries.

'On yer back,' a calm voice spoke, I turned round quickly to find my mother standing at the range heating her soft, supple hands, her dark, shiny curls ran down her back like a mysterious shadow. With amusement she noticed her delicious pasty whacked in half, 'Was someone hungry?' she laughed. I looked down at my grubby black leather shoes still filthy and giggled. 'Right,' she said, 'shall we fill these pies up and put some tea on?'

Nodding I began to gather the ripened succulent strawberries and filled each pie to the very top. Mother brought out two chipped cups and filled them to the brim with pumping black English tea, cool creamy milk was set at the side.

**Eiméar McKinstry (15)**
St Catherine's College, Armagh

# King Arthur - The Unanswered Question
# Part Of The Story, The Ugly Woman

This tale is about King Arthur the legendary King of Britain and his nephew Sir Gawain.

King Arthur and his knights were sitting by the round table when a young woman ran in with her clothes torn and shaking with grief. 'Help me King Arthur,' she cried. 'My husband has been stolen from me by a wicked knight.' King Arthur rose to the challenge and he went to find this wicked knight and slay him.

As he rode through the forest it started to get very cold and dark, his whole body started to tremble and his teeth chattered.

He finally found the castle the evil knight lived in. The knight rode out suddenly on a horse dressed in ugly black armour. King Arthur fell to his knees in fear. The knight approached him accompanied by a woman, the same woman who had sent him on the task in the first place.

It was his sworn enemy Morgan le Fay. She had magically disguised herself to trick Arthur. 'Please spare me,' screeched Arthur.

'Instead of killing you now,' sneered the evil knight, 'I will send you on a quest; find out what women most desire and you will be spared. Come back in one year with the answer or else.' He slid his finger across his axe.

When he returned he realised it was black magic that had scared him so much. King Arthur and his nephew then asked the question to every woman who passed. Jewels, fine clothes, money, a good family. These were only a few of the answers he received.

A year passed and they were unsuccessful. As they rode back to the evil knight's castle they met the ugliest, fattest woman they had ever seen. He stopped the lady and decided to give the question one last go. But before he could ask it the woman stopped him and said, 'I know the question you wish to ask and the answer, I will tell you on one condition I marry that charming young boy.' She nodded at Sir Gawain.

Was the life of the king worth marrying this beast of a woman? Did King Arthur find out the answer, you will have to find out for yourself.

**Nicola Hart (12)**
St Catherine's College, Armagh

# Best Friend!

There was nothing unusual when I woke that fateful Saturday morning, nothing untoward in the daily hustle and bustle of family life that was seeping gradually into my room, nothing to alert me to the momentous news that was about to descend upon me. Sunlight was peeking enticingly through the curtains, the delicate sense of freshly ground coffee wafted alluringly up from the scullery below and the happy chatter of my younger siblings provided a perfect backdrop for my musings. I luxuriated in my lavish bed, enjoying the peaceful surroundings, savouring the feeling of the well-being and tranquillity.

Just yesterday, Elizabeth and I had contemplated our future, a future that held unknown, exhilarating, twisting paths. Our anticipation bit at us like ridges. The world was our circus, which act we would perform was going to take a lot of happy exploring. Everything seemed achievable. We were at the crossroads of our life and the possibilities were boundless. Like a beautiful golden beach, untrammelled by human endeavours, our future beckoned glowingly. No footprints marred the glorious wilderness. We ached to set out into the world, to leave our individual mark on uncharted waters.

**Carina Oliver  (15)**
**St Catherine's College, Armagh**

# Water, The Median Of Life
*(An extract)*

I raised my hand to my brow, wiping off the beads of sweat that saturated my face. As my fingers moved across my sensitive skin, I could tell the sun had left its mark. I felt there was no escaping the blanket of rays, only the clouds above seemed to be able to control. The pain was uncomfortable, but disappeared quickly as I scooped up the cool water and splashed it on my face.

I knew that I could not drink the seemingly infinite volume of water which surrounded me, so I headed for the nearby stream. Kneeling down, I penetrated the stream with cupped hands and raised the fresh water to my dry lips. Unable to control the water, it sifted through my fingers and ran down my arms, as if trying to escape back to the stream. I licked my salty lips and drank. Never before had I tasted a more refreshing drink of water. This euphoric experience was one that I savoured, as I reached for a second handful.

There have been few experiences throughout my life that I remember more vividly than of that day on the beach. I often think about where the water would flow, and who would be the recipient of its aqueous forgiveness. This simple stream had been the solution to my unquenchable need for sustenance. My connection, as if umbilical, was met when I broke the skin of Mother Nature's body to partake of her life-giving substance. But, something separated me from that world which existed internally beneath the stream. This was the first spiritual encounter I remembered having with water. The thoughts of these experiences connected my innermost soul with the interaction of beauty and nature.

Not a nature that I fully understood, but an understanding of the line that connects the perfection of life to a spiritual world. Eventually all things merged into one, and I would understand both physical and spiritual, but until then I would be left untutored.

**Helen McCann (15)**
St Catherine's College, Armagh

# The Kitchen Window
*(An extract)*

Looking out the tiny rounded window, the rusty autumn-coloured leaves swirl past the pane of glass, the miracle of Mother Nature. The leaves, the most beautiful colours of deep red and orange, caught the wind and lifted me into the air. Like fairies, they used their precious wings to take flight. They twisted and bowed, almost showing off; until the time came that they laid to rest on the ground. Each blade of grass had stopped growing. Coldness edged its way through each blade. The sky was covered in a fluffy grey sponge of dull cloud. Every ray of sun was hiding behind the clouds, taking refuge from the harsh nip in the air.

Winter was coming; all the signs were there, unmistakable for me to see. All the beautiful shrubs and plants, which had once blown in the radiant summer sun, were now tucked up cosily, sleeping, protected by the soil. Large blusters of wind pushed their way through the almost bare branches of the trees, letting them know that winter was here, like a lion shaking its mane. I felt the chill of the wind through my frail body. Pulling my shawl tighter around my hunched shoulders, I wondered if this winter would be my last.

Rocking in my chair I looked around the magical garden I had played in as a child. The children's voices echoed in my mind. The games we had once played, the fun we once had was a memory; a distant memory. I looked around my kitchen. I recalled the scent of the freshly baked biscuits my mother would make. The smell would wade through the whole house, making my taste buds ignite.

My modest, mature house hadn't changed much since my childhood. The crabbit gas cooker placed in the same spot, the heavy, enamel sink still perched under the box window looking out onto the porch where my mother and father would sit; watching the sunset. The cool pantry still had the same shape and layout, petite but perfect. All the food sat neatly on the designated shelf, just like my mother had taught me. The same wooden table sat in the middle of the room and of course the weathered rocking chair had always been beside the rounded window.

**Katie-Mary Harvey (15)**
St Catherine's College, Armagh

# The Day The World Ended 4th May 2053

*(An extract)*

'Why do you spend so much time in the shower?' exclaimed Anthony.

'Oh shut up,' yelled Jenny storming off and slamming the door almost taking it off its hinges.

'No, it's true. When you are finished there is never enough hot water left for the rest of us,' shouted Anthony.

'Kids, please be quiet, I have a splitting headache,' cried Sophie, their mother, in exasperation.

A normal Monday: teenagers arguing and a racing mother frantically packing lunches and making a fry up for her impatient husband, Peter.

Peter was sitting at the table, like a big fat slob, licking his lips. Sophie staggered across the kitchen, two packed lunches in one hand, a high calorie fry up in the other. Leaving the hot, sizzling fry up down on the table, she gave her boisterous children their lunches, turned around and headed for the sink to wash some sodden breakfast dishes.

Out of the window, the darkness crept in among the white clouds, lurking and threatening. The sun, no longer shining, made everything eerily silent apart from her husband's piercing chewing habit. The only thing that stood out from the dark, overpowering sky was the Manhattan skyline. The skyscrapers' silhouette merged with the sullen sky.

She felt compelled to go outside. There was no wind, no nature breathing. Dullness and clamminess oppressively surrounded the tight garden space.

The sky suddenly lit up with balls of fire pounding down towards the Earth. Gusts of wind got stronger and stronger. Screeches of children echoed in the neighbourhood.

Sophie screamed and tumbled into the house, too shocked to speak. She just stood there. Trembling, Jenny heard the shrieks of people outside and Anthony gazed out through the window in amazement.

**Joanne Caraher  (15)**
St Catherine's College, Armagh

# Nobody's Girl

The leaves glistened with the glittery sprinkles of the rain as the dull mind-numbing grey sky screamed, as the thunder rolled. The mud sludged as I ran through it. Rain slapped my face as I got faster and faster. Wind sliced the back of my neck. My hands hacked away like wood. I jumped over a piece of sharp, silver, jagged barbed wire and minced my leg, blood pouring. I ran until I could run no more. I fell in a heap. As I lay there I thought of her at last. Why stick it so long? Would she ever be back? He pushed her away when I needed her most.

Malicious, obnoxious, revolting man. He was the Devil's work. Why? What was his problem? How could he have such repulsion toward people closest to him? He was a lion on the prowl, looking for anything with blood pumping through its body just so he could attack and watch its poor face as he pounced on it, scrabbling, tearing it limb from limb, helpless. Although my mum was far from the ideal, model mother, still no one, not even she, deserved to be treated like some kind of unacceptable, worthless, insignificant human being.

The sky was clearing but my head was not. The sun splitting through the clouds, shot its tendrils out to reach me, but it just couldn't. Like my mother when she needed me, I couldn't reach her. I was so pathetic, weak, helpless. Why was I such a disgrace? I let a short, hideous, obese piece of meat rule our lives for so long. Not anymore. Now I'm taking charge. It makes me gag every time I picture him with his satisfied smirk on his face.

I knew where I was going, to the old bridge. My mum and I used to go for walks there every Sunday afternoon. It was the place she went when she was 13; she told me that if you look in the water all your worries would just float away. I can remember when I was 4, it was getting dark, the sun was falling behind the distant hills as I held her delicate velvet hands. I have never felt so safe in my life. It was a nice peaceful spot in the country. Very few knew about it, it was a place you could go to be undisturbed. To get them to listen. To get them to realise I was part of a family but now thanks to him I'm not. I was on my own. I took the short cut across the green valley field. There was a trail behind me of flattened down grass as I hauled my leg along behind me. I was only five minutes away from the bridge. I could see it in the distance.

**Maeve Devlin  (15)**
St Catherine's College, Armagh

# Hallowe'en Town

*(An extract)*

As I wandered swiftly through the darkened wood, the sound of twisted twigs breaking beneath my feet sent a chilling shiver up my spine. I found it grievous to catch a breath; everything seemed serene, motionless, as if time had stopped.

The grass shot up like acute needles, the dew from the mist balanced and poised on its slender blades. The saccharine smell of nature reminded me of my grandmother, sweet, but it had that spice, a kick of excitement like a velvet blanket, deep and endless, the night's sky stretched. The moon, plump and cylindrical; shone brighter than a million stars clustered together, luminous, a touch of mystery. The freshness of October was coming to a close, the golden leaves were beginning to rot and three monotonous months were ahead, awaiting me, just like my mother back at the house.

Hallowe'en night was here, the most significant night of the year, in my town anyway, after all this is Hallowe'en Town. I made my way down from the steep slope at the side of the forest. From the peak of the hill I could see everything. In the centre of the town the immense auburn pumpkin was smoking proudly. People came from all ends to join in the celebrations; witches flew high above the stampedes of tall intelligent wizards, creepy long nosed goblins, walking animals and dancing children. The town was decorated exquisitely. Stalls set up selling cotton candy, toffee apples and large Hallowe'en lollipops. Bright fireworks filled the sky, setting off in co-ordination every three minutes. It was like a fairy tale, something you would see in a film.

As I cast my sparkling green eyes over the town, I glimpsed the shadowy figure of an unfamiliar member. Focusing on him I absorbed every detail. Scruffy and diminutive, his tatty, waist-length dirty blond hair hung. The deep dark rings around his electric blue eyes, one covered slightly with a leather patch made him look as if he was close to death. Extremely thin, with baggy torn clothes; the dirt on his snakeskin boots must have been there for decades, it looked like rust. The skin around his mouth looked irritated and crusty, however, nothing compared to his teeth. Covered in a yellow scum, many of them were pitch-black like coal and crumbling. As he spoke to the merchant behind the pumpkin juice stall his distant cockney accent irritated the fresh air. His gait was unusual, he looked intoxicated.

**Lauren Hughes  (15)**
**St Catherine's College, Armagh**

# The Calling

*(An extract)*

The whiff of the recently fitted pine drawers, cupboards and staircase invaded your lungs, with every intake of the air as you entered; its scent rose from every corner of the house - a weird, fresh fragrance. Early that day we had been eagerly trying to get everything moved in, cleared up, personalised. Yet boxes positioned themselves at the stylish, original front door, and already friends were arriving to glance and gawk, examine and explore the glamorous stainless steel kitchen Mum had bragged about for so long.

While they were nattering and shuffling curiously downstairs, I took myself up the newly arranged pine stairs that escorted me to my room. As I assembled my thoughts, I planted myself in bed. Rain bashed furiously against the double-glazed windows, disfiguring anything that may have lurked beyond it. Howling winds, fierce, fully eliminated the lavish, clean, contemporary greenery and everything else that lay on its trail. Branches, suppressed against the once beautiful gardens and decorative patios, now were disguised by an unsightly mass of debris. The whole world looked like it had been sealed in horrendous, overcast grey clouds. A malignant bolt of lightning sharply slashed its way through the wild, hazy night sky and with it came a virulent uproar.

The halogen spotlights began to flicker tremulously.

**Laura Hughes  (15)**
St Catherine's College, Armagh

# A Day In The Life Of A Pencil

I woke up to the rattling of my owner going to school, I was in her schoolbag. There were loads of pens beside me and I was the only pencil, I felt alone because the pens didn't talk to me.

My owner arrived at school and I felt a bang as she took out the pencil case. I wondered who she would write with, could my day finally have come?

I saw a ray of light as the zip of the pencil case swiftly opened, my lead thumped as two sweaty fat fingers picked me up. I was a brand new, shiny red HB pencil introduced to the world at last. Just as I was about to show them what I could do, I suddenly felt squeezed, there was pressure on my body and the tip of my lead snapped. The pain was terrible and suddenly to make matters worse, I saw the enemy of all pencils, *the chunky black sharpener*.

My owner stuck me roughly into the hole and turned me. I thought I was a goner as she twisted me round, I felt tired but she took me again and wrote for ages. A loud bell rang and she quickly grabbed the pencil case. I was glad as I felt exhausted, but, oh no, I fell to the floor. The door banged and I was alone … I seemed to fall asleep and awoke to the bristles of a brush pushing me along into a corner. A few minutes later a new class of giggling girls arrived. I was picked up and admired. My new owner quickly threw me in her pencil case. When I looked around it was full of pencils. I made lots of new friends and I was happy at last.

**Sarah Rath  (12)**
**St Catherine's College, Armagh**

# Starting

Riding in the school van with my softball team had always been invigorating. The blatant sound of music created a soft vibration under everyone's seat; the non-stop yelling and chatter; the whizzing by of the additional cars on the road made it seem as if we were all in a big blur of competition. As we came to a sudden halt, a wad of sugary sap saturated itself onto the back of my head. I turned around to face a freckly girl with flamboyant red hair, 'Oops! Ha ha, sorry,' she said half-heartedly. Her mouth never seemed to shut and there never seemed to be a time when there wasn't a piece of that sweet sap in her big mouth, except for now.

'Look!' squealed the girl next to me as she swung her arm, just barely missing my nose. 'There it is!' Seven heads turned to the right as we neared our rival's field.

It was some field. The sun seemed to hit it at every angle in such a gentle way, it was like the movies, everything constructed flawlessly. The grass was so green and crisp, the dirt so still and kept. The dugouts looked like they were just freshly painted, and so carefully carved and smooth, each imitating the other, like there was only one looking into a mirror and coming out the other side. The van stopped and my coach came and budged open the hulk of metal he called a door.

'Alright girls, freshmen get the equipment, the rest of ya get a move on, c'mon now!' he spat and it was me who had received all his tobacco smelling saliva on my face. We all clambered out eagerly like a pack of hyenas just spotting a juicy big deer and running to see who could get to it first.

**Natalie Toal (15)**
St Catherine's College, Armagh

# Innocent

*(An extract)*

'Innocent until proven guilty', that's what they say, isn't it? But what about 'innocent but accused guilty'? To those unfortunate enough to be blamed for a crime they did not commit, there is still hope. For the false evidence used against them, it's only true if you let it be'.

The book was entrancing the nation, 'Innocent'. A word of abundant meanings. But this one was different. This one was a cry for help. It was like time had stopped, been brought to a halt. These words were the most anticipated of their time, given immense thought by all the evading eyes that were gripped by the once despised man.

The queue on the road was caused by the woman who had halted, and the traffic that was brought to a standstill. The policemen were not out fighting crime, the old man who sat on the park bench no longer had his newspaper rested on his lap. People stopped their usual day-to-day tasks in order to listen to this man's voice. All of a sudden he had his chance to speak out, be heard. Little did he know that one handshake was all it would take for a life of distress, torment and outrage.

'Maybe we are meant to meet the wrong people before meeting the right one, so that when we finally meet the right person, we will know how to be grateful for that gift'.

**Natalie McCreesh (14)**
**St Catherine's College, Armagh**

# Dreams Can Turn Real!

It was a dark stormy, spooky night and the wind was blowing, but in this little old-looking house had lived a young girl and her parents, that little girl's name was Jane Platte. Jane was nine years old and was a very smart, pleasant child with blonde, straight hair and green eyes.

Every night before Jane went to bed she said goodnight to her parents and this is what she did.

'Goodnight Mum and Dad,' said Jane as she walked to her room.

'Goodnight Jane, see you tomorrow,' replied her mum.

Jane walked towards her bed and hopped in it, but as soon as Jane's head hit the pillow she was fast asleep.

But then disaster struck! Jane had found herself in this spooky looking forest, she screamed for help but no one was there! She heard the pattering of footsteps around the place, not only that, but whispering as well.

But when she went to look around her she found herself looking down a very deep pit! But then suddenly from out of nowhere a whirl of strong wind came blowing into Jane's direction. She couldn't keep herself upright so the wind had blown her into the pit!

As she was falling she noticed that there were lions at the end of the pit.

'Help please!' Jane screamed. 'Ahhhh,' shouted Jane.

'What's wrong honey?' asked her dad.

'I'm going to die!' whispered Jane.

'No you're not, you're at home in your bed!' her dad said.

'What?' said Jane.

'Get back to sleep,' replied her dad.

What had happened to Jane had not made much sense to her. She was very puzzled and confused about what had happened so she went back to sleep.

It just goes to tell that dreams could really become true!

**Michelle Devine (12)**
**St Patrick's Academy, Dungannon**

# Lauren And The Fairies

It was a beautiful sunny day and Lauren and her older cousin Niamh went for a walk in the forest.

Niamh and Lauren walked a long way into the forest, talking a lot before they come to a path.

'Shall we take the path?' asked Lauren.

'Yes, we will take the path and see where it leads us to,' said Niamh.

'OK, but I'm a wee bit scared,' said Lauren. They started walking on down the path.

Niamh and Lauren were walking when they heard a funny sound.

'Did you hear that?' asked Lauren.

'Yes,' said Niamh.

They heard the sound again.

'Did you hear that again?' asked Niamh.

'Yes,' said Lauren.

Then they saw a fairy. The fairy was afraid.

'Don't be afraid wee fairy,' said Lauren. 'We won't hurt you.'

The fairy flew over to Niamh and Lauren.

'Hi I'm Niamh and this is my cousin Lauren, she has always wanted to see a fairy.'

'What's your name?' asked Lauren.

'Kelarinda,' said the fairy. 'Do you want to meet my friends?'

'Yes,' they both said.

Then lots of fairies came and Lauren was so excited.

After chatting the fairies decided to have a big party for Niamh and Lauren. The fairies danced and sang. They showed Niamh and Lauren all their little baby fairies and their houses.

Niamh looked at her watch. 'Oh no,' she said, 'Lauren we must go, we have to get back before dark.'

'Yes,' said Niamh.

They all said goodbye and Kelarinda asked them both to promise not to tell anyone that they had seen fairies. Niamh and Lauren promised, said goodbye and rushed back home.

When they got back Lauren's mum was worried and asked where they were.

'Oh just trying to find birds' nests in the forest,' said Niamh.

'So what did you see on your walk then?'

'Oh nothing too exciting,' they both said.

**Niamh Doris (13)**
**St Patrick's Academy, Dungannon**

# United Pay The Penalty

Man United lost on penalties in the FA Cup Final.

United had all of the play in the first ninety minutes of the game and also with the half an hour of extra time.

Paul Scholes missed the penalty, which proved decisive. Patrick Viera calmly put away the penalty, which won the shoot-out and the cup for Arsenal.

Arsenal who had no shots on target in the first ninety minutes and ended the game with ten men.

Jose Antonio Reyes was fouled five times without a Man United player being booked and he committed two fouls and was sent-off.

It was harsh on Man United to have all the play in the game to lose by that awful one goal on penalties; on a scoreline of five to four. It was great for Arsenal because this was both teams only chance of silverware in the 2004/5 season.

**Corey Cassidy (13)**
**St Patrick's Academy, Dungannon**

# Man Knifed!

Yesterday evening a 33-year-old roadworker called Kieran Knipe was knifed by a man wearing a mask. This happened on Coke Street in London.

The attacker was described to be 6ft, wearing a black hooded top with a designer cap. He was also wearing a pair of navy tracksuit bottoms and a pair of white trainers.

He was armed with a 12 inch cooking knife. The masked man was then later arrested and was charged with attempted murder. The police have not yet found out his name.

As for the 33-year-old roadworker called Kieran Knipe, he was brought to hospital and still remains there. His condition is supposed to be stable but he has an 8 inch cut down his stomach.

Here is what one of the doctors had to say about his condition.

'He is badly injured but is in a stable condition. He should be fully recovered in about 2 weeks. He will be getting 12 stitches to his wound'.

**Aaron O'Neill  (13)**
**St Patrick's Academy, Dungannon**

# Dr Kent!

It was a windy, stormy Hallowe'en night and I had just settled in my new abandoned house. I was all alone in this spooky house but with me I had my terrific experiment. Outside there was lightning and thunder and I hoped it would come beside the house soon. I was really lucky to be able to see the lightning as tall trees surrounded the house and it was really foggy.

My experiment was in the far corner of the room beside the broken window. The best moment in my life was about to come. Oh! If only I could control the lightning I would bring it over here as soon as possible. *Suddenly,* I heard a crackle of lightning! It had to be near now! Suddenly the lightning hit the electrical wires leading to my experiment. The experiment twitched. 'It's alive, it's alive,' I shouted. The experiment rose and got up off the table.

'Wait a second, that's not a holy angel, that's a *monster!'*

The monster had yellow skin that was waxy and looked like a dandelion's petals and his skin was beginning to rot. His eyes were bulging with goo, his hair was covered in leeches and it was very greasy and matted. His face was covered in warts and there was wax pouring out of his ears! He smelt of rotten insides and his fingernails were bitten down to his rotting skin. His breath smelt really bad.

He grunted at me but I couldn't make out what he was saying. Then he started to walk. His movements were slow, stiff and big. Every time his feet touched the ground you could hear a loud thud. He was walking towards me like he was going to kill me. I was horrified and frightened; I was too young to die! I felt as though I was a tiny mouse and a huge cat was running after me. Although I was curious to know if he was going to hurt me or not, I didn't stay to find out. I rushed out of the room, slamming the door behind me. I locked myself in the bathroom and stayed there that night, worried that the monster might hurt someone else other than myself, because if he did it would be my entire fault. I wonder where that monster is now …

**Jamie Hughes  (12)**
**St Patrick's Academy, Dungannon**

# Fairy Tale Times

### Snow White's Silent Fight

Snow White, 34, one of our most favourite celebrity princesses, last night finally lost the plot after what was a traumatising life. As a child, her wicked stepmother always neglected her and she had a rough childhood when her stepmother sent her into the forest in her late teens to be killed by a swordsman who then, when he was driven to do the task, just couldn't do it.

The young woman who had been living in the Twinkle Forest for some time now was showing signs of a mental illness. She was confined in a small, poky cottage, probably sitting there day by day going insane by the minute. This led to a series of many unfortunate events. On the 19th day of January, Snow White, while making soup for the seven dwarfs, added a dangerous toxin to the mix which led to six of the dwarfs going into an isolation ward in fear of the spread of a deadly virus. Grumpy refused to eat the soup.

He said, 'There was definitely something pink in my soup. I guess I was a lucky dwarf'.

On the 22nd day of February, Snow White struck again. She had hacked all the dwarfs' beds up into the shape of a knife. It disturbed detectives as they were clueless as to why she did this. She made eight other attacks on a family's housing, who wish to remain anonymous.

The dwarfs all stated that the possible cause and kick-start of Snow White's madness was when she was sent to prison last year for attempted murder of her royal husband as he was 'too busy for her'. Her husband chucked her out of the kingdom claiming that she was in no fit state to be a princess.

Snow White did not talk through this whole period in her life, but kept a disturbing and aberrant smile on her face that worried the dwarfs; they had taken her in shortly after the split.

Snow White is now receiving professional help at St Bernard's Hospital for the mentally ill, and receiving the best support anyone could ask for from her fellow princesses, Rapunzel, Cinderella and Sleeping Beauty.

**Michaela Cullen (13)**
St Patrick's Academy, Dungannon

# Come Home Molly

'Have a nice day, Rebecca,' said Mummy.

Rebecca had started to walk to school as she always did, but she didn't know that her pet duck, Molly, was following her. Rebecca knew that Molly loved Quality Street sweets, but didn't know that Molly was following her because she had Quality Street.

When she got into school, she stopped to talk to Mrs O'Neill, her primary 4 teacher. Mrs O'Neill was getting her younger daughter out of the car when Molly sneaked into the back of the car without a sound amazingly.

Mrs O'Neill's daughter was shouting, 'I want that duck, Mummy. I want that duck, Mummy!'

When Rebecca got home from school she couldn't find Molly. Her friends and family helped her search everywhere, but she just could not be found. Rebecca cried for hours and hours. Rebecca had started to give up hope and went upstairs to her room with her friends.

'We should make a book about Molly with loads of pictures of her,' said one of her friends.

Suddenly she heard a knock at the door. It was Mrs O'Neill with Molly! She was so, so happy to be reunited with her pet duck.

**Ciara McGrath (13)**
**St Patrick's Academy, Dungannon**

# Viery Nice!

It was the game everyone had been waiting for. Man Utd vs Arsenal. The last ever FA Cup Final to be played in Cardiff at the Millennium Stadium. For both teams it was the last chance to add some silverware to their trophy cabinets.

A sea of red and white jerseys filled the stadium. Both captains, Roy Keane and fierce rival, Patrick Vieira, were keen to make their teams go home with the trophy.

The game was tense and physical with some players like Wayne Rooney and Thierry Henry playing their hearts out. Jose Antonio Reyes was sent off on a harsh decision by the referee.

After 90 minutes the game was scoreless. The game went into extra time. Still no score after two hours of play, so it was left to only one thing, a penalty shoot-out for the FA Cup. A terrible penalty by Paul Scholes saw Arsenal take the lead. It came down to the last penalty, Patrick Vieira vs Roy Carroll. Vieira stepped up and calmly slotted it away to see Arsenal win the FA Cup.

**Conor Campbell (13)**
**St Patrick's Academy, Dungannon**

# Blossom

Once upon a time there lived a fairy. She lived in a blossom tree at the bottom of an old lady called Dorothy's garden. Dorothy was very lonely as her husband had passed away and her children had their own families.

One day Dorothy went to collect her post and saw the fairy sitting there. She thought she was seeing things, but no! There really was a fairy there. Dorothy called her Blossom.

One day Dorothy went to see Blossom and noticed her wing was broken. Dorothy took her up to the house and mended it for her. They became best friends.

One night, Blossom noticed a lot of smoke in Dorothy's kitchen. She flew up to Dorothy's window and whispered in Dorothy's ear to wake her up. She saved Dorothy's life like Dorothy had saved Blossom's wing. (During the events, Blossom's wing got broken again.)

Sadly now, Dorothy has passed away and a new family has moved in. Now Blossom is alone again. She sits and watches the family every day, hoping and wishing they would find her. Her wing is still broken.

**Niamh McCann  (13)**
**St Patrick's Academy, Dungannon**

# Dracula Drains And Dries!

*Dracula's blood, bones and body bits*

Last night, Dracula was found draining and drying up a corpse of its last dribble of blood.

The 487-year-old, Dracula, was taken into custody on suspected murder, but then he was released on bail. Detectives cleared his name of murder last night. The corpse was found with bite marks under his neck and a plastic sucking tube inserted into the left side of his heart. Detectives are investigating the corpse which was found in an empty subway station by a member of the public. It was also discovered with a petrol can and matches.

The police spokesman said, 'It was clear that it was planned to burn the corpse, but we have no evidence so we can't convict him'.

We'll bring a follow up of this story next week in our next issue.

**Sean-Michael McDowell (13)**
**St Patrick's Academy, Dungannon**

# The Fairy Times

*Cinders For Cinders - Cinderella Flips The Lid*

Princess Cinderella was arrested last night for arson and attempted murder after her outbreak of revenge on her husband, Prince Charming.

Soon after it was revealed that the prince was having an affair with the ugly stepsister, Cinderella decided to strike back.

The 27-year-old princess from far, far away, broke into tears when she heard the awful news, but this soon turned to vicious laughter as she stood at the palace gates watching it go up in flames with the intention of it and everyone in it being burnt to a crisp.

After gulping down several glasses of wine, Cinderella fled from the palace, but returned soon after with petrol and matches. She forced her stepsister into a closet, saying, 'How do you like it?' then set fire to the great hall which went up rapidly and spread throughout like lightning.

Cinderella's stepsister has got severe smoke damage to her lungs and is in intensive care at present, fighting for her life. This could be a murder charge for the princess to add to her list.

Cinderella admits all charges against her and spitefully shouted, 'If I get my hands on that man, I will kill him on the spot, and as far as that ugly sister of mine, well she can rot in Hell'.

Kingsville Palace is now nothing but ruins and millions of pounds down the drain.

Cinders is her name, and cinders is what's left.

**Niamh McGirr (13)**
**St Patrick's Academy, Dungannon**

# A Day In The Life Of Cinderella's Mouse

Yesterday the strangest thing happened to me, well, I think it happened, or was it a dream?

I was very hungry. I was scampering around outside with my friends looking for some food. There wasn't anything around apart from a few pumpkin seeds and I was still starving. All of a sudden I smelt something absolutely delicious coming out of the little cottage. My stomach was rumbling and my mouth watering, so I thought, *what harm would it do just to take a look?*

I ran up to the house and jumped on the window ledge. I saw Cinderella stirring something in a large pot and she seemed to be crying. That didn't matter to me, I had my eye on the large pot where the scrumptious smell seemed to be coming from.

I found a little space in the door which I squeezed through and got into the cosy little room. I crept quietly across the floor towards the pot. I then spotted a piece of cheese, and thought, *that would go down well for starters.* I ran lightly towards the cheese, took another step forward to take a bite and *snap!* I was trapped! What was I going to do? Well, at least I wouldn't go hungry! I hadn't been trapped long when, out of nowhere, a lovely old lady with a silver wand in her hand appeared beside Cinderella.

She said to her, 'I am your fairy godmother, and you shall go to the ball, but first you must bring me one pumpkin, six mice from the mouse traps and six lizards.'

No sooner had she said that, Cinderella returned with all the things she had asked for. She had five of my friends in her hand and was coming to get me! She removed me from the trap, gripping me tightly, so I had no chance of escape. She set everything down on the ground just outside the door.

The lady said something, and then everything seemed to get smaller around me. I was the same height as Cinderella! I saw my reflection in the window, I was a horse! There were five more horses and we seemed to be leading a carriage that held the beautiful Cinderella.

We arrived at some large building and Cinderella got out. I then ate a few carrots and fell asleep. Then there was a loud sound which seemed to be coming from the clock and Cinderella ran down the steps of the palace.

*Young Writers – T.A.L.E.S. From Northern Ireland*

By the time she got to the bottom of the steps she was back in her usual clothes. Everything seemed to be returning to normal, even me! I was back to my normal mouse self! It was then I realised my extraordinary adventure was over, but at least life is better now. I live in a beautiful palace with all the food I could ever want!

**Sarah-Jayne Campbell (13)**
**St Patrick's Academy, Dungannon**

# It All Went Wrong

He used to be so energetic and springy like a bunny rabbit and he and I would play every day. I can remember on Wednesday we would go down to the beach and throw stones into the water to see who could get the most skims, but every time I threw mine it would land in the water like a sack of cement hitting the ground.

I can also remember on Fridays when I slept over at his house and his mum would make her beautiful chicken pie. The smell would fill the house and after we had dinner we would go out and play football.

Everything has changed now. My family are moving house. I wanted to stay but they forced me to go, so I packed my belongings and said my final farewells to John. They were dragging me out without even telling me where I was going.

Later that day we arrived at a nice little cottage in the countryside and unpacked our stuff straight away. Some locals greeted us and welcomed us to our new home. After this I started to get friendly with them and started playing with them.

I'm telling you this now because last week I looked at a picture of John and decided to go and see him. I arrived at his house and there was a hearse outside his house. His mum came running out and told me that John was dead.

It seemed like only yesterday I was playing with him.

**Christopher Price  (14)**
**The Abbey CBS Grammar School, Newry**

# Republic Attacks Onderon!

*Republic vessel attacks Colonel Tobin!*

Today a Republic capital-class vessel, known as the Ebon Hawk, attacked and destroyed six Onderonian Star Fighters, which started the space battle that lasted for several hours, before being destroyed by Colonel Tobin's and General Vaklu's forces.

The Queen denies that it was a capital vessel and that it started the space battle.

General Vaklu is now saying that Onderon should break away from the Republic and end Queen Talia's reign.

Many have already joined General Vaklu, but most Onderonians are supporting the Queen over the General.

Even though the Queen and the General are cousins, they fight like they only just met.

It looks as if this conflict between Queen Talia and General Vaklu might turn into an Onderonian civil war.

*Political Crisis!*

General Vaklu announced that he is now taking control of Queen Talia's council and that he will have direct influence on their decisions. The Queen is furious, but is powerless to stop General Vaklu from removing Council members.

'This will be very beneficial to Onderon,' the General told us in an interview.

**Brian McArdle (12)**
The Abbey CBS Grammar School, Newry

# The Lawnmower Man
*(An extract)*

'You can't fire me, I've been here for 6 years,' bellowed Rowan Johnson.

'I can and I will,' replied Agent W Peters.

'I have to pay bills. I'll get kicked out of my apartment, *please*, one more chance.'

'No! You are discharged from White House garden duty. You have two weeks notice with $5,000 compensation for your service.'

'You'll be sorry,' Rowan said. 'I will have my revenge ...' With that he walked out of the room nearly taking the door off its hinges.

The phone rang abruptly, ending the off-duty sleep of Colonel John Anderson. He answered in a groggy voice, 'Hello? I'm on my way.' He flung on a pair of jeans and a sports T-shirt of the New York Yankees. 6ft 7 inches, he had blond hair with a small scar underneath his left eye from one of his many battles. He was very muscular and fast. He raced to the White House in his Lamborghini Diablo, he was there is 15 minutes.

As he pulled up to the White House there were reporters and police all over the scene. Flashing his pass, he hurried through the spectacular hallways until he entered the President's room where the police were investigating. A man in a black suit lay dead on the floor. The carpet was stained with red blood. He had been shot in the head and the leg. John couldn't quite make out who it was. Suddenly a tall dark-haired man whisked him into a room. 'We have an agent dead and the President captured. You have to find him in less than 24 hours. Got it?'

'Yeah,' replied John.

It was five o'clock and John had one lead; a gardener who had recently been fired by that same agent, his name was Rowan Johnson. Word was he was quite angry at being fired and swore he would get revenge ...

**Jonathan Rafferty (14)**
**The Abbey CBS Grammar School, Newry**

# The Carpenter

Francesco Corlioni is my name, Verona is my hometown, my profession is simply a carpenter.

Now that I've informed you of my identity, we'll embark on why my book is called 'I Knew I Had To Do The Right Thing In The End'.

It all started two summers ago, I was witness to the Mafia carrying out a hit on Gian Luigi Maldini (The Wrench). I was working late on the 9th of July 1978 because I was refurbishing a piano for my local hero Andre Pichelle who needed it for theatre next week. I had just locked up my workshop when out of the corner of my eye, I noticed a stocky, shadowy figure complete with a top hat and striped blazer which was complimented with a black and silver waistcoat.

At first I thought nothing of it, but then all I heard was the whimpering of a man, around or just over the age of consent, who had no chance of fending off the stalky figure. He was being repeatedly stamped on and that's when I knew I had to intervene. Little did I know that this was just an average day in the life of Don Antonio di Vio.

**Christopher Duggan (14)**
**The Abbey CBS Grammar School, Newry**

# A Frightening Experience

The wind beat against the window and the rain smashed against the eastern side of the house. Eoin lay in bed shivering with his blankets pulled up against his face and a million frightening thoughts running through his mind. Lightning struck and he flinched and let out a quiet shriek. He pulled the blankets closer as if trying to seek comfort from them. Suddenly, *tap, tap, tap*, went his large oak door. He let out a quivering, silent laugh. 'Eoin, you're being silly. It is the wind and nothing more.' *Tap, tap, tap*, again went the noise from beyond his chamber door. His body shivered once more and a chill ran up his spine.

He put one trembling foot out of his bed, then the other. The floorboards creaked behind him as he walked. He drew nearer to the door and then, *smash!* A branch from an oak tree which was planted beside his house came crashing through his window.

He fell to the ground trembling. He stuttered as he spoke to himself, *g...get up Eoin and see what the noise was. Fix the window in the morning and sleep in the guest bed tonight.*

Eoin stood up and put a trembling hand on the door handle, turned it and opened the door. Nothing. He stepped into the hall and closed the door behind him.

The next day his wife returned home from a business trip. She searched the whole house but he was nowhere to be found. What appeared most strange was the locked door to Eoin's chamber.

Locked from the inside and nothing disturbed to provide a clue. I'm sure Eoin's disappearance will remain a mystery, even to me.

**Eoin Murphy (14)**
**The Abbey CBS Grammar School, Newry**

# 21st Century Uniforms

Uniforms: uncomfortable; uncool; impractical. The issue of school uniforms is very much a live one. Have uniform, have controversy!

Some pupils and teachers will argue that a uniform is one of the only traditions still alive within our school and they stand for the school's ethos, carrying our crests and colours. Uniforms also prevent bullying, minimise criticism amongst the students over 'fashion' and keep us neat and tidy; but do we really have to endure sweaty summers and freezing winters just to look presentable and equal? There is a solution - change the uniform!

A fleece, a polo shirt, believe me, anything is an improvement. A more comfortable, pupil-agreed and practical version will make students feel more relaxed about wearing a uniform and will undoubtedly be conducive to learning.

A new uniform will not only satisfy pupils but teachers alike. With the new dress code getting the approval of students, they'll feel less inclined to rebel against it, therefore teachers will not have to worry about rule breakers (as regards uniform anyway!)

Never again will we hear the infamous cries of teachers, 'Tuck in that shirt', and, 'Where is your tie young man?'

What we need is a uniform that is individual - cool in summer and warm in winter. Getting a sports brand like O'Neills or Gaelic Gear to design and sell the uniform would also be a good idea. A simplified uniform will mean a more affordable price - bound to be uniformly welcomed by parents!

**Cathal MacDhaibhéid (13)**
**The Abbey CBS Grammar School, Newry**

# Mr Tompkins

When I was a young lad, around nine years old, I had trouble mixing with my peers until we moved to a small village called Burren. The house we moved to was a fair size but that wasn't important because it was there that I met Mr Tompkins.

He was a kind old man and had been living there for roughly fifty years. He was now one hundred and nine. We got along very well and were practically always together. Every evening after school I would race home to see Mr Tompkins, so we could be on our way to the park where we would sit on the benches overlooking the lake. I would sit doing my homework while Mr Tompkins would tell me about the good old days when he was fighting for our country in the war. Some nights we would be there for hours before descending on our journey home.

One Friday after school I was in the usual hurry to Mr Tompkins, but when I got to his house there was no one there, so I sat and waited on his doorstep. After a few hours, I picked myself up and decided to leave.

When I got home my mum and dad were sitting at the kitchen table waiting for me. They told me to sit down and went on to explain how Mr Tompkins had gone away permanently. Because I was a young lad, I didn't understand fully what they were telling me until the next day, when I called for Mr Tompkins, and again I sat and waited, and it was then I realised that he had gone to a better place.

**Declan Price (14)**
**The Abbey CBS Grammar School, Newry**

# Snow White The Schizo

Hi, I'm Snow White, you may have heard of me. This is the story of what happened to me after I caught up with the Wicked Witch and battered her. It wasn't a particularly bad beating considering what she did to me with that poison apple; I mean she could still walk!

I had been arrested and the police were trying to interrogate me.

When I was interrogated as to why I had almost murdered that woman the police didn't believe that it was a wicked witch. Eventually my interrogator became frustrated and angry. He began to talk to the mirror, 'Get psychs in here, this girl's a raving lunatic!' I pointed out that the mirror couldn't hear him as it was not magic like the witch's.

'Have you ever watched TV?'

(I asked what a TV was).

'How many times did your mother drop you on your head and be honest?'

I did not reply.

A man with a long white coat came in and asked me many questions. With each of my answers he grew more puzzled looking. When he was done he took a look at his results and told me exactly why I did not know what TV was.

This is the end of my story. It turns out that there are no such people as the Seven Dwarfs or the Wicked Witch. The dwarfs were my multiple personalities and everything I ever knew was just a big schizophrenic illusion.

Now I live in a new house with padded walls and funky coats with no sleeves. The dwarfs visit me occasionally but then I get an injection and they go away. Now all I want is for that bloomin' six-legged cow to go away and stop asking me to play snakes and ladders.

**Dónal Daly (14)**
**The Abbey CBS Grammar School, Newry**

# Ireland On Monday

*Bullying: A Real Problem.*

Bullying has become a major problem in many schools across N Ireland.

There have been over 4,000 reported cases of bullying in N Ireland over the past year.

People can be picked on because of the way they look, their belongings or even because of their clothes. This is unacceptable.

Why? I ask you, the bullies, why do you pick on others?

Are you jealous? Are you lonely? You might have your own problems, that's none of my business, but what is my business is when you pick on some small defenceless child, that's just wrong.

How would you feel if somebody hurt you both mentally and physically for no good reason?

The fact is, bullying needs to be stopped, sooner rather than later!

*What Is Being Done?*

Many people don't know who to blame for the situation in hand.

The fact is we are all to blame. Parents, for not knowing what their children are up to, or maybe even bullying themselves and setting a poor example. Also, teachers, this point is aimed at children bullies. A 500 word essay is not a good punishment for destroying someone's life. Try suspension or even expulsion.

**Christy Carr (14)**
**The Abbey CBS Grammar School, Newry**

# Hunting

I remember that day as if it was yesterday. I remember the startling noises that forced us to leave a Sunday dinner fit for a king, grab our coats and ascend the steep muddy fields that led up to the fence that runs along the perimeter of the mountain. We walked briskly for two reasons, firstly because it was quite cold and secondly if you stayed in one place for too long you were likely to get bogged down in the muddy fields.

We neared the thin line of trees at the top of our fields. We could see the stone ditch on the other side and just before we reached it we heard a series of gunshots echoing around the open area. My heart was pounding. We ran the last five feet or so and looked around the open clearing.

It was at this point I noticed nine men, dressed similarly in army-style camouflage, boots and each had a gun in hand, standing in the corner of the field shooting what seemed to be a family of foxes. One man turned and looked at us with a blank expression such as if he was buying a tin of beans, not that of a man who had just killed an innocent animal. He stared at us for a few moments then turned, casually picked up the dead animal and sauntered away with the fox slung over his shoulder.

My father told me that there was nothing we could do but return home and finish our dinner. We descended the steep hills without saying a word. We relayed the story to our shocked relations who had already started to eat.

There was a look of disgust on each of their faces accompanied by an awkward silence broken by, 'Your dinners are in the microwave.'

Everyone else immediately forgot the story and carried on as normal but the scenes from that day will remain with me for a long, long time.

**Shane O'Hare (14)**
**The Abbey CBS Grammar School, Newry**

# Dreaming
*(An extract)*

It was sunset as David pounded another lap around the track, the sweat glistened like ice upon his forehead. As he neared the home stretch, his head, heart and legs quickly came together and he realised it was time to stop. The sun was quickly setting in the sky, like a raindrop making its descent to the ground. When he stopped, he was breathing heavily, the thought of the next day and its implications on the rest of his life running through his head faster than he himself had sprinted down the track. By the way, we'd better introduce our character ...

His name is David Mills. He would never deny that he was born and bred on the rough estates and alleyways of Manchester. He played footy on the streets, he drank on the streets, basically, he lived on the streets. He once even got a trial for Manchester United, but didn't even turn up thanks to a heroin overdose. Instead of standing in the glorified halls of Old Trafford, he was in the Manchester Royal Infirmary having his stomach pumped. He took this overdose on the streets, the ones he had vandalised and destroyed. His mum had kicked him out at age seventeen, so he even slept on the streets.

David came from a single parent family. His mum was always drunk, ever since he could remember ...

His mum would be down the pub or at her friend's, while he picked up the pieces at home. He had missed out on the simple things like holidays and morals and guidance. No wonder David turned out the way he did. David didn't even have an education, as he had been expelled from seventeen schools, even the private school his mum had scrounged the money for. David didn't have any prospects; he had no interest in life.

But things were better now because tomorrow David would be going to the Olympic trials in London. The reason? Sheer luck! While he was at a young offenders institution, he spent his time in the gym or simply outside running ... it helped him forget. There he met William, a dedicated scout for Team GB as well as a youth worker. So, David's skill commenced, and he hasn't looked back since. He has trained and trained, and now is his chance to prove himself to the world. Of course, this was just dreaming now!

**Conal O'Hare  (14)**
**The Abbey CBS Grammar School, Newry**

# How Could I Be So Stupid?

*Only a week to go!* I thought, as I sat at the back of the class. It was a week till the summer holidays and I couldn't wait. But the thing I *could* wait for was the summer exams.

The teachers were always giving off about me slacking away, getting low marks and having slovenly homework. But this time it was serious. I was going to be expelled if I didn't pass the tests. I'd never been so scared in my life ...

I wasn't afraid of the tests but of my dad's reactions. He was a lawyer. What I'd call the 'academic type'. Not anything like me. That's why I had to do what I did.

I was given advice from a tear-away friend. He suggested that I make cheat notes. And although my conscience told me otherwise, I was going to do it.

The night before the first exam I quickly brushed through my book like a lion after its prey. I jotted down brief notes and dates. You know the sort of stuff. It had been the first time I was prepared for a test.

I picked a good, juicy seat at the back of the class away from the prying eyes of the examiner. I opened my test and was finished in no time.

But just before I closed my test a mysterious gust of wind knocked the paper off my desk. The examiner took one look at me and sent me packing. I was humiliated.

I was sent to the headmaster's office. It was a place I wasn't a stranger to. The man in charge sat me down. He didn't beat about the bush. He lifted the phone and casually informed my parents that I wasn't to come back to school. I was expelled and all for the sake of a simple test.

The only lesson I learned was, *failing to prepare is preparing to fail.*

**David Fitzpatrick (14)**
**The Abbey CBS Grammar School, Newry**

# NV

I can remember the first time I went to the famous NV Disco.

I was out on the dance floor strutting my stuff when I began to get thirsty and went to the bar for a drink of water, and then I saw her. Wow, what a mini skirt! And as curvy as the waves of the sea! I tried to walk past acting tight but I tripped and fell; I felt like a fool!

About an hour later at 11.30pm I saw her again, but she was sitting in the corner crying. I said to myself, *this is your chance mate, do it for your reputation!* I cracked my fingers and my neck and walked over to squeeze in beside her. I asked, 'What's wrong?'

She said in a bitter voice, 'Nothing much, he just didn't show up.'

I said sarcastically, 'But I'm here!'

She said, disappointedly, 'Yes.'

We were walking out of the disco to get a lift home with my brother and his friend, so we had to sit in the back of the van. On the way home I found out that she was rich, and I wanted to ask for the money back for the chips I bought her! I obtained the all-important phone number as she clambered out of the van and possibly out of my life forever. To make matters worse, her dad had forgotten to tie the dog up and it jumped in and bit me.

*All I can say now is that love hurts!*

**Owen Rice  (14)**
**The Abbey CBS Grammar School, Newry**

# Survival In The Rockies

Alex, Michael and James had been white-water rafting in the Canadian Rockies for two weeks and were having a wonderful time. The sun was shining, there wasn't a cloud in the sky and the water was cool and crystal clear.

The trip had been a success so far and everything had gone as planned. They had navigated down the river, safely avoiding boulders and canyons but now came to a narrow stretch with some tricky, dangerous currents and reported hidden rocks.

The boys entered the dark, taunting gully and lost control of the boat. They were bashed about madly until finally, the boat was slit open on the sharp rocks. Immediately the boat began to sink and the boys were forced to bail out and let the current take over.

After a while they were washed up on the river bank and were pleased to find that the boat was washed up too. Alex assessed the damage and announced that the boat could be repaired using some string and wax. He told James to go and look for some fibres that could be wound together to make string and sent Michael to find a bee's nest to get the wax from.

Alex began to sew the hole in the boat so that no holes were left in it. Once he had sewn it all, he applied the wax just to make sure that the boat would be waterproof and in reasonably good condition to carry them on the remainder of their journey. They went to bed that night confident that the next day they would be on their way home again.

Sure enough when they woke the next day, their boat was sitting in the cove ready to be used. So they set off down the river ready to battle the waves and fight for their lives.

**Keith Mackey (14)**
**The Abbey CBS Grammar School, Newry**

# My Car

When I was a child my family and I lived outside the hamlet of Burren with a small white fence surrounding the house. The pigs, sheep and cows were all placed in the larger of the two fields and the horse in the other field. In the winter they were all put into the barn.

I remember my father had left to go to a farmer convention in Dublin. He would be staying a few days and returning on the Friday night.

On the Monday morning I left as usual but on the Tuesday something big happened.

It was very cold and a light blanket of snow lay over the land in all directions. My mum turned the car and left it running to heat up so when we got in it would be warm. She was going to go out and put her laptop computer in the car when she saw it speed off!

Outside there was a black Jeep with a Dublin number plate. It then drove down the drive like a knight on his horse going to rescue the princess. My mother wrote down the number plate and quickly telephoned the PSNI who were very helpful.

We were told that the car could be in France by nightfall.

My mother's friend from work came and drove us to school. She thought that the car would be still in Burren. When I went to school I had to tell all the boys the ordeal that had befallen me on that morning.

**Eugene McAteer (14)**
**The Abbey CBS Grammar School, Newry**

# It Was All My Fault

It was a gorgeous summer morning. The birds sang gracefully and the family were planning an enduring hike up Slieve Gullion followed by a picnic after. But this enchanting morning was about to go quite wrong.

We left the house and set off to our destination. We had to take a detour due to roadworks. Naturally the city was overcrowded.

As we sped down the country roads, windows down and sunshine blazing I felt exhilarated. Suddenly my brother shouted. I looked round and next thing I knew an old man was on the ground, maybe dead. All I could remember was the thud of the brittle bones crashing on the bonnet and the blood splattering everywhere. My heart pounded and next thing I knew I was going at 80mph.

The kids were dazed at what had just happened. I couldn't live with the blood on the windscreen and the sirens in the background. I dropped the kids at my sister's and went to think.

Flashbacks clouded my mind. All I could think about was that almighty thud off the bonnet. That was it, I was handing myself in.

I arrived at the police station, stained with blood. A young chap was sitting at the desk, dozing away. The only words I could choke out were, 'It's all my fault,' and I explained what I had done. Now four years on I'm still doing time for a crime I will never forget.

**Francis Agnew (14)**
**The Abbey CBS Grammar School, Newry**

# It Was All My Fault!

The gang. Jimmy, Fatso, Mitch and myself. We were the bad lads, the rulers of Shortland Street Flats, with 14 ASBOs each it's hard not to understand why.

As usual we were in the estate next to the flats on our BMXs when a hooded man approached us.

'Heads up lads,' I warned as the man drew ever closer.

He reached us and asked in a throaty, rasping voice, 'Wanna get rich?'

'Of course,' we all answered. 'Yeah why not?'

The hooded man continued, 'Be at Shortland Street train station at 9.25 tonight.'

The hooded man had soon disappeared from sight but not from our minds so as half nine approached, we started off for the station.

It was 9.25 when we reached the station and true to his word the hooded man was there standing too casually as if trying to conceal something. 'Good, you guys showed up,' he choked out, 'I was starting to worry.'

'What do we need to do?' quizzed an anxious looking Fatso.

The man's hand slithered out of his coat holding a gun.

I froze, transfixed by the glinting piece of metal.

'Don't stand there gawping, take it! There's a train on platform 13 just about to arrive, a man in a creased nylon suit will get out carrying a briefcase, take it, if he puts up a fight, shoot him! Do this and it's £200 each.'

Two minutes passed and we saw the target, about 50 with a bad suit and a briefcase. 'Gimme the case!' ordered Fatso.

'No!' the man defied.

'Gimme it!' repeated Fatso.

'No!' the man screamed.

*Bang!*

The man was now on the ground, a small hole in his chest with a larger patch of red on his shirt.

*'Run!'*

A police officer was running towards us through the barrage of people running to the exits.

I, being the slowest to react was caught by the policeman but I managed to wriggle free but only to knock over Mitch, as if in slow motion Mitch curved in the air and hit the tracks.

I remember a flashing white light and a deadly silence.

Mitch was dead, it was all my fault.

**David Digney  (13)**
**The Abbey CBS Grammar School, Newry**

# It Seemed Like A Good Idea At The Time

*Tick, tick, tick!*

'Half an hour left, you should be on question two by now,' shouts the teacher.

By the way I'm Paul and I'm doing my end of year examination and I just can't get the answer to question one.

*Tick, tick, tick!*

I can't believe how fast the time is zooming by. Well, would you look at that Mr Stew, George Harrison, is sitting right in front of me.

*Tick, tick, tick!*

He's the biggest stew in the whole school, maybe I could just sneak a peek and copy one of his answers and I'll be flying.

*Tick, tick, tick!*

Brilliant! He's got all the answers! I'll just copy them and change them a bit … there we go, I know I'll pass now.

The next few weeks flew by, before I knew it my report came flying through the door, I was so excited I just ripped it open expecting to have passed with flying colours but to my shock and horror I failed! I actually failed.

**Christopher Harte (14)**
**The Abbey CBS Grammar School, Newry**

# Homework Horror

Homework is a disgrace! In school we go through the day doing massive amounts of work and then proceed to go home and continue with endless piles of homework.

I am here to put an idea to you and it's that homework should be abolished! Now most people who are older than us think it's the only work that we do all day but a lot of things have changed since the days our parents were in school. Nowadays it's get into the classroom and listen while the teacher tells you what to do and near the end of a lesson he/she thinks that you will get it done in class.

Now I say to you, for all the children out there, we should have a homework-free society!

No endless nights of maths, English and science! Instead the plain, good old stuff of 100% fun! We are children after all and we are literally being thrown into the deep end without even a paddle. Imagine this: no children with bags under their eyes; just fun, happy, awake children who are learning steadily and growing up. I think the amount of homework should go with your age, if you are 18 you do 18 pages, that's what we should all do.

**Aidan Slevin  (14)**
**The Abbey CBS Grammar School, Newry**

# Randy

When I was young I had a pet dog called Randy. He was the best dog going. Randy was a very nice, tame dog that rarely barked and never bit anyone. Randy was a black and white collie dog. He was about seven years old. I had him since I was six. Randy and I were the best of friends. My mother said that we were like two peas in a pod. I loved Randy so much, he was like a brother to me.

It used to be that when I would get home from school he would be lying at the front door waiting for me and when I came he would jump up on me and lick me in the face. But one day that all changed. I came round the corner one day on my way home from school and I noticed that Randy wasn't there. At first I thought he was sleeping as he tended to do that a lot, as he got old. I went into the garage and found that he wasn't there. I ran into my mother who was preparing the dinner at the time. I began shouting, 'Where is Randy? Where is he?'

My mother told me to sit down. When she said this, all sorts of thoughts started going through my head like *oh no, he has run away,* and, *somebody has stolen him.* Those thoughts were nice compared to what happened to him. At least in those thoughts he was still alive.

My mother said, 'John, Randy has gone to doggie Heaven.'

I began to cry and then I asked, 'What happened to him?'

My mum said the milkman ran him over. I got up off the chair and ran down the hall into my room. I felt gutted and so angry. I reacted in a very strange way; I didn't drink milk for a year.

About 3 months later my mother got me a new dog. He was a collie as well but it wasn't the same dog. I had to get rid of him after 6 weeks because every time I looked at him I kept seeing Randy.

**John McAteer  (13)**
**The Abbey CBS Grammar School, Newry**

# It Was All My Fault

It was a normal Friday night and I was lounging about the house like a lion in the midday sun. Mum and Dad hadn't been out in ages and they decided that tonight was the night they were going to go out. 'Niall!' Mum shouted. 'Me and your father are going out, Kieran's at football so you have to mind Mark.'

*Ah great*, I thought, *the owners get to go out and I get to mind the demon* (my little brother).

After about ten minutes Mother and Father gathered their stuff and shouted a quick goodbye as they bustled out of the house. *Great!* I thought. There was no sign of the demon and The Simpsons was just about to start so I plumped up my cushion, threw my feet up on the sofa and stared blankly at the TV. Now you'd think you would hear Mark's loud mouth but my favourite show was on and I paid exactly 0% attention to him when he mumbled something about my aunt Jean's. I gave a meaningless grunt and he left …

Time passed by and feeling hungry, I dragged myself out to the kitchen. I hoked around the kitchen and wondered where the good stash of biscuits was hidden, the place where Mum thought was safe. Everyone knew that Mum was a bit slow! I hollered up to Mark, 'Where is the stash?' I repeated myself and wondered where he was. It was only when I had searched the whole house did I realise two things. One: I had lost my smaller brother and two: I was in serious trouble.

Panic set in. 'Oh why did I not listen to the child?' I thought out loud. I bounced onto my bike and cycled around hoping the air would clear my head. I checked all his friends' houses and then the miracle I needed occurred.

Mark was out playing on the street in front of my aunt's! *Dummy!* I thought and grabbed Mark by the scuff of his neck and dragged him home. Even though my parents never found out I will always know that it was all my fault!

**Niall McAteer  (14)**
**The Abbey CBS Grammar School, Newry**

# The House

Near where I lived as a boy, there was an old house which I was told was haunted. One night I was dared to go into the house. I was eager to make a good impression to my friends so I decided to accept the dare. Here's what happened.

The house was an old dilapidated Victorian house that was partly made of brick and partly of wood. There was wood over the door and windows to keep people out or to keep whatever was in there, in ...

There are a lot of stories about the house. Some people say this was where scientists performed weird experiments on people, others say it was Old Man Winters' house (the guy that moved from there to across the street).

From what I can remember there was a big brass door knocker and doorknob. There were hinges on the windows, probably for shutters. There were also painted letters on the door, which said, 'Nirvana - The world of the wizard'. Nirvana meaning absolute spiritual enlightenment, I guessed that hippies lived here.

The door was the only thing I kept my eyes on. The door. What would happen if I opened the door?

I slowly and stealthily walked up the door for fear of being seen. The cold sweat rolled down my back and I could feel my heartbeat getting faster. I put my hand on the cold doorknob and very slowly turned the doorknob. It was locked!

Now that I was standing in the garden the house looked scarier. The paint on the walls was peeling off. There were overgrown bushes all around the house. I could make out an iron fence.

I turned around to head back the way I had just come, when I saw a door which I thought may lead into the basement. The door was hanging off its hinges. I pulled it open and peered into the darkness ...

**Mark Rafferty  (14)**
**The Abbey CBS Grammar School, Newry**

# It Seemed Like A Good Idea At The Time

Tom Fegan was everyone's hero! He was on the football team; he was successful at school and never got into any trouble. But one fateful night that was about to change.

It was Friday night and Tom was waiting to get into the disco. He was in the middle of chatting up a cute blonde-haired girl, when the bouncer interrupted him. After an indignant 'no' to the inquiry as to whether he had any drink or drugs in his possession, Tom waltzed on into the disco where the radiant light shone on his face.

After he got used to his surroundings, Tom and his friends 'hit' the dance floor. About twenty minutes later he and his friends felt tired so they got a drink and sat down.

Tom had just dozed off when he was brought 'back to Earth' by someone calling, *'Tommy! Tommy!'* It was Joey, his rough, troublesome and sporting friend. 'Tommy, everyone has taken one of these.' Joey held out a hand with a white tablet in it, 'they're gonna give us energy!'

'Where did you get that?' Tom exclaimed.

'Chill out man! Everyone else has had one, it'll just give you more energy.'

Then Tom made the biggest mistake of his life. The words 'data boy' sounded in Tom's ears after he had done the deed.

Tom then had an urge to dance with the cute blonde-haired girl and with his new-found 'energy' he shouted, 'Let's dance!' But before long Tom's head had started to feel quite dizzy. He ran out of the disco, out into the pitch-black and heard the distant rumble of the winter wind rustling through the trees. Tom could no longer hear the bouncers calling him; he was in a world of his own. He wandered out into the middle of the road and before he could think of what he was doing, something very, very fast and hard hit him.

Tom awoke in a hospital, paralysed, thinking, *it seemed like a good idea at the time ...*

**David O'Hare (14)**
**The Abbey CBS Grammar School, Newry**